CANTUTA

CANTUTA

⇒ *Inca* ⇐

He who *has* more, *wants* more.
—Old Spanish proverb

Peru
500 years ago . . .

A NOVEL
SHEILA LEBLANC

authorHOUSE®

AuthorHouse™
1663 Liberty Drive
Bloomington, IN 47403
www.authorhouse.com
Phone: 1-800-839-8640

Published by AuthorHouse   04/26/2012

ISBN: 978-1-4685-9420-1 (sc)
ISBN: 978-1-4685-9419-5 (hc)
ISBN: 978-1-4685-9418-8 (e)

Library of Congress Control Number: 2012906904

Author's Note:

This is a work of historical fiction based upon a true story. Many of the names, characters, places, and incidents contained in this book are real and are depicted as accurately as possible based upon the references cited in the bibliography. The characters of Father Pedro, Don Alvarez de la Vega, Vira Yupanqui, Sapaca, Prince Coca, Father Sebastiano, Pani, Turi, and the *Amauta* Kusa Akchi are fictitious and were created by Ilona von Dohnányi. They are not real people . . .

For my husband, Jeffrey Wayne LeBlanc
In memory of my grandmother, Ilona von Dohnányi
With admiration for my father, Seán Patrick McGlynn
With affection for my daughter, Ryan Nicole Starling
Because of my mother, Helen Dohnányi McGlynn

There is nothing new under the sun . . .

Generations come and go but it makes no difference. The sun rises and sets and hurries around to rise again. The wind blows south and north, here and there, twisting back and forth, getting nowhere. The rivers run into the sea but the sea is never full, and the water returns again to the rivers, and flows again to the sea . . . Everything is unutterably weary and tiresome. No matter how much we see, we are never satisfied; no matter how much we hear, we are not content. History merely repeats itself. Nothing is truly new; it has all been done or said before. What can you point to that is new? How do you know it didn't exist long ages ago? We don't remember what happened in those former times, and in the future generations no one will remember what we have done back here.

—King Solomon, Ecclesiastes Chapter 1

PREFACE

Nearly 500 years ago, the Inca Empire in Peru was the last advanced civilization in existence that was completely isolated from the rest of mankind. They lacked the wheel (not a great asset to be missed in the rocky and high-elevation terrain) and writing. Because the early written record of events in Peru available to historians told the story as witnessed through Spanish eyes, not much was known about the Inca.

To set the stage, it is interesting to note that King Henry VIII sat on the throne of England at the time this story takes place. Spain was developing with explosive force during these years. Driven by ambition to emulate the discoveries of Christopher Columbus (1492) and Hernando Cortés (who conquered the Aztec in 1519) a Spanish conquistador named Francisco Pizarro sought to discover his own brilliant golden kingdom.

Our story begins in 1532 (480 years ago), shortly before Pizarro and a company of only 167 men defeated the Inca emperor Atahualpa and 80,000 of his Indian warriors in Cajamarca, Peru. Atahualpa, who managed an empire of over ten million Indians, had recently settled the dilemma of sharing a throne with his half-brother who he soundly defeated in the city of Cuzco. Just as Pizarro appeared on the scene, Atahualpa was settling down to enjoy his divinity as the Inca King, the son of *Inti*, the sun god.

But this is only the beginning of our story. The Inca did not surrender. Many years of fighting followed—brutal and savage—until the Inca civil war actually morphed into a Spanish civil war. Different tribes of Indians chose sides (for or against the Inca). Some tribes actually changed sides during battles depending on how the fighting progressed. Greed, ambition, confusion, deception, racism, and violence ruled the land where Indians and Spaniards tried to survive and triumph over the enemy. Therein, one may find the story of <u>Cantuta</u>, the national flower of Peru, a beautiful blossom that an admirer should never pluck from its stem.

CHAPTER 1

On the rugged, Andean slopes southeast of Quito, capital of the northern province of the divided Inca Empire, the silence of the desert was disturbed by the approach of humans. Mountain birds cried harshly as they were stirred, wings flapping, from their nests. Although it was early afternoon, a thick fog still covered the huge blocks of stone, skillfully cut and placed, which formed the massive stone stairway.

Faintly visible in the misty, blue-grey atmosphere, a vision resembling an immense insect slowly toiled upward. It was an enormous wooden *palanquin*, or litter, borne on the shoulders of ten muscular *Rucana* Indians. The two long carrying poles had silver puma heads on both ends. Although the curtains were plain and dark, the care with which the litter was handled by the Indians over the rough terrain showed that the passengers must be very important.

Upon a terraced platform, the bearers stopped and lowered their weight. The curtains drew apart and a man clambered to the ground. He was short and clumsy, clad in a grey, woolen cloak similar to the garb of the humble Indians. His higher rank was evident in his attitude of superiority as he instructed the bearers to set up the steps to the litter. His hard features melted into humility as he bowed very low and reached up to offer assistance to a man who descended the steps with elastic vigor.

This man, a commanding figure, was slender, of medium height, but also simply clad. He wore a scarlet and gold *llautu*, or headband, made of very fine *vicuña* wool around his head with a royal fringe hanging from the front of his circlet that covered his forehead. His features, as well as his whole bearing, revealed his high ancestry. His face was surrounded by glossy, smoothly combed, black hair that reached his neck. He could have been called handsome, were it not for his sharp penetrating eyes under slanted eyebrows. His domineering expression was accentuated by tightly closed lips and a prominent chin.

In spite of his otherwise plain disguise, anyone who had ever heard of Atahualpa would have immediately recognized him. He was *Lord of Life and Death*, Inca King, but sadly, only half a man, for he was forced to share his Empire with his brother, Huascar. Although Atahualpa had possession of the professional army, Huascar had the love and loyalty of the people. As he looked around, his assistant handed him a spear with a golden axe head attached to one end.

"Here is your *champi*, my Lord," he said in a deep voice that sounded like a bear's growl. "Although, I don't suspect you will need it in the Temple."

Atahualpa's lips drew into a sarcastic smile. They curved up bitterly as he reached for the golden weapon to fasten it to his jewel-studded belt.

"You are and will always remain an optimist, General Quizquiz," he said. His voice echoed harshly against the surrounding rocks. "Temples should be holy places. But as long as I share this Empire with Huascar, and as long as the holy priests remain loyal to him, who knows what might happen in a Temple? I am ready to defend myself, even against God Viracocha himself!"

He looked around and raised his arm to command his servants. At this, they threw themselves face down upon the ground, not daring to move until their master and Lord gave his command. One of the Indians, in his haste to obey, slipped over the rocky ledge and fell down into the abyss. The others dared not make the slightest move to help the unfortunate man, but waited breathlessly and still for the next command of the Inca, the Son of the Sun God.

"Follow me with the litter," he ordered, "Stop at the beginning of that narrow path and wait until I summon you." Walking up the rocky way as majestically as though he were ascending his throne, Atahualpa examined several paths which branched off from the main trail.

"The Temple is here somewhere, Quizquiz," he said to his general.

Quizquiz shaded his grave black eyes with his hands to scan the landscape. "There, my Lord! There it is! The Temple of the Sun! We're nearly there!"

Following General Quizquiz, they soon stood before a massive wall which emerged from the rocks. Immense gates carved with grotesque dog heads, serpents, and other mysterious monsters opened directly into the side of the mountain. The grey stone contrasted sharply with the green bushes nestled in its niches and the ferns that climbed its ancient gray walls.

Atahualpa paused to wipe perspiration from his forehead. In spite of the cold and biting wind, his uneasiness at reaching his destination was obvious. What would the Oracle say? What wise counsel would he receive? What would be his fate?

"My Lord," whispered Quizquiz, "Perhaps it would be prudent to offer a peaceful agreement to Huascar. Certainly he will surrender his rule to you. Why not make him an offer or trick him into submission. Ah, what about Vira? She's your most beautiful sister and he loves her dearly. I have been told that she is by far his favorite. Ask him for her . . ."

"No more marriages!" interrupted Atahualpa. "Marriages don't fix anything!" Atahualpa's eyes flamed with indignation. "What good would it do to get mixed up with another one of Huascar's *Qhapaq ayllu* princesses if he remains unwilling to resign his rule? I'm already ruining Coca's life, marrying him to Sapaca. Even after they wed, hostility will continue. Disagreements can only be mended with weapons, Quizquiz. You, a general, should agree with *that*!"

"My Lord is always right," Quizquiz capitulated. "But if so, still . . . it might be better to return without asking the Oracle."

"Turn back!?" shouted Atahualpa. "Remember that I, Inca Atahualpa, Son of the Sun, will *never* make a step backwards, not even if . . . not even if I should have to cross a sea of blood and lose my own head. Let's go, no more wasting time!"

Leaving the nine Indians behind to tend the litter, Atahualpa and General Quizquiz cautiously climbed the steps that led to the temple gate. They passed through the gate and entered a corridor illuminated by a mysterious light. They walked as far as they could until the light failed them and they stopped in pitch darkness. As their eyes adjusted to the dark, they became aware that they had entered a vast hall with a raised platform in the center. Standing in the middle of the raised platform in a majestic pose stood a life-sized, solid gold statue of Inca Huayna Capac, Atahualpa's father. The Oracle stood beside the statue and awaited Atahualpa's question.

As his eyesight adjusted to the dim light and he was better able to see the gold image of his father, resentment began to boil up inside him. This was the image of the man who, on his deathbed, divided the Inca

Empire into two halves. To Atahualpa, he gave the northern lands. And to Huascar, he gave Cuzco and its surroundings.

The two boys had been born to different mothers just two days apart. Huascar was the elder and had never missed a chance to torture Atahualpa with jealousy. Neither son was their father's first choice for crown prince. Unfortunately, the choice to divide the expanding empire between them was made when death came suddenly.

As Atahualpa stood facing the Oracle, he felt torn between the injury he had to suffer from his father's decision and the sharp anguish that shortened his breath.

"What do you want to hear, oh Atahualpa?" asked the Oracle.

More of a stern command than a question, the sound of the Oracle's voice startled Atahualpa back to his senses. He bowed his head in homage to the spirit of his father and then dropped down to one knee.

"I came to learn my fate." He said in a husky voice. "What has been decided for me by Viracocha, my eternal Creator?"

There was silence. Quizquiz trembled. His teeth chattered and he drew closer to his master.

"The omnipotent Viracocha frowns upon you," intoned the voice. "You did not resign yourself to the will of your father and your God. You will be bitterly punished for the attack you plan against your brother."

Atahualpa's anxiety turned into rage. He grasped his *champi* and shook it menacingly.

"How dare you accuse me?" he shouted. "There can be no promise of a throne among an Inca King's sons. My father chose badly and the wrong son was crowned King. I was *with* Huayna Capac. I fought with his army in the north! He promised the throne to *me*! It was your cunning, you priests who influenced him to crown Huascar. *You priests* made him divide this land between us!"

"I accuse you, Atahualpa, because I see your deeds! The marriage of your son Coca to Huascar's daughter, Sapaca, is a trick. You think to steal your brother's heritage through treachery."

"It is as it must be!" retorted Atahualpa. "As long as Huascar remains a King, I am only half a man. I rule only half a kingdom. Such nonsense never existed in the history of the Inca!"

"Oh Atahualpa, a curse is upon you!" proclaimed the Oracle.

Atahualpa was no longer restrained. In his rage, he lifted his *champi* and swung savagely at the white-robed priest. The Oracle screamed, "What are you doing?"

Atahualpa made no effort to curb his frenzy. He had suspected all along, in spite of his superstitious fears, that the Oracle would be a fake. In the dim light, he swung the *champi* again and watched the masked head of the priest fall off his neck and hit the flagstone floor with a thud.

Atahualpa threw down the bloody *champi* and grasped at both sides of his own head in anger. He knew this was sacrilege. He knew the people would be outraged by the murder of a holy *Amauta* in the Temple of the Sun. He turned and left the temple.

With Quizquiz at his heels, Atahualpa made it out to the Temple gate. The cold mountain air cooled his senses as he tried to regain his self-control. The priest's blood stained his cloak. With shaking hands, he unfastened his cloak and threw it over the edge of the rock cliff. Standing only in his white tunic woven of fine *vicuña* wool, he looked at Quizquiz. Quizquiz stared at him with quivering lips and watery eyes.

"What's the matter with you, Quizquiz? Scared out of your wits?"

"Please forgive me, my Lord. I do not fear for myself, only for you, my Lord." Quizquiz's head was bent low in subjugation to his sovereign. "The Temple, my Lord . . . the *Amauta* is dead! What will become of us?"

"I will become Inca King and you will be my finest General," answered Atahualpa with stoic certainty. "Do you question the authority of the Son of the Sun God, Inti? That *Amauta* was a mere man, a fake, an imposter! Emulate me, Quizquiz, and fear nothing."

Atahualpa was trying hard to have confidence in his own words. Quizquiz was his best general and closest comrade. Agreement and loyalty were necessary.

"In all my life, I have respected Inti and the laws of my country. Viracocha himself requested me to commit this bloody action in response to an unjust and untrue curse."

"So you reject the curse, my Lord? Or do you accept the words of the Oracle?"

"Of course, I reject the curse! And I do NOT accept the sentence of a false Oracle!" Atahualpa clenched his fists toward the sky. "I will fight my brother and everyone, even Viracocha himself, to gain control of my Empire!" Atahualpa gently lowered his hand to the shoulder of General

Quizquiz. "You believe that I am right, Quizquiz? You believe that I am the strongest and should rightfully inherit the Inca Empire?"

"You are strong and you desire *power*, my Lord . . ."

Atahualpa's fierce eyes flared up for a moment then he turned and started with slow steps toward the litter. He stopped once and looked behind him. Quizquiz followed dutifully.

"It is not *only* power that I desire, Quizquiz," he said, his voice sounded very soft. "I also want the contentment of my people. This land cannot exist and survive divided into two parts as it is now. It must have only one king. And Viracocha must know that if I possess the power, I will use it for good and for the welfare of my people."

Quizquiz made no more comments. Secretly, he pressed to his heart the tiny amulet he wore around his neck which contained the tooth of a llama and a lock of hair from the head of his dying mother.

CHAPTER 2

T he *Qhapaq ayllu* family and royal court of Huascar, King of Cuzco and the southern Inca lands, enjoyed a proud and happy lifestyle in the luxurious royal palace he built called *Cañaracay*. Located just east of Cuzco within the sacred valley, *Cañaracay* was in the warmest and sunniest region of the Inca lands. Huascar's estate included parks, fields, and beautiful gardens. There was even a secluded forest where he and his courtiers could hunt.

Indian servants had cleared irrigation channels and raised terraces to grow potatoes, corn, beans, cotton, peanuts, hot peppers and other crops. There was always plenty of *kachi*, or salt, to flavor and preserve their food and plenty of *chicha*, a fermented corn beverage, to drink at festivals and parties. The protective stone walls defied every challenge from the outside world.

One summer night, the palace was dark. Only one light filtered through the partly drawn curtains of a window to a room on the second floor of the women's wing. The light came from the room occupied by two young princesses, Sapaca and Vira. It was late in the night but the girls were wide awake and discussing Sapaca's wedding feast to take place the next day. It had all happened so fast. Only three days ago, Huascar pledged Sapaca to Coca, one of Atahualpa's many sons. Everyone hoped that this marriage between the children of rival brothers would bring peace to the Empire.

Sapaca and Vira lay on their broad couches leaning on cushions embroidered with gold thread. "Sapaca," whispered Vira. "I'm worried about you."

Although she was only 16 years old, Vira was very wise and insightful. She was also fully aware that she was Huascar's favorite. She was beautiful and had a sweet disposition. But she questioned *everything*! Because she was so clever, Huascar discussed issues with her almost as though she were his equal. She was named for the sea mist on the great Pacific Ocean, where Viracocha lived. Her face was long and oval and of aristocratic Inca mold, framed by coils of glossy black hair. Her lips, now gently parted, were of a bright strawberry color that contrasted with her unusually fair skin.

"I worry about you, Sapaca," she continued. "I mean, about your marrying Coca." Vira looked searchingly at her as if trying to read her thoughts.

Sapaca averted her gaze and stared off instead at their nurse, Pani, an old Indian woman. Pani was snoring peacefully on her pallet on the floor. When Sapaca finally raised her eyes to meet Vira's, there was no sign of anguish upon her somewhat plain features.

Sapaca was three years older than Vira. She had a broad face with full lips and a small, blunt nose. Her complexion was darker than Vira's and her figure much plumper. Although she was not considered beautiful, she had lovely dark almond-shaped eyes under expressive eyebrows.

"Oh Vira, why worry about me? I'm going to marry a royal prince!" consoled Sapaca with a husky, little laugh. "Maybe this marriage will bring peace to our families. What more could a maiden ask for from Viracocha?"

"You don't even know Coca, or what he looks like. What if he's ugly? You have to make *children* with him! What if he's a monster like his father?

Sapaca shrugged. Her lazy, peaceful spirit was too primitive to think and too comfortable to rebel. She struggled at times to understand Vira who was so smart and emotional. "I'll do whatever Father orders," assured Sapaca. "His wishes are laws. Nothing else matters."

"But it *DOES* matter!" rebuked Vira. She sat up on her mattress so that her blanket slipped from her shoulders to reveal the slender, delicately rounded outlines of her young body through her soft robe. "Have you never thought about lying in your lover's arms and giving him your chastity, your dreams, your soul?"

"You're rebelling again, Vira" cautioned Sapaca. "Why not settle down and accept what you cannot change? You know very well that soon, you also will be given away as a bride! I've heard rumors about King Chincha."

"Ha! I'll die before I marry that Indian brute!"

"I don't know what's wrong with you, Vira," chided Sapaca shaking her head. "He's a brave warrior. He's loyal to Father. And he's King of the Cañari!"

Vira sighed, it was true. She had only seen King Chincha once. But she remembered his dark, bony face with eyes that were ravenous with desire for her. She hoped Huascar would deny his plea for marriage.

"I just don't understand how Viracocha could go down into the sea and leave no sons here for us to marry! If only I could find a man like Viracocha with white skin, black hair, and a black beard!" Vira laughed with Sapaca. They both knew the Inca ways. Still she hoped for a handsome, noble, brave, gentle, fiery yet dignified man to whom she could give herself. There were no men among the Inca or the Indians that could ever fulfill her hopes.

"Maybe everything will turn out all right, Sapaca," comforted Vira. "Perhaps your wedding will make your father happy and he'll forgive Atahualpa.

Vira always spent a lot of time thinking. She often reflected upon the wise words of her father, Inca Huayna Capac, when he said "We cannot cross a chasm on a bridge that is broken in two." She remembered stories he told her about strange houses that floated upon the sea and were loaded with white-skinned strangers. Their faces were hairy like Viracocha's and their bodies were completely covered with clothes.

Vira thought often about her father's dark revelation: That the bearded, *White Strangers* would return to Inca lands to destroy his Empire. She tried to sleep. Sapaca was already breathing heavily, dreaming of her wedding, no doubt. But Vira couldn't sleep. Until her father saw the *White Strangers*, her people believed they were the sole inhabitants of the earth. She grappled with the idea of *strangers*. Were they really dangerous? Would they really return to destroy her world? What if her brothers were busy fighting each other when the *White Strangers* came back? Would it be soon or would her favorite brother, Prince Manco, be Inca by then?

With a heavy heart, Vira rose from her bed and walked to the open window. She breathed deeply of the refreshing night breezes. Sapaca stirred peacefully as Vira gazed up at the moon. And then she froze. She heard a noise in the dark outside her window. Was it a puma? No, it was someone approaching. Who would dare to approach the royal castle and venture so near the window of the King's favorite maiden sister? Vira gasped and took a quick step back into the darkness. Sapaca awoke, "What's wrong? Why aren't you in bed?"

"Shhh!" Hissed Vira, her finger over her lips and her body pressed flat against the wall.

"Princess Vira!" They both heard the deep voice from outside. "Princess Vira, listen to my song. It is the confession of my heart!"

It was King Chincha. Why would he defy a hundred deaths to come to Vira's window?

Vira remained silent. Had he seen her? Should she alert Pani to the presence of her night visitor? Should she hide? Then she faintly heard the music. It was the song of the *queña*, the flute, sweeter than the midnight murmur of soft breezes. The sound conveyed a heart wrenching longing, full of hope and yet so sad that the girl's eyes filled with tears. A faint *tam-tam* accompanied the *queña*, a sound one could feel rather than hear, made by a small wooden stick lightly beating the animal skin top of a small drum. As its mysterious delicacy rendered the secret serenade intensely moving, Vira drew the curtain aside to peer below. Then she heard the voice of King Chincha, soft yet ardent, as he sang the words:

> "Wonder no more, lovely nymph of the mountain!
> Your lover has come in the moonlight with song,
> I'll mingle my notes with the splash of the fountain,
> To lull you to sweet dreams all night long.
>
> Lightning, thunder, swift falling rain,
> Exist only to serve you from their skies.
> One cannot fathom the depth of my pain,
> To see tears fall from your beautiful eyes."

The song was over. *Tam-tam* and *queña* ceased. In the trembling silence, only the girl's breathing could be heard.

The voice came from so near that only the wall seemed to separate them, "Royal Princess, beautiful Vira!" stammered the King. "Don't be surprised to see me here. Do you think that I asked for your hand in marriage for nothing more than my political gain? It isn't that! I've loved you for a long time. I saw you at the feast of *Situa* standing next to the Great Inca. You were only a child, but so lovely already. I beg you to say a word in my favor to your royal brother!"

He stopped for a moment then he pleaded on, "If you agree to marry me, lovely Princess, the great King who is so fond of you will surely give his consent. If it is that you do not wish to marry me, then I will withdraw forever from the Royal Court. My wounded pride and great sorrow would accompany me to my death . . ."

All was silent. Suddenly, a light object flew in through the window from below and landed right at Vira's feet. She shrank back with a shudder and involuntarily drew the curtains tight and ran to the farthest end of the room where her old nurse lay snoring.

"Pani!" she gasped. But the woman slept deeply. "Pani!" she whispered angrily. Even this call went unheard. Vira kicked the mattress. This helped. The Indian woman, who had nursed Vira when she was a baby, sat up with a jerk. She rubbed her eyes that lay deep in their sockets with her wrinkled fists and lifted her dark-skinned face. Her face did not reveal her years but was marked rather by work and worry.

"What's the matter, little Princess?" she asked in astonishment. "Why are you awake? It's night."

"For you it could be night for ages!" Vira scolded her in her soft, gentle way. "Will you be awake at last? Come, King Chincha threw something in through my window. It's for me. Come lift it for me, quick!

Pani was awake now and rose as quickly as her tired muscles allowed. Still rubbing her eyes, she walked to the window, lifted the tiny object then, holding it in her palm, examined it carefully.

"It's a flower, little Princess. A cantuta," she said in her sleepy voice.

"A cantuta!" exclaimed Vira. She took the flower into her palm, and repeated mechanically, "A cantuta! I have never seen the like!"

"Of course not, my little dove, my *urpi*," Pani admonished, "such a flower is too rare! It's the choicest flower of the mountains! It's forbidden to move it from its place! Do you remember the legend?"

"I heard it long ago," interrupted Sapaca, sitting up in her bed, now fully awake. "Those who pick it will be punished with the most horrible fate. They say each blossom has the spirit of a fairy maiden!"

Vira bent over the petals, which curved in a way to form a blossom shaped like the head of a woman. There were two spots for her eyes and a dark line below suggesting lips.

"Oh," she whispered. "It's just like a woman's face! I heard the stories, sad and lovely stories."

11

"Poor Chincha," Sapaca remarked. "He defied Father's night watchmen and he even defied the Evil Spirits, just to win your heart!" She sighed. "Still, I bet you don't want him, even though you'd be his queen."

"I don't want to be a queen," Vira protested as she tenderly placed the fragile blossom on a table beside her bed. She tossed her head high in defiance. "I want to be *happy*. I want to stand beside a man who is bold and brave, kind and noble . . . and *handsome*."

Pani, who had returned to her pallet hoping for some rest, shook her head in disapproval. "I'm afraid, little Princess; you'll just have to content yourself with the man your brother chooses. Your dear mother had no choice but happy she was, very happy until the will of Almighty Viracocha called her forth." Pani wiped a tear from her eye as she remembered her adored mistress who died giving birth to Vira. "But don't worry about King Chincha. I overheard your brother tell General Chalcuchima during the evening meal that he was sending King Chincha away because you don't wish to marry him."

"Why didn't you tell me that?" reproached Vira, although she was unable to hide her joy and relief.

"I never repeat words that were not said for me to hear," answered Pani respectfully. "But I can't watch you suffer this way, my little dove."

"You dear, sweet, woman!" Vira rewarded the faithful old servant with a gracious smile.

Just then, the whole room swayed and shook the women back to reality. The earthquake was small but frightening. Vira leaned back against the stone wall for support and hid her face behind her hands. Sapaca fell back upon her cushions and drew the blanket of soft alpaca wool over her head. "Come, Vira, climb into your bed. It might be safer!"

As the motion ceased and everything grew quiet again, Vira silently thanked her brother for having the good sense to build the palace with such large stones. These earthquakes were so scary.

Vira dashed over to Pani and actually grasped her by the shoulders as she sat on her pallet. "I can't stand it, Pani," she cried. "Bring Manco to me. I must see him now."

Pani was accustomed to Vira's outbursts and whims; however, this time she shook her head with disapproval. Although she was aware of how much Vira loved her brother, Pani knew that their relationship must change now that Manco had been chosen as Crown Prince. He completed military school at Yachahuasi College in Cuzco and was now a general in the army. Vira had to grow up. Pani decided that she would not go running around the palace in the middle of the night.

"Little Princess," cooed Pani. "You know your brother sleeps. You know he's not allowed in the women's quarters. Please, go to sleep now, little one."

"Pani, we just had an *earthquake*, Manco and everyone else in this palace is awake! Go and bring my brother to me!"

"You know, Vira," chimed in Sapaca. Manco is a man now and he's going to be the king one day. He's not your little playmate anymore. You really should treat him with more respect!"

"You both know full well that Manco is always ready to come to me. Even if he has to fight off pumas or wear a disguise, he'll always come to me when I need him. And anyway, I'm giving you a command, Pani, so go!"

There was nothing Pani could do. She struggled to her tired feet and tripped her way through the dark palace to summon Manco. She knew he wouldn't mind. He always indulged Vira's whims. A mysterious midnight excursion to the women's quarters would most assuredly appeal to his sense of humor.

CHAPTER 3

Vira wanted to chat with Sapaca while she waited for Manco; however, much to her chagrin Sapaca was already snuggled up and fast asleep. Vira shivered and wrapped a soft throw blanket adorned with hummingbird feathers around her shoulders. She could hear the hustle and bustle of servants running around to check on the condition of the palace. As she picked up her gold brush and began to brush her hair, she thought about the wedding to take place in the morning.

She was happy that she would get to see Kusa Akchi tomorrow. Kusa Akchi is the Priest, the holy *Amauta*, who taught her all about the Gods. He taught her how to pray to Viracocha and told her that, after the Great Flood, Viracocha told the sun, the moon, and the stars—all of the holy eyes of light, to release their light and brighten the sky for Imaynana and Toqapo, his man and woman. When Viracocha wept over the sins of his people, it was his tears that anointed the first Inca King.

Kusa Akchi always took the royal children to their confession and taught them to speak only the truth. Vira was taught to respect all that is good and noble and to despise all that is false or evil. Yet, as much as her deep faith in the gods comforted her, Vira was still lonely. Her father had tried his best to give her the love of both father and mother. But he had been an important man and had many activities to oversee. Now she lived with her brother Huascar. He was Inca King of half the empire and had very little time to dedicate to Vira. Pani helped, but she was just an Indian. Pani taught her everything she needed to know to be a proper Inca Princess. But she was not her mother.

Vira sighed. It was Manco who was truly closest to her heart. How they played as children. It felt like ages although it was only just over a year ago. So much had happened. Ever since Ninan Cuyuchi died so suddenly from that terrible rash and fever and then Huayna Capac died from it also, well, everything just fell apart. If only Ninan Cuyuchi had lived to become the new Inca King, then Huascar wouldn't be fighting with Atahualpa. Why did they always have to fight? There was so much tension. Before Huayna Capac died, the men used to fight *together* against troublesome Indians. Now they fought each other. Vira felt vulnerable. Where *was* Manco anyway, what was taking him so long?

Finally, Vira heard footsteps in the corridor. The door opened and Manco breezed into the room. He was a fine young man, tall and slim with sun-browned skin and dark eyes. Even in his night dress he looked like a king. His black hair, cropped short in the back, fell in soft waves over his forehead. His face, long and narrow, wore an expression of mock severity. Only his large gold ear plugs revealed his rank.

"What's the matter, little sister?" he asked Vira. He broke out in a big, white-toothed smile as Vira ran to him and flung her arms around his neck. "What net of intrigue has captured you this time? What is so urgent that it can't wait until morning?"

"Manco, I'm so lonely, I just longed to be near you," Vira cried in relief.

Just then the door opened again and in walked Kusa Akchi. He was tall and grim and wore the long white robe of the priests over his angular frame. There was something almost supernatural in his bony face. Grey hair framed keen eyes set close together in caverns that were dark in contrast to his pale skin. His fierce penetrating eyes and long hooked nose made him look more like a bird of prey than a wise and holy man. Regardless of his looks, the Indians adored Kusa Akchi and the Inca showed him deep respect. His dignified manner was accentuated by his modest behavior except for one aspect: Kusa Akchi thought he was able to see into the future.

Vira stared at him in surprise but quickly remembered to bow deeply and touch the edge of his robe with reverence.

"Welcome, *Amauta* Kusa Akchi," she whispered. She glanced questioningly at her brother and gave him a look that begged the question, *why on earth did you bring him here?*

Manco could read his sister's face well. "I had to bring him with me, Vira! I can't come to the women's quarters at night by myself!" Manco chuckled at his beautiful little sister. "Change that look on your face, it doesn't become a Princess!" he chided.

Vira was uneasy to share her feelings in front of the priest. "Manco, I'm sorry. What with the wedding tomorrow and the earthquake, I don't know, I just needed to speak with you."

Kusa Akchi was perturbed. "You know how your father felt about fear. You are an Inca Princess. You must learn to master your fears!" scolded Kusa Akchi in a dark, gruff voice.

Vira feared disappointing him more than she feared the earthquake. "All right," she confessed. "I sent for you because I'm worried about Sapaca. What's to become of her in this marriage? She's just a sweet, little thing of a person. How is a naïve, young girl supposed to bring peace to the Inca Empire?"

Manco smiled, Kusa Akchi winced, Vira fretted, and Sapaca slept. "Vira, listen, it's a step in the right direction. Sapaca doesn't mind. And Coca is a good man. Remember, I told you I met him at school. Really, it's going to be fine."

"And you wouldn't question the order of King Huascar, now, would you?" added Kusa Akchi. It was more of a threat than a question. "One day, you'll do the same as Sapaca and marry the man chosen for you."

Vira groaned as her shoulders slouched in despair. "I thought we would all be together forever. Why can't *you* marry Sapaca instead?"

"Vira," continued Manco in his most charming and soothing voice. "Look, we have to do everything we can to forge peace. Remember Father's warning about the *White Strangers*? What if we're so busy fighting Atahualpa that we don't see them return!? All we can do is hope that Atahualpa will be satisfied with Sapaca for Prince Coca. At least we're trying!"

"Well, Manco, since you know everything and are so wise and all, what if the *White Strangers* turn out to be good and kind? What if they return as friends and bring us fine gifts from their lands, wherever they're from? What if we *like* them?" argued Vira.

Manco's eyebrows furrowed with real concern. "I will never trust an intruder, Vira. If the *White Strangers* return and they are weak and helpless, well, then they will deserve our protection. But if they are strong and have the weapons Father told us about, I'm afraid I will have to fight them to the end."

Sapaca stirred on her mattress and woke up, "Oh, hello Manco! Greetings, *Amauta* Kusa Akchi!" Sapaca jumped out of bed to kneel before the priest and touch the hem of his robe to her lips. "What on earth are you two doing in our room at this hour? Oh yes, Vira sent Pani to fetch you! Did Vira tell you that King Chincha was outside the window singing songs and throwing flowers?" blurted Sapaca.

Vira gasped, Kusa Akchi bristled, and Manco was outraged as he turned to face Vira. "What?! What does she mean? Chincha was *here*? After Huascar sent him *away*?"

Vira bit her lip and swayed on her feet. "Oh that," she laughed and waved her hand through the air, "it was nothing."

"He even gave her a *cantuta* flower . . ."

"Sapaca! Go back to sleep now!" Vira begged nervously.

"Chincha picked a cantuta blossom?" Manco shook his head with dark foreboding. "Listen Vira, if King Chincha approached you in any way, if he laid eyes on you, if he *touched* you . . ."

"He didn't *touch* me, Manco!" assured Vira. "Please, just let it go, the poor man's heart is already broken. He's in love with me! You should have heard the words he sang to me . . ."

"He was singing?" Manco was outraged. It was a crime punishable by death to approach an Inca Princess.

"Please Kusa Akchi! Say something! You taught us to be kind and compassionate toward the Indians. And remember, his people, the Cañari, are our friends now!"

"She has a point, Manco," Kusa Akchi announced slowly. "There's no need to send Chincha's people over to Atahualpa's side right now. King Huascar does not need to know of this incident. Let Chincha go back to the Cañari. Tomorrow there will be a wedding. We must go now."

With that, Manco pressed his sister's hand affectionately and the two men quietly exited the women's quarters.

"Is everything all right now, my dove?" asked Pani as she came back into the room. With one look at Vira, standing dejectedly with her head downcast, Pani knew it was not.

"Oh, this won't do, this won't do at all! You'll worry yourself sick with all of your *what-if's* and *might-happens*. Did King Chincha's words really stir you so? Just sleep, my darling, and Pani will watch over you and sing a song for you."

17

Vira reclined on her mattress and allowed Pani to arrange her pillows and cover her with the blanket. As Pani hummed some old Indian lullaby, Vira finally fell asleep. And as she dreamed, her lovely lips curved ever so slightly into a smile.

CHAPTER 4

P ani woke Vira up the next morning. "Little Princess," she cooed. "It is time for your bath. It is already day time and the sun is up. Wake up now."

Vira walked sleepily with Pani to the marble pool located in one of the palace gardens. They were alone. As Pani removed Vira's night clothing, Vira stared into the cobalt blue waters of the pool. While she stared, an image took shape. It was the face of a stranger, a man. His eyes were dark and his lips were full and sensual. His brown hair waved and framed a face that was strong and caring. Vira dreamed of this face. She dreamed that his mouth would speak to her and say, "I love you" and call her away to a life of adventure and companionship.

"Pani," she murmured, "is it possible for a woman to fall in love with an image created by her own heart?"

"Well, I suppose so," she answered. "You're just longing for a man to love, Little Princess."

"It feels so strange. Do you think there is something wrong with me?"

"Probably, now get into the water and bathe your pretty little body."

As Vira walked down the steps into the pool of purifying water, the ripples she created blurred her lover's face. She fell forward headlong into his eyes as the image washed away around her.

When she came up finally for air, she asked, "Pani, do you know if anything bad happened to King Chincha because of last night?"

"King Chincha went away last night as he was told. He's gone."

"How terrible he must feel," said Vira with a sigh. "I wonder how badly it hurts to love someone who doesn't love you back."

CHAPTER 5

The wedding was scheduled for high noon when the sun pours down like honey to please Inti, the Sun God. Inca nóbles and their servants traveled from all over the Sacred Valley around Cuzco. Atahualpa's family traveled south from Quito. It was a perfect day for a wedding.

The wedding feast was prepared in the courtyard of Cañaracay, Inca Huascar's palace in Cuzco. There was a variety of dishes prepared with potatoes and corn mixed with the meat of birds and llamas. There were side dishes of *Qinwah*, a grain cooked and served like rice along with platters filled with colorful peppers, squash, baby broad beans, and fruits such as guava. Some of the mountain Indians brought guinea pigs that were prepared along with offerings from the coastal Indians that included fish, shellfish, and seabirds. Although the dishes were tempting and artistically arranged, the wedding guests were far more interested in drinking *chicha* and dancing.

The lords and ladies were dressed in their finest woven alpaca mantles and gowns filigreed with silver and gold. The men's mantles reached their knees and heavy gold belts were tied at their waist. They wore sandals made from llama leather that were fastened to their feet with ribbons decorated with colorful gems. They wore scarlet headbands that held beautiful parrot feathers in place and large golden ear plugs. The women wore long alpaca wool robes of either white or pale colors that reached down to their ankles. Shells from the sea and beads were used to adorn the robes. With every movement of their arms, their many bracelets tinkled like little silver bells.

Members of the Inca royal family were in attendance. Many of Huayna Capac's widows with his sons and daughters and their children were there to celebrate the marriage of Sapaca and Coca. Paullu, one of Huayna Capac's sons born to the daughter of a non-Inca Indian chief from Huaylas, was there with his brothers Inquill and Huaspar.

Long ago, *Amauta* Kusa Akchi had told a story to Vira about a beautiful young maiden who had a pure heart. Because of her kindness, she consented to marry an old and ugly king. The king was so grateful to her that he gave her a coat made of pure gold. When the maiden died, she came back to life as a *vicuña* so the grieving king forbade anyone in his kingdom to harm a *vicuña*. Only the royal Inca family was allowed to wear clothing woven from the lustrous and silky fleece of the *vicuña*.

The wedding guests were ushered through the enormous festival hall where over 1,000 people could be seated and into the private audience room of Inca Huascar. He was seated upon his throne of pure gold wearing a cloak woven of hummingbird feathers and gold thread. His heavy gold ear plugs were as large as saucers and stretched his earlobes down to rest on his golden shoulder decorations. His crown of macaw tail and wing feathers was adorned with emeralds and other jewels and the royal tassel covered his forehead. In his right hand, he clutched his golden *champi*, his spear with the axe head that all Inca rulers carried. He was magnificent. His face was proud and stern with the fierce eyes of a hunting puma.

The wedding guests formed a long line and, one by one, came before the throne to bow and touch the edge of the Inca's royal robe to their lips in reverence. An expression of fatherly affection passed across his face as he recognized his relatives who had come to celebrate with him. He lifted his hand to give them his blessings and called out to some of them in greeting, "Thanks to Viracocha that we have come together once more."

Once all the guests had passed before their king, a side door opened and *Amauta* Kusa Akchi entered. He wore his usual plain white, priest's robe. Kusa Akchi approached the King's throne. Inca Huascar rose to greet him and slowly descended the stairs from his throne.

"Is Atahualpa coming? Is there any report of his whereabouts? It's his *son's wedding*! What is wrong with him?"

"He's still a day away, my Lord, and it was rather short notice" soothed Kusa Akchi. "At least his family has arrived safely, thank Viracocha."

A long procession of court ladies, all dressed in white, walked slowly toward the Inca. Behind them came the Inca Lords of highest rank led by Prince Manco with Prince Coca, the groom, at his side. And then Princess Sapaca entered the hall. She was beautiful in her long white robe that fell past her golden slippers. Her head was covered with a fine soft scarf adorned with precious gems. Vira walked beside her. Pani had parted Vira's hair down the middle, combed it smooth, and left it in two long braids that rested on her shoulders. She wore a crown of white bird feathers.

The Inca gave a sign for the bride and bridegroom to approach him together in front of the throne. They bowed their heads and fell to their knees in front of the Inca. Huascar placed a hand on each of their heads and quietly bestowed upon them his blessing and special prayers for wealth, happiness, and fertility. When he was finished, he motioned for them to rise, he joined their hands, and he touched their foreheads with his royal lips.

He then motioned for *Amauta* Kusa Akchi to come forward. The holy priest, prayed to God Viracocha to unite the young couple forever. No human would have the power or the right to separate them.

Kusa Akchi prayed, "Oh Creator without equal, you are at the ends of the world. You gave life and valor to mankind saying "Let there be man" and for the women, "Let there be woman." You made them, formed them, and gave them life so that they will live safe and sound in peace without danger! Where are you? By chance do you live high in the sky or below on earth or in the clouds and storms? Hear me, respond to me and consent to my plea, giving us perpetual life and taking us with your hand. Receive our offerings wherever you are, Oh Creator!"

The wedding ritual was complete. The new couple withdrew to one side of the hall to receive the congratulations of their friends and relatives. As all attention was drawn to the young bride and groom, Inca Huascar looked over to his friend the *Amauta*.

"Thank you, *Amauta* Kusa Akchi. You serve me well" praised the king.

"I serve you with a loving and faithful heart, my Lord" assured Kusa Akchi.

"I have wanted to commend you for your loyalty," continued Huascar. "I haven't yet told you how honored I am that you decided to dedicate your life to the preparation of my lovely little sister, Cura Ocllo, as *Virgin of the Sun*."

"She is very young but I have taught Cura Ocllo to perform her duties well," answered Kusa Akchi. "Cura Ocllo is ready."

Huascar sighed. "I saw her this morning in the Temple of the Sun and she asked for you, Kusa Akchi. I'm afraid she's nervous. She seems to cling to you."

"It is only that I have spent so much time with her in preparation," answered Kusa Akchi. She is wise for her years and craves knowledge. She will grow accustomed to the rules of her commitment."

The Inca and Kusa Akchi looked over at the bride and groom as they continued to greet their wedding guests individually. Vira was kissing Sapaca's cheek.

Under his breath, the Inca muttered one last prayer, "Be happy my daughter. May God Viracocha bless your marriage with peace . . . and may He bless my Kingdom with the same."

CHAPTER 6

Long before the wedding feast had ended, Vira and her cousin, Cusi, a girl of short stature with vivacious dark eyes and a sweet smile, led Sapaca into a bedroom specially prepared for her wedding night. They chatted excitedly about the wedding as they struggled to remove Sapaca's wedding gown and accessories. Together, they helped Sapaca into a diaphanous, nearly transparent, nightgown that was beautifully dyed with geometric patterns representing fantastic birds. The nightgown reached the soft carpet on the floor; however, it left her arms completely bare. It was exquisite.

"Of course you're crying again, Vira. What on earth is wrong now?" huffed Sapaca.

"Aren't you scared?" Vira asked as she wiped her eyes. "Aren't you nervous? What if it hurts?"

"Don't be silly, he's my husband now. I belong to him. It doesn't matter if it hurts or not. Anyway, I heard it only hurts a little the first time. I'll be fine. Quit crying."

"Sapaca's right, Vira, quit crying" echoed Cusi.

"Well, at least make Coca promise to have no other lovers but you, Sapaca. Don't let him marry hundreds of others and have babies all over the place!"

"You really *are* crazy," gasped Sapaca as she slowly shook her head in disbelief. "I should forbid my husband from taking more wives and keeping concubines? I cannot do that even if I *wanted* to. Vira, what are you thinking? You and this idea of love (Sapaca drew out the word like it was something delicious to eat) you've gone way over the mountain with it. Anyway, who wants to stay pregnant all the time? Maybe his other women will keep him busy and give me some time to myself!"

"Well then you just can't possibly be in love with him," pouted Vira.

Sapaca lifted her face to look blankly at Vira. "It's not about love. It's about my father and *his* father. It's about being an Inca Princess." There was no suffering or abhorrence in her voice or on her face. Sapaca was quietly resigned.

Pani finished brushing Sapaca's long black hair. She left it down to fall freely below her shoulders. Sapaca was ready. One by one, Pani, Vira, and Cusi placed loving and respectful kisses on Sapaca's forehead and cheeks. Together they showered her with praises and encouragement. Pani led the way to the door and Cusi grabbed Vira's hand to gently drag her from the room.

CHAPTER 7

When Vira awoke late the next morning, Haicapata Square was already filled with revelers to celebrate the annual *Situa* Festival. The holy *Amautas* had been busy all night setting up the holy idols from the temples along the path that led to the palace gates. A royal throne hewn from granite was located at the end of the path at the top of a hill. It was also decorated with golden, silver, and ceramic idols. From Quito, Atahualpa's home, to Chilé, people who belonged to the Inca Empire came to celebrate in their most festive attire.

No king had busier tailors than an *Inca* king. Only Huascar's specially chosen women, called *mamaconas*, were allowed to make his clothes. He never wore the same tunic or mantle twice and his clothes could not be washed. When he disrobed to bathe, which he did often, his beautiful clothes were ceremonially burned. Each costume he wore was new and made just for him.

Next to the royal granite throne, on low wooden stools, sat the forefathers. This was the special area dedicated to the Inca Kings who had died. Their dry and shriveled mummies were brought from their estates located all around the sacred valley near Cuzco. Yahuar Huaccac was brought on a litter by his entourage from Qhapaqkancha. Pachacuti Inca Yupanqui was carried from his estate in Ollantaytambo. The mummy of Huascar's father, Huayna Capac, dark and sinister, traveled south from Quispiguanca with the *Hatun ayllu* family.

There were eleven mummies present for the festival all seated on low stools and dressed in their best Inca clothing. Each one wore the large golden ear plugs and the kingly fringe across their forehead that identified them as an Inca King. As they sat on their low wooden stools, women gently fanned away the flies with beautiful feathered fans. Indian servants served them *chicha* in ceremonial bowls. Beside each mummy stood an Oracle, a person who knew the deceased ancestor's thoughts and could answer questions for him. For the Inca people, these ancestors still lived.

It was noon. The sun's rays radiated from the golden roof of the Temple of the Sun. Atahualpa had still not arrived. The gigantic wooden gate to Huascar's palace opened and Inca Huascar appeared in his new ceremonial cloak and scarlet headband, sitting atop his golden litter. In his right hand he carried his *champi*. When the litter reached the throne, Huascar, Son of the Sun, a god himself, took his royal position on the granite throne. His courtiers sat around him on low seats.

Behind the nobles amassed an endless crowd of humble and devoted subjects, the Indians. They wore colorful checked cloaks and had bare feet. Most of the Indians were farmers who had only two options in life: They could pay homage to the Inca King through labor or by providing vast amounts of gold and silver. Most of the natives were; therefore, forced to provide around three months of labor for the Inca every year. Their homes were simple and small, made of stone with thatched roofs. But none of them were homeless. They toiled relentlessly to raise crops from the dry soil and gave most of their harvest to the Inca King's administrators, but no one went hungry.

Crimes were punishable by death (or punished so severely that the punishment would end in death anyway). So there were no jails and nearly no crime. Who wanted to have their hands or feet cut off? Who wanted to have their eyes gouged out? At least the Indians knew that the Inca was fair. If a noble or courtier transgressed his rules, the punishment would be the same. It was a very civilized crowd of revelers.

As the choir accompanied by *tam-tams*, bells, and flutes completed the bars of their hymn, with *Amauta* Kusa Akchi standing reverently beside the granite throne, Inca Huascar began his dedication speech to the crowd. "By the grace of our god Viracocha and magnanimity of Inti the Sun god, we assemble ourselves once again to request the assistance of all the gods to banish all plagues, earthquakes, landslides, avalanches, floods, droughts, and all other misfortunes that may befall us. I invite you all to this *Situa* Festival and . . ."

Before Huascar could complete his opening speech, there was murmuring in the crowd. The crowd split to allow passage of an impressive entourage. The man who dared this disrespect, punishable by death, was

Atahualpa. The nobles immediately made way for him to pass, their expressions shifting between fear and resentment.

Atahualpa was even more fabulous than Huascar. His golden litter was decorated with golden idols and beautiful feathers from condors and parrots. His litter carriers were taller and more muscular than Huascar's carriers. As their eyes met and locked, the difference between the two brothers was obvious. Atahualpa was a soldier. He was lean and strong, proud and solemn. He wore a savage and determined expression as his litter halted before the granite throne. Huascar rose to greet his brother. They leaned toward each other to kiss.

As Huascar touched his lips to Atahualpa's cheek, Atahualpa whispered in his ear, "You should not have attacked me in Quito. As Pachacuti did to the *Chancas*, I will turn your world upside down! You will lose again, my brother." His lips never touched his brother's face.

A gilded armchair was presented to Atahualpa by one of the nobles. Atahualpa climbed down from his litter and sat in the chair. As his entourage found a position behind him, he motioned to Huascar to let the festival resume. He had made his entrance. Knowing the fun had only just begun, he was more than pleased with the looks of dread upon the faces of the nobles.

The celebration continued. *Amauta* Kusa Akchi led the musicians and priests in songs and prayers, dances and games. Huascar motioned for his special military forces to present their show of force. They marched in colorful procession and situated themselves in columns surrounding the square: One hundred faced north, one hundred south and one hundred also faced east and west. After the troops of Inca Huascar had settled in their formations, additional warriors were observed filling in the gaps: Warriors clad in full battle armor.

Huascar leaned toward Kusa Akchi and stated nervously "It appears as though Atahualpa has brought General Chalcuchima and his army. Priest, you better pray to Viracocha now that this is merely an unusually large escort."

As though nothing unusual had occurred, the gates of the Temple of the Sun opened to reveal many white-robed *Amautas*. Huascar and Atahualpa walked together, followed by their chief officers, to preside over the holy *Amautas* as they offered ceremonial sacrifices to the Sun God.

The four regiments of Huascar's special military forces marched in precise formation behind Prince Manco who led them toward the Sacred

River, the Apurimac, for the annual ritual purification. As they marched along the broad road paved with huge stones, people who were too feeble or ill to attend the festival shouted out encouragement and blessings to them from their doorways.

"The moment of purification has arrived!" shouted Manco to the troops. "Let the waves of the river wash away every impurity so we may better serve our King!"

As Huascar's special militia bathed naked and unarmed in the river, Atahualpa's army conquered Cuzco.

Amauta Kusa Akchi, suspicious from the moment of Atahualpa's rude arrival at the festival, had prepared a message for Prince Manco. When Atahualpa's warriors became aggressive, he sent the messenger to find Manco at the river. As Manco was being dressed by servants, the messenger approached. He bowed deeply and touched the hem of Manco's cloak to his lips with trembling hands.

"What is it? What do you want?" ordered Manco.

"I have an urgent message for you from *Amauta* Kusa Akchi, my Lord" gasped the messenger. "You must run to the mountains. Cuzco has fallen to Atahualpa and his 10,000 warriors. It is no use to fight. Huascar has been taken prisoner. You are to hurry away from the city with the troops! It is your duty to your people to save yourself, Prince Manco. *Amauta* Kusa Akchi said you have no choice. Go swiftly!"

Water dripped from Manco's wet hair in streaks down his face. His eyebrows knit together and the hairs on the back of his neck stood on end. As the horrid news disclosed by the messenger began to sink into Manco's heart, his muscles became as taut as the string on a drawn bow.

"I run from no one. I am an Inca Prince, heir to the throne. I was taught to fear nothing. Run? Impossible!" he stated with finality.

Manco clenched his teeth. Slowly he raised the *champi* in his right hand to gain the attention of his troops. Hundreds of dizzying thoughts crowded his brain: What about Sapaca and Vira? Was Huascar hurt? Was Coca a conspirator with Atahualpa? His mind raced, but he would not. He was determined not to quicken his steps to spare his own life. In a slow and dignified gait, he marched his troops solemnly away from Cuzco.

CHAPTER 8

M anco led his troops high up into the mountains. Night had fallen long before and the scouts he had sent out reported back to him with word that Atahualpa's warriors were not pursuing them. In fact, Atahualpa's soldiers were still in Cuzco. The scouts also told Manco that two litters were approaching. As the troops rested and waited, Manco waited and watched for the two litters. He was told that in one litter rode Prince Coca, Sapaca, Vira, and Pani and, in the other litter, much smaller than the first, rode *Amauta* Kusa Akchi and Cura Ocllo.

By the time the two litters caught up with the troops, it was midnight. Manco was delighted that Vira and Sapaca were safe. "Manco," yelled Vira, as she leapt out of the litter nearly tackling him to the ground in joy. Tears streamed down her lovely face as she kissed him again and again.

"Hello, Vira, my sweet sister. Thank Viracocha you are unharmed," said Manco between kisses.

Sapaca poked her head out from between the litter curtains. "Sapaca, what a lovely wife you make. Hello to you too!" he greeted his favorite niece.

And then Prince Coca, Atahualpa's son, Sapaca's new husband, appeared from behind the curtain. Manco wasn't sure how to respond to his presence. He stood there staring at his nephew.

"Manco, I'm glad to see you. Please, there's room in the litter for you to ride with us," offered Coca. Coca leaned forward to place a kiss on Manco's cheeks but Manco backed away. "Please don't blame me. Please don't be angry. I had no idea that this would happen. Thank Viracocha for your tutor, *Amauta* Kusa Akchi. It is as though he knew about the attack in advance. It was he who arranged our safe escape. I'm forever grateful to him."

Manco's expression softened. He was so tired. What was supposed to have been a day to drink, feast, dance, and celebrate, had turned into a horrific disaster.

The second litter was carried by only four Indians. The carriers stopped and set up the steps for *Amauta* Kusa Akchi to descend. "Manco, my dear, there is little time," he uttered in haste, "you must go with Coca to his estate near Quito. You must stay there in hiding until I send for you."

Manco's attention was distracted by a rustle when the litter curtains parted on the small litter and a dark little face peered out curiously into the darkness.

"Is that Cura Ocllo?" asked Manco.

"Yes, it is Cura Ocllo. Atahualpa's warriors attacked before our retinue could depart into the mountains to sacrifice her to Inti. She's a Sun Virgin; I didn't know what else to do. I couldn't leave her in Cuzco. Atahualpa's forces will leave no survivors from your side of the family."

Manco stared as Cura Ocllo, who had been treated with special reverence in preparation for her great sacrifice, smiled at him. Manco felt an odd sensation in his chest. It was strange for him, for he was well accustomed to beautiful women. But there was something different about Cura Ocllo. Perhaps it was simply that he could not have her. Only an Inca King is allowed to touch a Sun Virgin. Perhaps it was that he knew Sun Virgins were specially prepared from early childhood to please Inti sexually. It seemed impossible for him to avert his gaze from her.

Kusa Akchi immediately noticed the Prince's interest in Cura Ocllo. He walked to the litter and gently pushed her head back behind the curtains and closed them with an abrupt motion of his arms before he walked back over to speak with Manco.

"I will take Cura Ocllo to Lake Titicaca. I hope to find a safe place there for her until the next *Situa* Festival. If we are pursued, I will take her to the coast. You must go with Coca. Take your troops with you and may Viracocha watch your every step. May the footing of your bearers be secure upon each mountain precipice." Kusa Akchi said goodbye in his usual stilted way, unable to say he loved him but equally unable to hide it.

Kusa Akchi turned away and strode sadly to the small litter. Manco watched as the litter slowly turned to carry Kusa Akchi and Cura Ocllo south toward Lake Titicaca.

"Come on, Manco," called Vira. She extended her hand to him and accompanied him to the large litter. Manco followed Sapaca, Vira, and

Coca and watched them ascend the steps to join Pani in the enormous palanquin.

"I can't," muttered Manco. "I can't go with you. I'll go to the mountain forests. I need time to think." Manco looked lovingly at Vira. "*Qamña allinlla*," he said as he smiled weakly, "and now you be good."

"Go!" he yelled to the litter bearers. In horror, Vira watched Manco through the curtains as the carriers, whose lungs were somehow able to breathe the rarified air of the high mountains, started the long journey to Coca's estate. Her tears continued to fall long after Manco was well out of sight.

Manco couldn't believe he was really leaving Cuzco. The shame he felt for leaving Huascar a prisoner gnawed at him. He was trained to fear nothing. But he was also trained that his life was not his own, to end as he may choose. He would wait and watch. He would be ready at the next opportunity to avenge his brother. Aside from the thought of Cura Ocllo's smile, this promise he made to himself was his only comfort.

CHAPTER 9

For many long weeks, the three Spanish ships rocked upon the Pacific Ocean along the western coast of South America. The Governor, Francisco Pizarro, informed the crew more than once that they were near the town on the Peruvian coast where he had landed three years before to discover a country of great wealth. He told them fabulous stories about the land which possessed vast gold and silver treasure, enough to fill the gaping privy purse of His Majesty, King Charles of Spain, with plenty left over to fill the pockets of each ex-prisoner, outcast, and criminal who had gained absolution by joining his expedition.

There was still no sight of land, not one floating branch upon the water and no seagulls. There was only the hint of transparent clouds overhead, like a thin fog, and through this white veil, the rays of the sun scorched the galleys with a burning heat. The Spaniards didn't know that the country they were seeking was called the Empire of the Sun. What they did know was that the sun was so bright and so persistent, that it had nearly faded the red crosses, the symbol of their God, from the ships' white sails.

The lead vessel was a light, broad-beamed ship with a double tower at the stern and a single one in the bow. It was like a wine cask sawn in halves lengthwise and raised up at both ends. The deck was almost empty on this particular day at noon. Most of the half-naked crew had withdrawn into the cabins which, although they offered little comfort, did, at least provide shelter from the sun's burning rays. The men peered out desperately and anxiously toward the east.

"We'll never find Tumbez," growled a bearded soldier named Lopez. He sat on the deck chewing a slice of stale, dry bread. A red scarf was tied around his forehead to protect him from the brutal sun. His face was lean and haggard; his malicious eyes squinted into the glare. Fleshy lips curved into a grimace as he continued, "*Banta Maria*, how he boasted of high mountains called *Andes* and golden palaces filled with treasure! Snails and tortoise shells is all we get! Sickness, sweat and hunger are all we have! I'm dying of thirst while surrounded by water, nothing but water!" He spat furiously onto the wooden deck planks as though the words tasted rancid in his mouth. His audience, crouched around him, nodded in resentful agreement. In Madrid, Lopez had been arrested for thieving and pillaging. He was pardoned when he agreed to join this expedition. During the long journey he had become a leader and had earned the respect of most of the crew.

"Cut it" warned one of the sailors in a whisper, "Vega's coming."

Lopez glanced from under his half-closed eyelids at the tall, young officer walking toward the ship's bow. He shrugged his shoulders and muttered under his breath "Don Alvarez de la Vega, now there's a real caballero, a real gentleman. Well, what do we care for Officers? We risk our necks the same as they do. Don't we all want the gold? Don't we all want some heathen Indians to sell in Spain?"

Nevertheless, when the young Spanish hidalgo passed in front of them, they all fell silent. For, although they did not fear him, they respected him.

Don Alvarez de la Vega was a strikingly attractive young man, about 23 years old with black hair that had grown out to cover his temples in soft waves. His features were regular and strongly masculine, his eyes dark and brilliant in his sun-tanned face. In spite of the heat, he was in full uniform, black and close-fitting with long trunk-hose that emphasized the perfection of his slim build. In accordance with the avowed aim of the expedition, there was a scarlet cross embroidered on the left side of his jacket just above his heart.

When he reached the bow, he grabbed hold of the heavy rope and gazed for a long while over the endless waves of the ocean. As if he had been waiting for an answer that didn't come, he sighed dejectedly and continued his way toward the cabin of Governor Francisco Pizarro. Don Alvarez made a fist and knocked lightly four times.

"*Adelante*," he heard through the wooden door.

He opened the door to see the Governor sitting on a wooden bench, cushioned with blankets, wiping the sweat from his bare chest and forehead with an old handkerchief.

Francisco Pizarro, Governor and Captain-General of Peru and Commander of this expedition, was an illiterate, goat herder born in

Extremadura, Spain. He spent the past 30 years fighting Indians and living in Panama where he had become a wealthy landowner. As the bastard son of a Spanish nobleman who abandoned him at birth, military conquest provided his only window of opportunity to climb the ladder of success. He was a man with no heritage and no family influence, but he had a royal license granting him the right to conquer Peru.

He was a tall and sinewy man already past his prime at 54 years of age. He had a long, narrow face with hollow cheeks. His nose was big and crooked like an eagle beak, under which his thin, brown beard was trimmed short on the sides and honed to a pointed goatee. His large eyes were set under high, wide brows and revealed little emotion except for a ruthless ambition that was hard and inflexible. He was an adventurer and had already trampled over the lives of innumerable victims to reach his goals.

At the moment, Pizarro was discussing issues with the Priest, Father Sebastiano, who sat opposite him at the small writing table, scribbling notes on paper with his fat fingers. Father Sebastiano had come under orders of the Church to stand officially at Pizarro's side to represent the interests of the clergy. He had no interest in treasures of gold and silver. He hungered only for souls to convert to Christianity.

His face was round and his head was bald but Father Sebastiano's tiny twinkling eyes were clear and suspicious. He was ready and eager to perform his task thoroughly and he kept a watchful eye on Pizarro. He had no reason to doubt a soul so deeply devoted, a soul who never missed a chance to celebrate the Mass. It is just that he knew Pizarro was under enormous stress as Commander. Father Sebastiano would make sure that the Governor would not forget to perform his duties toward the Church.

Don Alvarez entered the cabin, sweat dripping from his brow and temples. Pizarro halted his conversation with the Father and frowned at the uninvited visitor. The Father nodded in greeting, exhaled loudly, and pushed his chair away from Pizarro's desk. It was obvious that he did not welcome his presence.

"*Bueno*, Don Alvarez," said Pizarro. He gave a bored wave of his hand to indicate where Don Alvarez was to sit. "Well, I can tell by your woeful countenance that you haven't spotted land."

"I'm sorry, Señor," apologized Don Alvarez. "I require orders." Don Alvarez stood up to deliver his status report. "The death toll has now reached 50 souls. Our number is down to 168 fighting men. There's no sign of land. The crew doubts that Tumbez exists."

"Show respect to your Commander, young man," yelled Father Sebastiano. "Remember to whom you're speaking! Do you dare to doubt the word of your Governor? He risked his life for this expedition, a life, I may add, worth more than the combined lives of all the bastards on this boat!"

Don Alvarez gasped at the Priest's outburst and Pizarro scowled angrily. Alvarez didn't understand why the Priest, who held a position of great authority on the ship, disliked him. He was just doing his job. But like him or not, Don Alvarez was competent, and Pizarro knew it.

"I assure you, Don Alvarez," interceded Pizarro in his rasping voice, "if I say that I anchored a ship in Tumbez three years ago, then it's true. It's lucky for you that I had to return to Spain to meet with the King because now you're with me for my victorious return. *Por Dios*, I tell you we're close. And this time I have the men and the weapons to take what I want! Stick close to me, Don Alvarez and you'll get your share. And don't worry, Father, you'll have lots of savages to convert!"

Pizarro lifted the tension with a crooked smile at the Father. "*Santa Maria*, Father, didn't I just say that any time now we'll be gazing upon the Promised Land!?"

Don Alvarez struggled hard not to show his contempt. He was in charge of the crew and the crew was suffering. Again, he was just doing his job. He continued to stand. "We're almost out of water and the men, especially the sick, clamor for more water," reported Don Alvarez.

"*Water*?! It's terrible to drink in this heat! The more they drink, the more they'll sweat! Tell them to pray! Tell them to be strong and not to give in to the weakness of their flesh" ordered Pizarro.

"Sir," reported Don Alvarez, they need food and water."

"*Sir*," mimicked Father Sebastiano insolently, "what the spoiled heathen criminals on this ship need is *discipline*."

"Watch it, Father." Pizarro looked directly at Father Sebastiano as he restrained his agitation. "We are fortunate to have this crew. I know you don't approve and think of the men as brigands and bastards. I know you wanted friars and missionaries to assist you on your *Quest*. Just remember, this is *my* expedition and we are about *my* business. It's only because of me and my brothers that you have a chance now to be about *our Father's* business."

The Father was silenced. He bit his tongue, angry at himself for forgetting again to exclude Pizarro's half-brothers from his criticisms of the crew in general. But he couldn't help the way he felt about Don Alvarez. A man of noble birth who could forget his upbringing and sink to the depths of sinning against God was especially repugnant and would *NEVER* gain his respect. He shouldn't have been spared judgment and released just because he was willing to accompany Pizarro on this expedition. The priest would *never* accept Don Alvarez's authority.

Pizarro cleared his throat. "Finish your report, Don Alvarez."

"Some of the black and Indian slaves have collapsed from hunger, Señor" he stated gravely.

"Throw them overboard" said Pizarro.

"It's Felipillo and Martinillo, the two you brought back on your last voyage to Peru. They're the ones I've been teaching Spanish and they're the only ones familiar with the land we're searching for. They're very weak, Señor."

"Then give those two extra rations, I might need them soon . . . Throw the others overboard!"

Just then there was a knock and Father Pedro peeked in as the door creaked open.

"Am I disturbing you, Governor?" asked Father Pedro. Father Pedro had impeccable timing for entering every scene at just the worst moment. He was a friar, a shy and modest servant of God. It's all he wanted. He didn't want gold or promotion. He just wanted to love God and to serve Him and his children kindly and gently.

Father Pedro was only about 40 years old but his face was already lined with wrinkles caused by sorrow and worry. His dark eyes were wells of kindness and understanding. His purity had a wonderful affect upon everyone with whom he came into contact. No one lied to him. Tensions and troubles would dissipate upon his arrival. Although he was small and weak, he was the first man to volunteer for dangerous tasks.

Father Pedro looked upon each of the three men in the Governor's cabin. He felt compassion for each man knowing that each was daily confronted with the terror of failure. He watched silently as Don Alvarez slowly sat down in a chair.

"Come in, Father Pedro," welcomed Pizarro. "Please, sit down." Pizarro arose and placed a wooden chair beside Father Pedro.

Father Sebastiano and Don Alvarez greeted Father Pedro with nods as he took his seat in the chair with a pleasant smile on his face.

"Well, go ahead, don't mind me. I'm only here to visit" said Father Pedro as he encouraged them to continue their conversation.

There was an awkward silence.

Don Alvarez cleared his throat again and turned to Father Pedro. "I was asking the Governor for orders regarding some of the black and Indian slaves. I reported that many have collapsed from hunger and are very ill. Although they are not quite dead, the Governor has ordered me to throw them overboard." Don Alvarez kept his eyes on Father Pedro but he could feel the glares of Pizarro and Father Sebastiano trying to kill his soul.

Father Pedro shifted in his chair and straightened his back. "Doesn't King Charles require that cooperative Indians be treated like our own soldiers? Wouldn't it be appropriate for Don Alvarez to confine the slaves and provide food and water as needed?" asked Father Pedro. It was, of course, a rhetorical question. Father Pedro was a student of diplomacy and knew how to speak to men in ways they could understand. Don Alvarez suppressed a smile.

"If we treat cooperative Indians as our own soldiers, Father Pedro, then what right did Don Alvarez and his men have to brutalize the women of Púna? Those Indians were cooperative to say the least. Are cooperative Indian *women* not to be treated as soldiers? Does the King allow orgies and rape as part of conquest celebrations?" asked Father Sebastiano sardonically. He snorted air out of his nose as he shook his head in disgust.

Don Alvarez's hand made a slight move toward the hilt of his sword and then quickly relaxed. He could not raise his hand to a priest. He rose again to his feet. "I'm a Knight, Father!" he exclaimed with indignation. "I cannot endure such insults against my honor! Not even from a servant of God."

"Oh, such honor of a *Knight*! Yet you fornicate and rape? You are no *Knight* and no *Christian* for that matter!" yelled Father Sebastiano.

"Gentlemen, please," soothed Father Pedro, "my friends, please, calm yourselves. We must not quarrel now, not when we're so close to our destination. It is hard to stop a quarrel once it starts!"

Don Alvarez, barely mastering his indignation at the whirl of accusations that chafed his anxiety, bowed stiffly and turned to leave the cabin.

"You're not at court anymore, Don Alvarez," Pizarro said to his back. "You're in military service. You're on *my* ship. Remember that."

Don Alvarez walked out and shut the door behind him. "I don't know why you pick on him," Father Pedro said to Father Sebastiano. "He's only as guilty as every other sailor on this ship. So he used to be *somebody*. So he has gotten into trouble. Did we not publicly declare absolution for every man that joined this expedition?"

"It's the hypocrisy," sneered Father Sebastiano. He thinks he's superior. He sinned against God and was found guilty. Yet he acts so high and mighty."

"Haven't we all sinned against God? Anyway, don't worry. If it is his punishment you desire, I believe he punishes himself far worse than you would be allowed. I have seen his face at times when he thinks he is alone. He grieves deeply, I can see it in his eyes" sighed Father Pedro.

"What sort of penitent knight in shining armor rapes helpless females and partakes in orgies?" raved Father Sebastiano.

"*Do not judge lest you be judged yourself,*" warned Father Pedro. He looked at Pizarro who remained quiet, glad that he didn't have to compromise his orders. "As I already stated, the entire crew was complicit in that outrage. Who among us, except for us Priests, would dare to boast of having come only to serve the purposes of God?"

"I am here to conquer the souls of a conquered land, not just to search for riches," claimed Pizarro in his own defense.

"All right, Governor. You are correct. The difference is this: I have come to accomplish this mission armed only with love, not with spears and guns."

Pizarro, tired of so much blather and philosophical debate of right and wrong, spoke with finality, "We have troubles more important than that silly Don Alvarez with his worthless scruples. Whatever he did or didn't do is none of my concern. I could care less what is done with a bunch of dying Indians. Get out, all of you; I have work to do."

As Pizarro turned back to his writing table and leaned over a tattered map covered with zigzag lines, Father Sebastiano and Father Pedro quietly walked out of the Governor's cabin and closed the door.

CHAPTER 10

E vening descended over the great waters and covered them with twilight. The ships, loitering as they were, bobbed around in hope of finding Tumbez. In the dark, bluish-black sky, from which the veil of clouds slowly cleared, appeared stars: Not the Bears Great and Little, not the familiar 'W' of Cassiopeia, or Sirius, not even Polaris. These were unknown constellations scattered about. The moon shone with a light strangely different from that which silvered the towers of faraway Spain.

"We have come to another world" murmured one of the soldiers as he lay upon the deck surrounded by a group of his companions. They were enjoying the light night-breeze. "It's a world of fairy-tales."

"*Por Dios!*" grumbled Lopez. "To me it seems rather that we're lost and can't even find the gates of Hell!"

In the open doorway of a small ship's cabin sat Don Alvarez with his legs just over the door sill. He was completely absorbed in his own thoughts, which must have been bitter ones, for he wore a severe frown upon his face. He almost looked old as he stared up into the unfamiliar sky.

Disturbed by the sound of approaching footsteps, Don Alvarez turned to see Father Pedro approaching. He made a move to stand out of respect to the priest, but the Father motioned him gently to remain seated. Don Alvarez scooted over on the wooden bench and Father Pedro sat beside him.

"You are far away again, Don Alvarez," he remarked gently. "What is it that grieves you so deeply and torments your heart?"

His reflexive response was aggravation at the nosy priest. But then Don Alvarez inhaled deeply from the evening breeze and exhaled in a loud sigh. "When I joined this expedition" he answered sullenly, "I was given absolution for my sins."

"That is true," agreed the priest with an encouraging smile. "I'm not here to reprove you. I'm only here to see if I can offer you the rite of confession. I can see that you suffer and I hope merely to ease your burdens."

Father Pedro's voice was soft and felt like balm upon the troubled soul of the young officer. Don Alvarez was overcome by a desire to talk.

"I know I must carry my cross, Father, just like everyone else," he began. "But, well, I hoped my cross would not feel so heavy if I sailed forth to new lands to save lost souls for God. Now, as I see that I am expected instead to impose war and cruelty on unsuspecting barbarians, well, I'm afraid that my cross has become too heavy to bear."

"I understand," soothed Father Pedro, not wanting to stop Don Alvarez from talking but wanting to show him that he had his full attention. "So you see yourself as more of a missionary than a soldier?"

"Yes," he answered. "And I don't like the fact that before I can help the pagans to *see the Light*, I will have to conquer their savage tyrants and brutally murder many of their brothers and fathers. What kind of *Deliverer* can I be when I have blood spattered all over my hands and face?" As tears blurred Don Alvarez's eyes, he searched in the eyes of Father Pedro for an answer.

"You care so deeply, Don Alvarez . . ."

"I do," he interrupted for emphasis.

"Then may I ask you a question?"

"Yes."

"How were you able to rape those native women in Púna? Do you have an alter ego? How do wanton depravity and sexual perversion fit into the construct of a noble knight on a quest to win souls for God? I don't understand."

There was silence. The ship heaved and pitched. The two men sat side by side and stared out at the new stars. Father Pedro feared that he had pushed too hard. He started to get up to leave, but Don Alvarez grabbed his arm and pulled him back down to the bench. "I think, Father, that you'll have to take my confession after all."

Father Pedro smiled into the sad eyes of Don Alvarez as he began, "Forgive me Father, for I have sinned . . ."

"I swear to you, Father, and to God above, that I have never purposely injured any man except in battle. But in regard to women . . . to injure a woman, well, I don't consider that a crime anymore."

Father Pedro repressed a gasp. "Are not women weak and defenseless creatures? Is not a knight committed to the laws of chivalry? What do you mean?"

Don Alvarez rubbed his forehead nervously wondering if a holy man could ever understand what had happened to him. "Women are mean and abominable beings who use men for their gain and abuse children for their sport!"

Don Alvarez rose suddenly. He was close to losing his composure. He rubbed his hands together and breathed fast. In his own defense he offered the argument, "What can you know of the vileness of *women*, Father?"

"Tell me what happened, Don Alvarez. There is time, try to relax."

"All right," he continued. He was impressed that Father Pedro had not walked away. He knew his words were hard. But the priest had sat tight. He even seemed calm and sincere. He would go on. Don Alvarez sat down again beside the priest.

"I was from a good family . . ."

"Was?" asked Father Pedro.

"My mother died when I was five."

"I see . . . go on."

"I was raised by a stepmother. I was nothing more to her than a pebble in her shoe. I was a constant aggravation to her and she loathed me just for living." At having spoken these words, Don Alvarez's eyes once again blurred with tears. "Well, anyway" he continued sniffing and wiping at his eyes with his shirt sleeves like a little boy, "she's dead now too. Died birthing a baby that wasn't my father's! My father never found out, of course. The baby died too." Don Alvarez breathed deeply to control his emotions.

"You must have been terribly lonely growing up without your mother" stated the Father.

"She's the only good woman I ever met" answered Don Alvarez. He shook his head as if to shake away memories.

"My father was a Marquis and Counselor to the King and, because of his influence; I became Knight of the Queen and held a position at court. After my father died, I felt truly alone. And that is when I met her: She who ruined me and causes this torment you see on my face."

Don Alvarez's eyes darkened. Twilight had passed and the night was setting in. The waxing moon was nearly full and cast its glow upon Don Alvarez's handsome and tortured features.

"Go on" said the Father.

"Her name . . ." Alvarez paused as if he wasn't sure he'd actually be able to say the name out loud. "Her name was Doña Elvira." He gasped at having really said it. Again, he breathed deeply from the night air and exhaled slowly, his lips pursed. "Doña Elvira, she was the Queen's Maid-of-Honor." He spoke muskily and his hands trembled. "I loved her, I loved her so much. She was so beautiful." His throat tightened and he couldn't finish the words. He looked at Father Pedro with a pitiful yet angry expression. After a moment he continued.

"She meant the world to me. I thought she loved me. One night we met in the park. She kissed me with her red lips and held me tightly. She unlaced the bodice of her gown so I could kiss her breasts." Don Alvarez blushed and so did Father Pedro. "Anyway, I couldn't resist my desire, I had to have her. I had her right there in the grass with nothing but the darkness to hide us."

It was all Father Pedro could do to sit still and not shake his head in disappointment. This was not the behavior he expected from a knight. But he wanted to hear the rest of the story. So he remained silent and kept his opinions private. "Did you ask her to marry you?" he asked hopefully.

"No, I never got the chance. I barely saw her. And when I did see her, we were never alone. Then, a week later, I was able to meet her again in the park. She asked me to challenge her step-brother to a duel. She told me he was enormously rich and that she would inherit all his wealth. She even had a plan. She would invite us both to a party and mix a sedative into his drink. With his senses muddled and his strength diminished by the drugs, I would be able to defeat him easily."

Father Pedro's forehead knitted into deep creases. Don Alvarez stopped talking.

"Did you challenge her proposal?"

"Of course I did, but she considered my argument an insult. I knew I couldn't do her bidding. I certainly knew I wouldn't marry her. So I left. I told the Queen I was ill and I left Court so I wouldn't see her. I went home to my country estate. But Elvira wasn't finished with me. She felt as though she had paid her part to seal the deal between us. I knew her plan now and could witness against her. So she hired men to attack me on my own property. I killed three of them, but the others got away after wounding me. I was stabbed through my right shoulder. It still hurts, especially when I fight." Don Alvarez stretched out his right arm and flexed his fingers with a grimace.

"As I recovered in my bed, a friend came to me to report that Doña Elvira had denounced me to the Queen (who was her cousin and best friend) for "*having slain her valuable servants who had gone to deliver me a kind message.*" The law was dispatched right away and the dead men were found at my estate for I hadn't yet instructed my servants on what to do with the corpses. It all happened so fast."

"I didn't know what to do. It was as though something in my head snapped. I was furious. There was nothing for me in Madrid anyway, nothing but bad memories. So I left. I headed to Seville and that's how I ended up on this filthy tub full of angry, greedy, heartless men."

That was it. The confession was over. Father Pedro had nothing unique or inspired to offer or tell Don Alvarez except for the obvious.

"You must put the past behind you. Have you repented?"

"Repented? What for? I didn't do anything wrong! I should have killed *her!*" Don Alvarez pulled on his shirt collar. He stood up and then sat down again.

"Well then you'll just have to forgive *her*. And then you'll have to forgive your step-mother and your mother as well. You'll just have to forgive them all for the harm . . ."

"My mother was a *Saint!*" interrupted Don Alvarez angrily. "What do I have to forgive *her* for? She was good and pure and she loved me. She . . ."

"She died and left you here all alone when you were just a little boy, Alvarez" interrupted the Father. "She left you. And after she left, your step-mother came and hurt you."

Father Pedro put his arm around Don Alvarez's shoulders. Don Alvarez dropped his face into his cupped hands and sobbed. "Why did she have to die? Everything would have turned out so differently had she lived." He couldn't speak anymore. He sobbed. He turned toward the Father and put his wet face on the priest's shoulder. As Father Pedro held him, his sobbing continued. After a few minutes, Don Alvarez became still and took a deep, ragged breath. He wiped his face with his hands and used a handkerchief, badly stained, to blow his nose.

"But I *hate* them, Father" he slurred in an exhausted voice. I *hate* my step-mother for what she did to Father and me. I *hate* Elvira for making me love her, for offering such beauty to me, and then using me as a pawn in her game. No woman is innocent, Father." Don Alvarez's anger was returning. "When I did what I did in Púna, it felt *good*. I saw the face of Doña Elvira on those women and I gave them what they deserved. It is my only revenge."

"*Vengeance is Mine sayeth the Lord*, Don Alvarez" admonished the Father. "The Lord is your avenger. What *you* must do is *forgive*. You have judged all women by the behavior of two evil ones in your life. Do you not remember our Virgin Mary? Do you not recall what you learned about our saintly women in Heaven? There are many beautiful and good women in this world, Don Alvarez."

Father Pedro paused in thought. "You can make a new beginning, Don Alvarez. You are a Knight, an Aristocrat, and a polished *Gentleman*. You are a *Christian*! Start anew, right now! From here on out, live your life so that it will be pleasing unto God."

"My distaste for women will not be easily shed, Father. A woman hurt me when I was just a child. A woman made a fool of me. A woman took away all that I ever had. A woman broke my heart. I will never be the same again."

"No! You will be better than before" smiled Father Pedro. He knew what to say. "If you were injured in a battle, what would happen if you stayed in bed and never tried to walk again?"

"I suppose I would become an invalid," answered Don Alvarez.

"That's right! Even though it would hurt and ache and you would yearn to lie down again, you would still get up and walk through the pain, correct?"

"Correct, it is the only way to heal."

"You are wounded in your mind and in your heart." As Father Pedro spoke the words, he pointed to Don Alvarez's head and heart. "I know it hurts, but you must get up and walk through the pain. You must make your mind and your heart strong again. You must re-dedicate your life to *God* and let *Him* be your avenger and let *Him* restore you to a full life. *With God, all things are possible!*"

"Do you pray, Don Alvarez?" asked Father Pedro.

"I try, Father, I try . . ."

"I don't mean the prayers from your books. What I mean is do you *talk* to your Father in Heaven? You must do something soon for this hatred will destroy you. Try to pray, Alvarez. Pray in your own words—the words from your heart and mind. Then wait for your miracle. I feel that it is not too far off in the distance."

CHAPTER 11

"Mountains. Mountains! *Land!* I see ***Land!***"

Everyone on the ship heard the call to glory. The rosy hue of dawn calmly stole over the ship and a favorable breeze stirred the sails. The sick and weary sailors crept out from below deck, bleary-eyed, with incredulous smiles of hope on their faces.

"Those are not clouds," called Hernando Pizarro, "those are *mountains!*"

Hernando was a big man. The journey had taken a toll on his body and he had grown lean but his rugged features still displayed his shrewdness. He wore a pointed goatee like his older brother, Francisco. He had suffered for weeks aboard the vessel with illness and was leaned on a short walking stick for strength and balance.

A murmur of excitement began to grow among the crew. As the men gathered facing east, the murmur grew to whoops of joy. Francisco hurried onto the deck with Father Sebastiano at his heels.

"Diego! Diego, come quickly!" he yelled at the top of his lungs. Many of the men embraced each other and jumped and danced for joy with the little energy they had left.

Diego de Almagro came running. He was short and ugly and wore a black scarf around his forehead to cover the place where his eye had been.

"I knew we'd find it. I knew it was only a matter of time," he said with confidence. "Oh, the King will be pleased, yes, very pleased indeed." He laughed happily and clapped Francisco on the back in triumph.

Francisco looked at Diego and smiled. He was not only a business partner, he was his friend. They had been through so much together and Diego never let Francisco get discouraged.

Within minutes, the crew gazed upon a white line of breakers and, beyond the breakers, to their extreme relief they saw the steeples and cupolas of tall buildings.

"Land! Land!" they continued to shout with delight. For they all knew they couldn't have waited much longer. Many men fell to their knees and gave thanks to God that they had lived to see the shore.

The celebration quieted as the men continued to look at the city ahead. They had finally found Tumbez. It was even grander that Francisco had described.

"Put on your armor. Take up your weapons. Dress the horses in armor. And say your prayers." Francisco spoke the orders as he wondered about the red tint that glowed from the steeples.

"Shouldn't we approach as friends and read them the *Requirement*, my Lord?" asked Father Pedro respectfully.

"I've been here before. They know about us. We must be prepared for anything," answered Francisco.

Just loud enough for Don Alvarez to hear, Lopez muttered "Get ready to swallow our spears you red-skinned bastards!" He grasped a half-empty bottle and drained its last drop letting some of the liquid pour down his shaggy beard. "I'll not dry up like an old woman! Come try to eat *me*, you damned cannibals, I'll fill your mouths with my fists!"

The men around him roared with laughter. Lopez smiled like a hero.

"Put on your armor, Lopez," warned Don Alvarez. "And wipe your face. If a cannibal gets a bite out of you, he'll drop to the ground drunk and poisoned."

The men laughed again, but not as heartily. Awkwardly, the crew dispersed while Lopez glared at Don Alvarez. Grumbling something under his breath, he turned and went below with the others to prepare for the landing.

The excitement aboard the ship was tangible. The scraggly, emaciated men crowded together and marveled at the contours of the superb buildings that could be distinguished through the fog. Each man dreamed and boasted out loud of the booty he would take home to Spain.

Francisco Pizarro was too agitated to utter a sound. His brows were furrowed and wore a troubled expression on his face as he stared into Tumbez.

"I don't understand the fog, there shouldn't be so much fog" he murmured to Don Alvarez.

47

Don Alvarez cupped his hands over his eyes to get a better look into Tumbez. He felt an icy chill in his spine and his enthusiasm waned. "I don't think it is fog, Governor, I think it might be *smoke*."

"Smoke!" the commander called out in astonishment, louder than was wise, "Why should there be so much *smoke*?"

As the ship drew closer to Tumbez, flames could be seen bursting through the heavy cloud of smoke that covered the whole town.

"It's burning!" yelled Don Alvarez, "the whole city is on fire!"

The vessel grated against the deserted landing pier. The strongest of the men that were still able, leaped out and fastened the ship to the dock with sturdy ropes. A ramp of heavy planking was pushed out from the ship and was dropped to the pier with a loud bang. Francisco Pizarro rode down the plank on a superb, black mare. He wasn't much of a horse lover, but he wanted to make an impressive entrance.

Close behind Francisco rode his half-brothers. Although he was older and was in charge of the expedition, his brothers had something Francisco would never possess: Their father. Hernando was the eldest and, unlike Francisco, had been educated. But there was not enough polish in the world to make him shine. He was a rough and brutal conquistador who, in spite of starvation, had not lost the sharp edge of his ambition. Juan and Gonzalo were hardly more than boys. They rode on fine stallions behind their big brothers with looks of awe and fright on their faces. Behind the Pizarro brothers rode Father Sebastiano, coughing and wheezing from the smoke.

One by one, the officers and soldiers disembarked. The men and horses were mere shadows of themselves after a year aboard Pizarro's ship. Of the 160 men who departed from Seville, only 70 were still alive. No one spoke. The horses bumped each other and whinnied with excitement to be outside on solid ground. The men looked around in wonder at the splendid paved roadway, the monumental ruins of the scorched buildings, and the remnants of carved and molded stonework. There was so much stonework, that only the thatched roofs and wooden overhangs had burned.

"It's amazing, look at the size of those building blocks" exclaimed Don Alvarez. "These are not primitive dwellings, these are impressive!"

"They're not impressive to me unless they're filled with gold," snarled Lopez just loud enough for his friends to hear.

Francisco sent Juan to fetch Felipillo and Martinillo, the two Indian slaves. They came trembling with fear to have been summoned by Francisco, riding together on a mule. Don Alvarez had tended to their needs during the night and they were feeling a little stronger.

"Stay close to me," he ordered. "I may need you to interpret for me. "Juan, keep an eye on them and don't let them run away."

"*Run* away," laughed Juan, they can hardly *walk*!" Juan shot his trademark mischievous boyish grin at his big brother and promised to watch over the two sick Indians.

When all the men were lined up and ready to ride into the smoldering city of Tumbez, Francisco lifted his arm to give the marching order. Very quietly and cautiously, the men rode into Tumbez. The dark ruins looked like tombs in a cemetery. Father Pedro whispered a blessing for the souls that perished in the fire. It was almost impossible to breathe and the air stung their eyes and noses.

The small army rode through the worst of the smoke and ashes and found themselves in an open square. At the far end of the square stood a tall, elaborately carved tower with a roof of solid gold plates. This was the spire they had seen shining brightly from the ship. Because of its location near the huge open square, the structure had not burned.

"It must be a temple of some sort," mused Francisco.

He got down from his horse and strode over to the building. Hernando, leaning on his walking stick, and Father Pedro who had been riding on a mule beside Father Sebastiano, followed him on foot. Although the gates were thrown wide open, the three men hesitated at the entrance. Greedy curiosity drove the Pizarros forward past the grotesque figures of snakes and dogs carved in the stone pillars. Francisco motioned for Juan to follow with the two Indians. Don Alvarez also dismounted from his horse and followed behind. He turned to motion to the others to wait and watch for signs of trouble.

The temple hall was dark except for a dim light which flickered in a corner and faintly illuminated a beautiful golden altar on a marble platform. There was a soft sound and a white robed figure emerged from the darkness and strode forward toward the men. The two Indians fell to their knees, put their faces down on the flagstone floor, and trembled.

"Seize him!" yelled Francisco, wondering what was wrong with his Indians. Hernando and Don Alvarez hesitated, not sure how to seize the tall and obviously unarmed figure. In the white robe, it seemed more like a ghost than a man. Just as they grabbed him, the sound of a shrill, feminine scream pierced their ears and another white-robed figure, this one much smaller, burst out of the darkness and grabbed the larger figure, clinging to him. The men were shocked and frightened by the outburst and let go and backed away quickly. It was hard to tell which white-robed figure was protecting which.

As their eyes adjusted to the darkness, it became evident that the tall figure was an elderly man and the smaller figure, although heavily veiled, was a woman. Hernando reached over and pulled the veil from her face. As her hands flew up to cover her horrified expression, the men could see that she was young and beautiful.

"Don't touch her," yelled the man as she tried to hide in his chest. He put his arms around her protectively. "*White Strangers*, I knew you would return. Please, we are not armed."

"What did he say," yelled Francisco at the two crouching Indians.

Both of the Indians stayed low but looked up at Francisco Pizarro with nervous eyes. The younger of the two, Felipillo, crawled over to Francisco and whispered. "He say no touch lady, he call you *white stranger*, he say you back, please no kill, no sword."

"I'll touch whatever I want to touch," answered Francisco angrily as he stared at the beautiful, dark eyes of the frightened girl. "Ask him who he is and what happened here."

Felipillo crawled over to the robed, elderly man and respectfully touched the hem of his white robe to his lips. In Quechua, the official language of the Inca Empire, the meek Indian presented Francisco's questions and received a lengthy answer.

"Señor, him *Amauta* . . . priest like Father Pedro." Felipillo pointed to Father Pedro for clarification. "He name, *Amauta* Kusa Akchi. Lady name Cura Ocllo, she Sun Virgin, Señor, no touch, die bad if you touch, much curse, she for Viracocha!" Felipillo bowed low to indicate to Pizarro that he was only a mere messenger, a translator, and was not giving an order to the Governor.

"Por Dios," exclaimed Hernando "how appetizing! It's been ages since I held a woman." As sick as he felt, he was still man enough to lust after a supple young virgin.

With an angry gesture, Francisco motioned to his brother to be quiet. "What happened here? Who destroyed Tumbez? Tell him I might spare his life and that of the girl if he tells me the truth."

Again Felipillo spoke to *Amauta* Kusa Akchi reverently and, again, he received an answer. *Amauta* Kusa Akchi's voice was low and sonorous and the sound of it resonated with authority throughout the empty hall.

Felipillo rose to his feet at *Amauta* Kusa Akchi's urging and spoke as follows:

"This land Empire of Quechua people. Inca Atahualpa now king, he burn city and take from brother, Inca Huascar. Now for Inca Atahualpa, Son of Inti the Sun God, he God. Viracocha give now power to Atahualpa."

"Ask him who he serves" said Francisco. "And ask him where I can find this Inca Atahualpa."

Felipillo turned to *Amauta* Kusa Akchi who kept his arms tightly around the shoulders of Cura Ocllo. As she wept quietly, he asked the old man Francisco's questions.

"*Amauta* Kusa Akchi now loyal to Inca Atahualpa. But he not know where to find."

This answer did not please Francisco Pizarro. He didn't have time to waste in this burned-out village. He didn't have time to coddle old sorcerers. Don Alvarez looked at Father Pedro. Both were fully aware of how the Pizarro brothers got answers from people who kept secrets.

"Let me try," said Don Alvarez to Francisco. "I learned some words during the voyage. Let me try," he asked again.

"Go ahead," said Pizarro. "You can try. And then . . . I'll try *my* way."

"We help you. No more Inca King, we make you free," said Don Alvarez while using every hand sign and pantomime he could think of to help the *Amauta* understand.

Amauta Kusa Akchi *did* understand and he answered, "We love our Inca King! We serve the Inca King *freely*. Viracocha was angry at his people and sent a great flood upon them. Only one single island remained above water in Lake Titicaca. Only one man with one wife lived on the island. They had white skin and were very wise. The man became the first Inca King. Inti, the Sun God, threw great light upon him and told him that he will be the ruler of his people. The tears of Viracocha fell on him and made him Inca King. We will *always* serve our Inca King," answered Kusa Akchi. He then added, "We do not need *help* from *White Strangers*."

As Francisco Pizarro listened to the *Amauta's* translated answer through Don Alvarez, he began to lose patience.

"Where is Inca Atahualpa," he asked again.

Don Alvarez cringed as *Amauta* Kusa Akchi answered, "I don't know."

"All right then," said Francisco. "Tie them up and bring them along. If they don't cooperate when *I* interrogate them later, we'll burn them."

Juan Pizarro wiped the sweat from his young brow and pushed his auburn hair away from his eyes. He would never understand his oldest brother's anger and cruelty. He swore to himself that he would never let his own heart grow so cold.

Pizarro led his entourage and prisoners into a building that had not burned located next to the temple while his soldiers thoroughly searched the temple for treasure. They found some golden idols around the altar but, other than the altar itself and the gold plating on the walls and ceiling, there was little they could take for themselves.

The building next to the temple was adequate for temporary lodging. Francisco, accompanied by Hernando and Father Pedro checked all the rooms and motioned for Juan, still guarding Felipillo and Martinillo, and Don Alvarez respectfully holding *Amauta* Kusa Akchi and Cura Ocllo in rope bindings to follow. Finally, Father Sebastiano and Diego de Almagro pushed their way in.

Inside the house they found beautiful pieces of wooden furniture with animal skin seats. There were paintings of parrots, macaws and exotic birds and animals as well as gilded and carved figures on the stone walls and wooden beams.

"Put the shaman and his woman in here and guard the door," he ordered Don Alvarez. "Don't let them out and, unless he wants to tell us where to find Inca Atahualpa, don't let him talk."

Don Alvarez led *Amauta* Kusa Akchi and Cura Ocllo into a side room and motioned for them to sit down on chairs. He loosened their bindings, nodded kindly to them, backed out of the room and closed the door.

Francisco found a large woven basket filled with a fruit plant he didn't recognize. "What is this?" he asked Felipillo.

"Good to eat, sweet fruit, Señor," he answered, happy to at last provide some good news. "It name *pacay*."

Francisco, practically starving like the other men, cracked one open against the stone wall. Inside he found a white, cottony mass. In a rage, he flung it at Felipillo's face hitting him hard. He grimaced in pain, bowed low and covered his head with his arms in fear of further reprisal.

"You liar!" he yelled. "What possessed me to think I could trust an Indian for a single moment?"

Martinillo, eager to help his countryman, crawled over to the cracked and discarded *pacay* and stuffed a handful of the white mass into his mouth and chewed. Timidly, he held it out to Francisco who took it with great hesitation and touched it with his fingertip. He licked his finger and discovered that it had a sweet and delicious flavor. Everyone in the room grabbed a *pacay* and cracked it open on the wall to expose the white fruit. It was unbelievably good to eat and to taste something other than hard, stale bread.

Francisco walked slowly to a large window and looked out at the embers of Tumbez. The smoke and ash still hung in the air stinging the nostrils and throats of his men. No one spoke. The only sound they could hear were the shouts and hoof beats in the distance of the conquistadors and their horses as they searched the remnants of the town. It was now early afternoon.

"Governor, Governor!" came a man's call from outside of the house. Francisco strode to the door with large steps and threw it open to reveal Lopez holding a rope tied to an Indian's neck.

"Look what I found on the beach, Commander," he shouted for all to hear.

The Indian, a fine young warrior, stood proud and unflinching before the Commander. Blood oozed from a wound on the side of his head that, due to the swelling and discoloration, looked as though it had been caused by a blow from a heavy object.

"Bring him in and let's see what he has to say," said Francisco skeptically.

As Felipillo spoke Quechua with the new prisoner, every eye was glued to him. He was tall and strong although obviously exhausted and in pain. He informed them that Inca Atahualpa and Inca Huascar were brothers who shared the rule of a divided empire. He explained to them how Inca Huascar attacked Atahualpa's army in Quito in the north and how, in retaliation, Atahualpa's army attacked Cuzco and took Inca Huascar prisoner. Since then, Atahualpa and his army have traveled around the kingdom to find and to kill his remaining brothers and to subdue Indians that claimed loyalty to Huascar.

"A civil war," exclaimed Francisco. "We, the *White Strangers*, have walked into the middle of a damned civil war."

CHAPTER 12

Night descended slowly. The soldiers camped in the roofless houses near the shore where the smoke was not so suffocating. All slept the deep sleep of exhausted and disappointed men except for Don Alvarez and Father Pedro who kept vigil at the gate of a small cottage. Francisco had moved *Amauta* Kusa Akchi and Cura Ocllo to the cottage and appointed Don Alvarez and Father Pedro to guard them. They were appointed four soldiers to assist them with their task; however, all four of them slept soundly on their backs snoring.

The night air was balmy but the land breeze blew away the insects and provided respite from the smoke. The pointed helmets of the conquistadors along with their chest armor and weapons lay scattered about the sleeping men. Don Alvarez paced the length of the cottage with his shirt off holding a large knife in his right hand. Father Pedro sat on the stone steps muttering prayers. Barely audible in the distance they could hear the waves gently splash against the shore.

Inside the only room still covered by a section of roof, a night lamp was burning. The *Amauta* sat in a corner whispering words of comfort to the maiden who listened quietly. As Don Alvarez peered in at them, he noticed that the veil which covered her lower face was wet with tears. What moved him though, was not the wet veil. It was the courage of the old man. He had no sympathy for the female, she was probably just as mean and wicked as any other woman. It was the dignity of the man and how, although he was obviously important, he was able to show such care for an insignificant girl.

As his pacing brought him close to the submissive figure of Father Pedro in prayer, Don Alvarez heard him say his name. "Don Alvarez, what do you think about our prisoners?" In the light of the waning full moon, Father Pedro looked almost mystical.

"I don't know, Father, I suppose they're just a couple of pagan Indians that will be tortured and burned at the stake for withholding information from the Commander. I don't know, Father," he said again as his shoulders dropped.

"What if we rescue them for our Lord? And I don't mean Señor Commander!"

"What are you saying? That's treason," whispered Don Alvarez angrily. "Pizarro would torture and burn us too if he heard you right now!"

"Well," smiled Father Pedro with glistening eyes, "they're asleep," he nodded toward the sleeping soldiers, "and there's a balsa raft on the beach loaded with supplies. There's a man waiting to take them to an island where they can hide."

"What man? One of our men?" whispered Don Alvarez incredulously.

"Almagro himself," smiled Pedro.

"Are you joking?"

Father Pedro smiled and rocked back and forth on the step happily. Don Alvarez sat beside him and shook his head. He also smiled. They smiled together in total silence.

"If any of us are caught," added Pedro, "We'll share in the punishment. I'm quite certain that Francisco can't afford to do without you right now, he needs every man he has . . . so how badly would he dare to punish you?"

Don Alvarez jumped up. He checked on the sleeping soldiers. None of them were stirring. He looked at Pedro who nodded at him. Quietly, he walked into the room and used his pocketknife to cut the cord bindings around the wrists and feet of *Amauta* Kusa Akchi and Cura Ocllo.

With a smile on his face, Don Alvarez backed away from the prisoners and pointed at the open door. "You free, come," he whispered in badly accented Quechua. But *Amauta* Kusa Akchi and Cura Ocllo understood. The girl gasped and clapped her hands together. Don Alvarez could not see behind her damp veil but he could tell that her eyes were smiling. *Amauta* Kusa Akchi stared at Don Alvarez as though he sought to penetrate his secret thoughts. He didn't move. Don Alvarez motioned with both arms sweeping toward the open door, "free," he repeated hoping it was the right word. *Amauta* Kusa Akchi held out his right hand. Don Alvarez straightened up and looked at the *Amauta*. He extended his right hand to grasp the hand of the priest. They stood in silence staring into each other's eyes shaking hands: Two men from worlds so far apart.

"You have the blessing of Viracocha," said Kusa Akchi as he bowed. "We thank you."

"Thank our Christian *Amauta*," whispered Alvarez as he pointed at Father Pedro. Pedro smiled and waved shyly. "Come, run," directed Alvarez as he led them in a fast jog through the trees and down to the beach where he could see the silhouette of the balsa raft and a lone figure standing ankle deep in the water.

Kusa Akchi and Cura Ocllo climbed aboard the raft and Alvarez pushed as hard as he could to move them off into the gentle surf. There was no time to say farewell. As the balsa raft moved away from shore, Almagro pressed his index finger to his lips. Don Alvarez nodded his consent, waved one last time, and ran back to the cottage quietly.

"Good job," whispered Pedro with a wink and a soft pat on the back. Don Alvarez felt as though his broken heart had been bathed in healing waters of comfort.

CHAPTER 13

T he superb palace of Prince Coca stood on an Andean slope beside
a lovely brook that swelled into a river every spring. Surrounded
by a stone bastion, it was more like a fortress than a palace and
looked capable of resisting every potential assault. Certainly no enemy
would be able to storm this rock palace with arrows, clubs, spears or any
weapon used by Indians.

It took months for Prince Coca and his new family to get there but,
once they arrived, he was sure that he would live undisturbed behind these
thick walls forever. He feared no one, for his father was Inca Atahualpa
who now ruled the Inca Empire—by himself.

As time passed, Vira and Sapaca resumed their daily lives of leisure
and comfort customary of Inca Princesses. Sapaca, expecting her second
baby to be born any day, was exhausted by the strain on her body and lay
wearily on her couch. She groaned now and then and breathed heavily.
Weeks of heavy rains had raised the humidity of the region to a point at
which the air was stifling.

Beside her sat Vira, who dipped a soft cloth into a bowl of cool water
and placed it on the heated brow of her miserable niece. Vira had stayed
with Sapaca ever since her brother had been so viciously captured during
the *Situa* Festival. She had found refuge here, almost a home. She had
often worried about Manco who refused to accept Coca's hospitality and
went into the mountains east of Cuzco. There had been no news of what
was happening around the Empire.

It was a moral dilemma for her to live in the palace of Atahualpa's
son, and even though Coca was always friendly, even affectionate, she felt
depressed and sad. She found consolation in the fact, however, that she

could be of use to Sapaca. At the moment, she was tenderly patting her niece's forehead hoping to soothe her.

"Pani, open the curtains," she ordered her Indian nurse. The room was stuffed with furniture carved from brown oak and decorated with gilded figures. "There might be a breeze by now since the sun is setting."

Pani hurried to obey her mistress and yanked aside the heavy rugs that covered the main window. As the light of the sun began to fade, a refreshing breeze penetrated the room to fan Sapaca's sweaty face. She began to breathe more easily.

"That's better, much better," she murmured.

"Vira," she said, touching Vira's shoulder. "Why aren't you happy here? What do you need?"

Vira raised her eyes questioningly. She was 18 now and had developed into a beautiful woman. Her figure was still slender but her childlike athleticism had been replaced with soft, feminine curves. Her face was still delicate but her features had gained an irresistible sweetness from caring for Sapaca during her two pregnancies. Maita, Sapaca's first born son was already eleven months old.

It was Vira's eyes that were most captivating. They were bright and clear with obvious intelligence yet tinged with an ever-present melancholy. Although her eyes smiled out from behind a black veil of dark eyelashes, the sadness they contained was alarming.

"Are you wishing for a family of your own? If my father were here, he surely would have found a husband for you by now. I wish you could be with Manco."

Vira's eyes hardened as her brows knitted together. "Your father isn't here and I can't be with Manco. Watching you suffer doesn't exactly make me yearn to get pregnant, Sapaca," answered Vira with finality.

"So you won't marry Atahualpa? If you married him, you could stay here with me forever."

"I'll die first," answered Vira through a tight-lipped, sarcastic smile.

"Vira, you'll marry him if it's what he wants! When he returns from the baths at Konój, he might order you to marry him!" Sapaca fretted that Vira would fail to obey the Inca King's orders. She worried that she might end up losing her hands and feet before she would agree to marry as directed. Sapaca groaned.

"I'm content to live here quietly with you and Maita. He's the sweetest little baby I've ever seen, Sapaca. I wonder what you'll have this time.

Maybe you'll have a lovely little girl! What will you name her?" Vira tried to change the subject as usual.

"You should have a baby of your own," urged Sapaca, "a beautiful little prince or princess!"

"Atahualpa ruined my life, Sapaca! He took Huascar away, he chased me from my home, and he even threatens Manco's right to wear the *llautu* . . . for what reason would I possibly agree to marry him?! As long as I live, he'll get nothing more from *me,*" stated Vira with a dramatic wave of her arm. "Anyway, it's only a matter of time before Manco kills him and becomes Inca King. I'll wait for Manco!"

Just then Prince Coca entered the room with Maita. He greeted Vira cheerfully and his gaze lingered long on her lovely face. He had grown to love his wife and he was a good husband. He would be glad to marry Vira as well so he could take his time admiring her beauty. But that was up to his father.

He turned to Sapaca and kissed her forehead lightly. He placed the baby prince on her lap—what little was left next to her swollen belly. Little Maita clung to his mother and embraced her neck with his tiny arms. Then he reached out to Vira.

"Maita adores you," said Sapaca as she handed the smiling boy over to Vira. Vira embraced him warmly and pressed her lips to his silky cheek. Her face was radiant with tenderness. Sapaca watched Vira hold her son and thought that Vira was the most beautiful woman she had ever seen.

"You're my little sweet potato, my *apichu,*" giggled Vira as she cuddled Maita.

Coca paced the length of the room nervously.

"Something happened," said Coca. "There's news from Father."

Both women looked up at Coca expectantly.

"When my father arrived at the hot mineral baths in Konój, his scouts reported that there were intruders nearby. They wore clothes made from the silver tears of the moon goddess and rode on top of animals taller than me. They have strange weapons."

Vira sat up straight and put Maita on her lap. She looked intently at Coca and asked "Do they have white skin?"

"Yes, their skin is white and they're tall and hair grows on their faces. How'd you know they had white skin?"

"It is just as my father and *Amauta* Kusa Akchi said it would be. The *White Strangers* have returned with magical weapons."

59

Vira spoke as if she were asleep. She secretly prayed to Viracocha that they'd kill Atahualpa and restore Huascar to the Inca throne. Of course, she couldn't let Coca know her true thoughts. Vira turned away, ashamed that she had accepted hospitality from her brother's enemy.

"They landed in Tumbez," continued Coca. "Father's army burned it because the leaders there failed to cooperate with his negotiators. The *White Strangers,* as you call them, rode south on their huge animals to Cajamarca to find Father. It is rumored that they want to be allies with Father."

Vira felt as though she had been pierced through the heart. Her god-like deliverers of whose re-appearance she fantasized were here—and they decided to ally themselves with *Atahualpa?* This could not be. She needed air. Quickly she arose and handed Maita back to his mother against his protests. She nodded to Coca as she almost ran from the room.

Vira's apartment was next to Sapaca's and faced the mountains. Through the open windows she could feel only a slight breeze. The room was cozily furnished with warm colored rugs, two comfortable couches, a gilded bench against the wall, and a huge gilded case of dark wood in a corner that contained her jewelry and precious ornaments. The faithful Pani was arranging perfumed mountain flowers in brightly-colored clay vases.

"Pani," she burst out passionately as she sank down upon a couch and stared up at the gilded ceiling, "do you know what I just heard? The *White Strangers* from Father's prophecy have come. They're in *Cajamarca!*"

Pani clapped her hands together in surprise and stared at Vira. Then she pressed her hands to her heart and, with a groan, uttered a prayer, "Oh mighty Viracocha! Don't let them destroy us completely!"

"They won't harm us, Pani. They say they're going to ally with Atahualpa and help him to *finish* claiming the Empire!"

Pani shook her head. Her primitive but shrewd mind had learned much about the nature of men during her years among the powerful elite.

"Can *White Strangers* be so different from our own men? I assure you my dove, just as it is certain that sparks fly upward from a fire, a man seeks friendship for favors and wealth. Atahualpa should beware."

"You're worried about *Atahualpa,*" asked Vira angrily. "I wish he'd return as a mummy!"

Pani bowed low and kissed the feet of her angry mistress. With wise eyes she looked up into the lovely dark pools of emotion.

"Vira, I see that this occurrence is monumental to you. Leave your worries in the care of Viracocha. He will see to your needs. Calm yourself, there is nothing you can do right now."

Nobody knew better than Pani how Vira longed for a man to love. Her childhood fantasy of a tall, strong warrior with love in his eyes continued to haunt the young woman. Pani did not know how to comfort her.

"It's all right, Pani. I'll be all right." Vira placed her left hand gently on Pani's head and spoke as though to herself, "Oh Pani, how can you understand? You never were married or in love with a man. But you're the only mother I've ever known and I have no one else to talk to. I'm sorry. Now the man I've waited for who looks like Viracocha Himself is here. My lover with the fair skin and dark hair, the one I've dreamed about is here, and what does he do? He joins forces with my *enemy*. Everything is ruined."

Vira buried her face in her hands and wept. All hope was lost. Pani held her mistress and rocked her lovingly in her arms. But she wondered at Vira's ignorance. What did Vira know about Pani? How could Pani have wet nursed Vira if she had never known of men? There was so much that Vira didn't see.

Meanwhile, outside, the clouds grew thick and a thunderstorm rolled in. Hardly did one blast of thunder end when the darkness was split by a fabulous array of light. The thunder occurred simultaneously. Heavy rain began to fall and splash loudly into the open window.

Vira rose and hurried to the center of the room. She watched Pani draw together the heavy curtains. She was a brave young woman—except when it stormed. She was taught as a child that storms occurred when the gods were in a rage. She wrapped herself in a soft feather cloak. As another round of thunder shook the room, she heard knocking at the outer door of her apartment. She motioned to Pani to see who was there.

When Pani returned she was accompanied by *Amauta* Kusa Akchi and Cura Ocllo. It was dark in the room and their cloaks were wet from the rain, but Vira recognized them immediately.

"*Amauta* Kusa Akchi, it's you, what are you doing here?" she exclaimed, forgetting about her anguish for the moment. With an outburst of joy, she moved toward him, bowed low and kissed the hem of his wet cloak. She smiled and looked at Cura Ocllo. She barely knew her youngest sister although they had grown up on the same estate in Cuzco.

"You remember your little sister, Cura Ocllo, don't you?" said Kusa Akchi formally. "She has matured quite a bit since you saw her last. She accompanies me on long errands now as my eyes and legs are getting weak."

The *Amauta* lifted his right hand to bestow a blessing on Vira. Cura Ocllo made a slight curtsy.

Vira noticed that Kusa Akchi had aged greatly in the past two years. His once silver hair was now snow white. His face was covered with deep wrinkles and his eyes were even more deeply set into the dark hollows of his face. His hands trembled and he seemed unsteady on his feet.

"Welcome, Cura Ocllo. Pani, help them with these wet clothes. Please, sit down. Pani, get them something dry to wear."

Cura Ocllo lifted her wet veil with a graceful gesture to reveal a face of rare beauty. She reminded Vira of an idol she had seen in a temple of the goddess of the moon. She had fine and perfectly chiseled features with skin as smooth as sanded stone. Vira was enchanted by her loveliness and yet felt estranged by her rigidity.

"Thank you for your kindness, Vira," said Cura Ocllo. Her voice was deep and smooth and each word was pronounced with great care. "We need to discuss terribly urgent matters with you."

Vira was startled by the abruptness of the girl. She must have an iron spirit to go along with her strong body to be able to bear the hardships of life with *Amauta* Kusa Akchi. Vira dismissed Pani.

"Is it news from Huascar?" asked Vira impatiently.

"Princess Vira," announced the *Amauta*, "Huascar is dead. He is with Viracocha now."

"What? No!" wept Vira as she grabbed at the collar of her robe. "Did Atahualpa kill him? What happened?" Vira wept but maintained her dignity.

"We don't know exactly what happened," answered the *Amauta*. "But we do know that the *White Strangers* have taken Inca Atahualpa captive in Cajamarca."

"Captive? But Coca just told me that the *White Strangers* are Atahualpa's *allies* and are going to help him finish taking the Empire from those loyal to Huascar!"

"They tricked him, Princess. They lured him into a trap and took him prisoner. Thousands of his warriors were slain without killing even one of the *White Strangers*. Atahualpa's entourage was not even armed. They were to meet as friends and have a celebration. Instead it was a terrible slaughter."

"Maybe Pani is right. Maybe the *White Strangers* are no different from our men. Well, Atahualpa got what he deserved. That's just what he did to Huascar." Vira looked at Pani and nodded to show that she recognized the wisdom of her old nurse.

"Their leader is a cruel and harsh man named Francisco Pizarro. He has no mercy for Indians or Inca. Cura Ocllo and I were captured in Tumbez by the *White Strangers*."

"What were you doing in *Tumbez*?" asked Vira.

"It was just another place we sought refuge from Atahualpa's armies," answered the *Amauta* in a very tired voice, "but Atahualpa destroyed Tumbez as well. Pizarro demanded that I tell him where to find Inca Atahualpa but I didn't know where he was. I answered truthfully but he wouldn't believe me. He thought *I* would *lie*! He arranged for me to be tortured, Cura Ocllo too, and he was going to burn us to death if we wouldn't tell him where to find Atahualpa. Imagine the horror, Princess, that Cura Ocllo and I would be burned and never be allowed to find our way to Viracocha!"

Vira and Pani gasped. She had heard of men burning to death in accidental fires. Without their bodies, they were not able to journey to Heaven. There was no worse fate that Vira could imagine. She reached out to Pani and clasped her hand.

"Fortunately, one of Pizarro's own men smuggled us to safety during the night. With the assistance of three of the *White Strangers*, we escaped torture and death. It has been a long journey from Tumbez, but we are here now to warn you and to help you and Sapaca escape."

Kusa Akchi paused to catch his breath. Cura Ocllo sat beside him and rubbed his back lightly with one hand. They both looked so tired.

"Sapaca has a son and expects the birth of her second child any day now. She's so happy here. Oh, *Amauta*, are you hungry?" asked Vira not knowing what to say. "What can I do for you?"

"Nothing," answered Kusa Akchi. "This Pizarro is not like our Inca Kings. His men ride into a village on their huge beasts they call *horses* and kill everyone. Our Inca King welcomes cooperative Indian tribes into the Empire and leaves them in peace requiring only occasional labor and gold. But Pizarro—even when people try to cooperate, he orders bloody conquest. He will not negotiate. I fear we will all be killed or made slaves."

"Have you seen Manco," asked Vira.

"Yes, we met him in the mountains," said Cura Ocllo. A slight blush touched her cheeks as she continued, "He asked us to tell you that he is well."

"Thank Viracocha! What else did he say?"

Kusa Akchi began, "He worries about you, Princess, and asked me to protect you from . . ."

"He's making a terrible mistake," interrupted Cura Ocllo. "He wants to fight Atahualpa and was preparing to do so when the *White Strangers* returned. Now, instead of fighting the *White Strangers*, he's waiting to see what they do with Atahualpa!"

"So? Why should you disagree with him?" asked Vira.

"I think our leaders should unite against these *white intruders*, Vira. Our armies don't understand their weapons or their animals. What if they take the throne away from the Inca forever? Manco will never be Inca King if he refuses to join with Inca Atahualpa's armies!"

Cura Ocllo looked around the room. "Princess Vira," she asked in a secretive tone, "can you hide us for a while?"

Vira wondered at this girl who seemed intricately familiar with military strategy and the preservation of life and limb.

"Of course! You are welcome to stay here forever! You do not have to hide. You must eat and rest. You're exhausted. Your litter bearers must rest and eat as well."

"We're on foot."

"On foot? *Amauta* Kusa Akchi, at your age? With a *Sun Virgin*? This is insanity!"

"It's the only way we can be discreet. Cura Ocllo helps me, I lean on her shoulder."

Although the thunder had died down, a new sound was heard through the covered window. It was similar to thunder, but it didn't roll away. Kusa Akchi frowned deeply.

"What is it? What's that noise," asked Vira.

Kusa Akchi and Cura Ocllo stared at each other with raw fear on their faces. "It sounds like the *White Strangers*," answered Kusa Akchi. "That sounds like their beasts running. Come Princess, now we must all hide."

"I won't hide," protested Vira. "You're the one who taught me to fear nothing, not even death! I won't run and I won't hide, you can't make me," said Vira with complete conviction.

Cura Ocllo panicked. "I'll go, *Amauta*, I'll tell them to bolt the gates, wait here!"

But just as Cura Ocllo stood up, they heard banging at the palace gates. They heard the loud crash of splintering wood. They heard Coca's servants protest outside that they were welcome and they didn't need to wreck the palace. After all, they were allies of his father. The sound of the horses and men shouting frightened the women. But Vira had a strange desire to see the *White Strangers*. Her curiosity was greater than her fear of the *Viracochas—the men who looked like God*.

"There are far worse things than death, Princess," warned the *Amauta*.

Shouts and heavy thuds were heard through the window. Pani rushed in and grabbed her mistress' arm. "Coca and Sapaca are calling for you, Mistress. But I think we should run. Come now and be a good girl, let's go through the tunnel, at least we might have a chance to get away."

"Let go!" yelled Vira and yanked her arm out of Pani's grasp. "Go all of you, run to the tunnel. I'm staying here with my Sapaca. Have you forgotten about her? Pani, where is she?"

"I think she must be in the great hall, my dove." Pani was so scared that her eyes were as round as saucers.

"Go, Pani, take *Amauta* Kusa Akchi and Cura Ocllo to the secret stairway that leads to the tunnel. Run as fast as you can and hide. I'll send help for you all as soon as I can."

Vira smoothed her hair, covered her head with a light blue veil, and quickly made her way to the great hall. She wondered if Coca knew that his father, Inca Atahualpa, was a prisoner of the *White Strangers* and that they had lured him into a violent trap with false offers of friendship. She wondered if they would bring ruin to the Inca Empire. She wondered if they would be handsome like Viracocha with wise eyes and compassionate souls.

CHAPTER 14

P rince Coca assembled his court in the Gala Hall of his palace. He sat on a gilded arm chair with Sapaca at his side. Baby Maita sat quietly on his mother's lap. They waited in courteous expectation for the unusual guests to arrive. A dark cloud of dread filled the hall. The late evening visit was strange and to crash through the palace gates was totally unnecessary. There was a strange terror in Coca's heart.

Vira entered the hall and headed toward Coca to inform him of the latest news from *Amauta* Kusa Akchi and Cura Ocllo. But, just then, the visitors were announced and it was too late to approach Coca. Vira sat down in an arm chair among the other noble ladies. Her hand maidens gathered around her to arrange the pleats of her feather cloak and light gown before settling down upon soft cushions at her feet.

The main entrance doors to the Gala Hall opened and the *White Strangers*, clad in their silver war armor and carrying lances and swords, clattered in two and three at a time. Most of them wore pointed metal helmets with feathers sticking out of the top. Some of the men wore helmets that covered most of their faces. They were a frightening vision as they entered and gathered together in the hall.

Vira sat bolt upright in her chair and watched. She looked most closely at the men whose faces she could see. What little bit of their skin that Vira could see was not what she would consider *white*. It was definitely lighter than the skin of the Inca and the Indians, but it wasn't *white*. Most of their face was covered by dark hair which looked completely alien in contrast to the bare faces of her people.

Vira was terrified at last. She shuddered and sat back in her chair as far as possible. She prayed to Viracocha that Pani, Kusa Akchi, and Cura

Ocllo were far away and well hidden. She wished that she had listened and hidden with them. It was too late.

Then, among the tall, silver warriors, she saw a small man wearing a brown robe tied at the waist with rope. He didn't have any hair to cover his head or face. There was only a little ring of hair around his scalp that looked like fuzz. Vira watched him closely and felt her terror slightly dissipate. This man was different. The expression on his face showed concern.

A tall soldier marched into the center of the hall and called out in a deep voice: "Don Alvarez de la Vega!"

A warrior stepped forward. Vira thought he was their king. As he stood there in front of the others, he removed his helmet. Vira gasped. It was *him*, the man she dreamt of since her earliest youth. He was beautiful like a god with large, expressive, dark eyes. He looked intelligent and wise, kind and strong. Yes, he must be their king. Vira's heart beat even faster as she watched him.

Prince Coca stood to face Don Alvarez. "Welcome to my palace. Please introduce yourself and state the reason for your visit."

"Honored Prince," began Don Alvarez in his heavily accented Quechua. "I introduce for you, Hernando Pizarro who brings greetings from our chief—Francisco Pizarro, *Governor and Captain-General of Peru and Commander of our expedition.*" Don Alvarez spoke Pizarro's title in Spanish as he had not been able to learn any Quechua equivalents.

Hernando stepped forward and removed his helmet. Vira was stunned that Don Alvarez was not their king. From what he had just said, he wasn't even a chief.

"Our Chief delivers to you a message from our prisoner, your father, Atahualpa" continued Don Alvarez very formally.

Prince Coca shook his head. "My father is Inca King and, as I have been informed recently, your ally. Why do you say *prisoner*? Who is your king?"

Hernando sneered and shook his head. He spoke quietly to Don Alvarez who nodded.

"Our King is King Charles of Spain. For the freedom of your father you will pay: A room to fill with gold. When the room is full, your father will be made free."

"I must pay for my father to be free? You want gold? Of course, you may have all you want." Coca was terrified but greatly relieved that all they wanted was gold. There was plenty of gold. One room full of gold was nothing. He also felt a false sense of authority to learn that these men were not kings and not even chiefs. These were merely runners, messengers on a mission. Coca relaxed. He looked around the room at his courtiers and smiled. As his eyes settled for a moment on Vira, Don Alvarez followed his stare.

From behind her light blue veil, Vira's eyes met the eyes of Don Alvarez de la Vega.

"And how do I know that you are telling me the truth?" asked Coca. "Señor Don," asked Coca, but Don Alvarez was still looking at Vira. Hernando hit him on the arm with his gloved hand and Don Alvarez, startled and embarrassed, directed his attention back to Prince Coca. Vira blushed under her veil.

"And how do I know that you are telling me the truth?" asked Coca once again.

Don Alvarez handed him a *quipu*, some knotted strings the Inca used to keep a record of measurements. It was the closest equivalent to writing they possessed. Prince Coca reached out to accept the *quipu* from Don Alvarez's extended hand. He looked at it carefully and turned it over in his hands.

"Where is this room to fill with gold?" asked Coca.

"In Cajamarca," answered Don Alvarez. "We are here to carry it to Cajamarca."

"That is far and there is much gold. How big is the room?" asked Coca.

Don Alvarez spoke quietly to Hernando. As though it was painful to deliver the answer, Don Alvarez said slowly, "Too big for all that you have to fill it."

Coca shuddered. His momentary sense of authority and bravery vanished.

"What we cannot carry, you will send to Cajamarca," said Don Alvarez.

Hernando grinned as he watched Prince Coca's smile disappear to be replaced with a tight-lipped grimace. He could tell the Prince finally understood.

No one moved. Prince Coca looked from Hernando to Don Alvarez and around the room as though this wasn't really happening. Don Alvarez wondered if he had used all of the right words and if Prince Coca had understood. Hernando leaned over to Don Alvarez again and spoke to him.

Don Alvarez looked at Hernando and swallowed hard. He turned back to face Coca and said, "Now, Prince Coca. You will get the gold now."

Coca motioned to his guards. They came to him to receive orders and then motioned to Don Alvarez de la Vega to follow. Instead, fifteen of the *White Strangers* followed Coca's servants to the Royal Treasury. The tension in the Gala Hall was palpable. It was dark outside and the hall was poorly lit. It was hot and humid and the soldiers sweated in their armor. Hernando leaned casually on his oversized sword but held a small shield in front of his heart.

Vira watched Don Alvarez. He didn't look cruel and merciless to her. He looked down at the floor and then over toward the place he had seen Vira. Their eyes met again. For Vira, it felt as though lightning flashed between them. She breathed fast and her heart raced.

Don Alvarez looked away and Vira's world seemed drained of color. Everyone waited in silence. Only Maita was heard making little baby noises, oblivious to the trouble around him.

Finally, heavy footsteps resounded in the corridor and the *White Strangers* returned carrying enormous sacks. With the loud clatter of metal hitting metal and stone, they threw the sacks in the middle of the Gala Hall.

Hernando's eyes flared open in rage and he hissed words to Alvarez in such a torrent that he could barely translate. "Not enough, bring more," said Alvarez almost apologetically.

"There is no more," defended Coca.

"You lie!" shouted Hernando in Spanish.

"There must be more," said Don Alvarez. "Bring silver and jewels to add to the gold," he said hopefully knowing how the men would behave unless satisfied.

Hernando walked toward Sapaca like a wolf. He reached out his dirty gloved hand, almost touching Maita on her lap, and yanked at the gold and emerald necklace she was wearing.

Prince Coca raised his *champi* as a signal for his men to use their weapons. All the servants, guards, and nobles drew their weapons and lunged at the *White Strangers* bravely. Coca swung his *champi* at Hernando but he ducked. As he straightened up, he plunged his sword through Coca's heart.

Lopez grabbed Maita by the leg, tore him from his mother's arms, and slashed off the baby's head. Everyone in the hall went mad. The men were fighting and slaughtering one another and the women were screaming.

Vira ran toward the bloody, headless body of little Maita as two men dragged Sapaca away. As most of the men of Coca's court were dead, the Spaniards started to attack the women. After tearing away all the gold and jewels they could grab, they began to tear the clothing. Some of them slipped in the blood that spattered the floor.

Before Vira could reach Maita, two Spaniards grabbed her from behind and pulled off her veil. They grabbed violently at her necklaces and bracelets. Frantic with terror, Vira bit one of them on the hand but he didn't even notice.

Suddenly, the men let her go. She stood there facing Don Alvarez de la Vega. He used a large knife to cut the thick gold and silver chains from Vira's neck and threw them at the feet of her attackers like meat for dogs. As Hernando Pizarro watched, Alvarez picked Vira up and ran from the hall. He then headed down a very dimly lit corridor.

When he had run far enough that the screams from the Gala Hall were barely audible, Alvarez entered a side room and set Vira down on a couch. He backed away to look at her and to catch his breath. As she sat there, Alvarez began to remove his armor and clothing. He never took his eyes off of her. At first, she looked at him appreciatively. Up close, he was even more handsome than a god.

Free from his burdensome apparel, Alvarez grabbed Vira tightly by the arms and pulled her to him. Vira thought about protesting—no one was allowed to handle an Inca Princess in this manner. But she knew this man was too strong for her. Anyway, she had awaited his arrival for so long. There were no rules anymore.

With one hand Alvarez tore the front of her robe downward but it was well made and didn't tear. He pulled out a large knife and cut her clothes away from her body. His large rough hand held one of her breasts and he and clasped her to himself for a rough kiss.

Vira's head was spinning. Waves of joy engulfed her and her body yearned with desire. She put her arms around him and kissed him in return. He broke away from her and looked at her as though she had lost her mind.

"Not afraid?" he asked her in a husky voice.

Vira didn't answer. She kissed him and rubbed the dark hair on his chest. Everything about him amazed her. His skin really was white, only his face and hands were darkened by the sun. She was overwhelmed with emotion until he reached between her legs.

Vira screamed. "No, let me go, no, you can't!"

Don Alvarez laughed at her. "I am."

Vira pushed and twisted with all her might, which was considerable, and managed to squirm out of Don Alvarez's hold. She dashed naked, wearing nothing but a gold chain around her ankle, to the far corner of the room but *not* toward the unlocked door.

"Wait," she begged as Alvarez chased after her wearing only his stockings and boots. "Wait," she said again as he cornered her.

"I dream about you. I knew you were coming! My father told me the prophecy. I've seen your face before in my mind!"

He stared at her. She was the most beautiful woman he had ever seen. "What? What is *dream*? What is *prophecy*?"

Vira spoke too fast for Don Alvarez and used words he didn't know.

Vira pantomimed for him. She had his attention now and he stopped chasing her. She came out from behind the chair in the corner and placed her hands together. She put her hands on one side of her head and closed her eyes to feign sleep."

"Sleep."

Vira continued. She moved toward him as graceful and stealthy as a puma. She framed her fingers around his face and pointed to her head. "I see your face when I sleep," she said slowly.

Don Alvarez smiled. He could grab her again if he wanted.

"Who are you?" he asked.

"I am Princess Vira, sister of Inca Huascar," she answered sadly but proudly.

As she spoke, Don Alvarez saw the torture in her dark eyes. As his mind grasped the deeper meaning of her words he backed away slowly.

"No," she said and stepped forward. "You saved me. I thank you."

Don Alvarez remembered his confession to Father Pedro. He recalled the joy he felt when he assisted the old priest and the girl to escape torture and death. "I'm sorry," he said. I won't hurt you."

"Your men hurt me. You saved me."

Don Alvarez turned around and started to dress himself as quietly and quickly as possible. He handed Vira her robe although he had cut it almost down to the waist. As they both dressed as fast as they could he asked nervously, "Is there somewhere you can hide for a few days and be safe? You must get away from here before you are found."

"Can't you keep me safe?" asked Vira.

"No, I am nobody," answered Don Alvarez.

"I think you must be a king," said Vira sadly.

"No, I'm nobody," he repeated.

He reached into his pocket and withdrew a small, pearl-handled pocket knife and held it out to Vira. "Here," he said, "take this so you can defend yourself."

Vira reached into a pocket sewn into the side of her robe and withdrew a larger knife. "It's poisoned," she said.

Don Alvarez laughed again, but not at her this time. This time they laughed together. "Why didn't you use that on me?" he asked.

"You are my *dream*," she said, and she pronounced the new word slowly and carefully so Don Alvarez would understand. "I will not let my *dream* die."

Alvarez opened the door to the side room and checked left and right in the dark corridor. It was empty and quiet. "Go now, Princess. And God bless you."

Vira looked at him as she clutched her robe together. She wondered if she would ever see him again. She walked to him and put her hands on his face. She looked into his eyes and kissed his lips. A tear rolled down her cheek as she backed away and ran from the room. She ran down several dark corridors in her bare feet until she arrived at the stairway that led to the secret tunnel. Down she ran as fast as she could fly. She felt as light as a feather.

She hadn't gone far through the musty tunnel in total blackness when she saw the faint glow of a very small light ahead. To her utmost joy she discovered that they had waited for her: Pani, Cura Ocllo and the *Amauta*.

"We must run," panted Vira. "All is lost. Go, we must go as fast as we can!"

The odor of dampness and decay enveloped them. After a short while, they stopped to rest for a moment.

"Do you think we're safe now Pani?" asked Vira in a whisper.

Vira leaned on Kusa Akchi's arm and the *Amauta*, in turn, leaned on Cura Ocllo. They rested for only a few minutes until fear drove them on. Cura Ocllo led the way along the narrow, slippery steps. They felt their way along the moldy walls and waded through patches of ankle-deep water. They went on and on in the darkness.

"Will I be poor now Pani, like the Indians? Do you think I'll ever ride again in a litter and have hand maidens and wear jewels? Do you think they'll make me labor like the Indians?"

As Pani removed a pin from her dress and used it to close Vira's torn robe, Vira looked hard through the darkness at her nanny. "Maybe I'll be a child's nurse, just like you, Pani," she said with a sad smile.

Finally the tunnel curved and they saw rays of moonlight penetrate an opening through which they finally reached the mountains. They slowly climbed upward breathing freely from the mountain breeze. The night was dark and the road was wet and slippery from the recent storm. They ascended a gentle slope followed by a downward path into a valley. Cura Ocllo and the *Amauta* walked in front, followed by Pani and Vira. They had trouble staying on the narrow, stony track which led through the thick undergrowth, and often stumbled over wet ferns which covered the ground.

They headed southeast toward Cuzco knowing well that there would be no one and nothing waiting there for them except for perhaps hard struggles and deprivation. Although they were fairly certain that Cuzco was still free from the *White Strangers*, they knew its capture was eminent. All that they had which gave meaning and routine to their lives had been lost.

Vira stumbled along, lost in her thoughts. She remembered the trip she made, hardly two years ago, in a litter to the castle of Prince Coca. Now she was returning to Cuzco: Barefooted and brokenhearted. She was scared for her very life. The fact that she was not alone gave her strength. And for the first time in her life, Vira did not lean on Pani. Once they exited the tunnel, she stopped leaning on *Amauta* Kusa Akchi as well. He had enough trouble bearing his own weight. It was the first time in Vira's life that, if she slipped in the mud or tripped over a stone, no one tried to catch, steady, or comfort her.

"*Amauta* Kusa Akchi," asked Vira, "when you were held prisoner by the *White Strangers*, did you meet a warrior named Don Alvarez de la Vega?"

"Yes, Princess," he answered as he stopped to catch his breath, "he is the one who set us free."

A flush crept into Vira's cheeks and her eyes slowly filled with tears. She extended her arms toward the sky in speechless gratitude to pray. A spark of triumph ignited in her heart.

"Thank you, Viracocha," she prayed silently, "thank you for letting me be right: He is as good as I dreamed he would be."

What is it my little dove," asked Pani as she watched Vira curiously.

Vira smiled at her, "I saw a lovely flower, Pani, the most beautiful flower I have ever seen."

CHAPTER 15

Atahualpa and his court, a fabulous entourage of Inca nobles and Indian Chiefs, and over 40,000 warriors traveled to Konój to enjoy the hot mineral springs. Konój was located in the beautiful and fertile Cajamarca valley only a few miles from the town of Cajamarca itself. It was here that Atahualpa and Francisco Pizarro were destined to meet.

Francisco and his army of 168 men arrived in Cajamarca while Atahualpa's army camped peacefully in lovely colorful tents surrounding his Konój estate. General Quizquiz was occupying Cuzco and General Chalcuchima was with his army in Jauja. Atahualpa was seeking nothing more than rest and recuperation after his successful campaign to take the Inca Kingdom from his brother, Huascar.

It was a serene atmosphere. Atahualpa dined under an open tent. As he sat on a low stool, he pointed to a ceramic bowl filled with llama meat. Inés, one of his many lovely sisters, retrieved a bite-sized portion and fed it to him with her delicate hand.

"Forgive me, my Lord," she said in horror, "but a drop has fallen on your tunic. Please, come with me." She held out her hand to assist Atahualpa to his feet. He smiled gently and took his sister's hand.

As Inés and the other women helped Atahualpa into a new robe made from the velvety skin of vampire bats, Atahualpa spoke lovingly to his sister, "You are becoming a lovely woman, Inés. Of all my sisters, you are the most charming and kind."

Inés blushed and smoothed the garment over Atahualpa's broad, muscular shoulders. They returned to the picnic and, to whatever dish Atahualpa pointed, the woman closest to that bowl retrieved a tasty morsel and fed it to him with her hand. There was peace within his heart.

"We'll soon meet the leader of the *White Strangers*," he spoke while chewing. "You can all have your choice of the men for servants and guards once they're castrated. But I certainly won't castrate their beasts, no, those beasts are *wonderful*. I'll breed them and we'll not need litters and carriers anymore! We'll ride majestically on the backs of those *horses*—I think that is how they are called. How does that sound?"

Atahualpa surveyed the lovely faces of his women, "They are better than jewels, aren't they?" All the women giggled at Atahualpa's sly smile. None of them doubted for a moment that he was a god.

Atahualpa stood as the women gathered the remnants of his meal. "I promised the *Hernandos* yesterday that I will go to Cajamarca to meet their Chief. I find it odd that there should be two of them with the same name. They are not kings! One is *Pizarro* and the other is *DeSoto*, do I remember that correctly? Can you imagine, the *Pizarro* one calls me *brother* and offers to help me subdue my Kingdom? If he knew how I felt about my *brothers*, he would not offer himself as such!"

"I will castrate the *DeSoto* one first. I don't like how he tested my courage with his beast. Imagine letting his animal approach me so I could feel his breath upon my sacred royal fringe. I think he meant to frighten me!" Atahualpa loosed a joyous belly laugh while his women giggled heartily.

"What uncivilized barbarians these *white strangers* are," continued Atahualpa.

"Why did they bring you no gifts?" asked Inés. "Usually your visitors bring us such lovely presents."

"I think they must know nothing of how to approach a King properly," answered Atahualpa. "They looked right at me and showed absolutely no humility. They have much to learn!"

"Come, ladies" Atahualpa smiled at his lovely women, "make yourselves beautiful for the parade and the celebration!"

At noon, Atahualpa's warriors assembled to escort their king to Cajamarca. They wore checkered uniforms and walked slowly in front of Atahualpa's litter removing leaves and sticks from his path. Atahualpa's silver-plated litter was carried by dozens of Indian nobles dressed in fine royal blue tunics woven from the wool of baby alpacas. King Chincha, lovesick and filled with bitter resentment toward Huascar, was carried on a fine litter behind Atahualpa.

There were no curtains to conceal Atahualpa's glory as he sat on a stool upon his litter. The parade was so large that it covered the valley. From Cajamarca, the conquistadores watched their progress and waited for their arrival. It was late in the afternoon before Atahualpa and his entourage finally reached the town.

The conquistadors hid in ambush. Hernando DeSoto commanded the sixty conquistadors who had horses. They were mounted and ready to charge. Lopez was so scared of the approaching mass of Indians that he urinated in his armor. No one spoke a word or made a sound. They had been ordered to capture the Inca King. They could do nothing now but wait in silence and pray.

Atahualpa's litter entered Cajamarca but not one *White Stranger* was visible. When he scanned the square and saw no one, he looked down at his escorts and asked, "Well, where are they? Are they so afraid of me that they hide?"

After much hesitation, Father Sebastiano forced himself from his safe refuge and approached Atahualpa with Felipillo, the young and uneducated Chimú Indian who was expected to interpret.

"You are invited, Señor, I mean King Atahualpa, to join Governor Pizarro for a meal in his quarters," stuttered Sebastiano nervously.

Felipillo, having never in his short lifetime come face to face with an Inca King, froze in terror. Father Sebastiano shoved him forward and in true horror, Felipillo did his best to translate the invitation without fainting.

"They made *you* their spokesman? Are you the best they could find? asked Atahualpa with a fierce chuckle. Atahualpa became serious once more, "Tell them I'll not eat with their *Chief* until he returns the gold and treasures his men stole from me."

Felipillo fainted. Many of the nobles in Atahualpa's retinue laughed nervously.

Not sure of how to handle the situation, Sebastiano proceeded to read the *Requirement* to Atahualpa. Juan sent Martinillo to throw a bucket of water on Felipillo to rouse him. As Martinillo ran away, Felipillo scrambled to his feet wiping his face frantically with his hands. Rousing him was of little use; however, as Felipillo did not know any existing Quechua words to explain to Atahualpa that the Pope of the Holy Roman Empire required his cooperation and recognition of the Church or that he would suffer dire consequences. Sebastiano formally explained that the Spanish Royal

Council had appointed him to reveal the Christian religion to the Inca and to tell him about the things of God.

Sebastiano handed his book to Atahualpa. Atahualpa turned it over and around but was unable to open it. Sebastiano reached over to help him open the book but Atahualpa slapped his hand away.

Finally, Atahualpa opened the book and leafed through the pages. He had never seen anything like it and was impressed by the intricate designs and swirls. But he didn't understand it and didn't grasp the importance of the object. His face darkened, he stood up on the litter and tossed the book down to the ground.

The moment had come. Francisco launched the ambush. With thunderous noise, the canon and harquebuses, a type of musket mounted on a tripod, were fired into the masses of Indian warriors. The conquistadors, dressed in full battle armor, charged on their horses into the crowd of unarmed natives. Trumpets blared and the rattles attached to the horses made a terrible din. The Indians panicked.

Pizarro pushed through the crowd of his own men and grabbed Atahualpa by the arm but he couldn't pull him off of the litter. His men killed the litter bearers one by one, but as soon as one would fall, another Indian took his place. The Spanish soldiers, trying to bring the litter to the ground, sliced off the hands and arms of many of the Indians but they would use their shoulders to keep the litter high above the ground. They would not let their King fall.

It finally took seven mounted Spaniards to pull down the litter. Atahualpa was captured and his nobles and warriors were slaughtered. Many of the Indians ran away. In less than two hours 7,000 of Atahualpa's nobles and warriors were killed. King Chincha was among the dead.

Atahualpa was taken prisoner and was confined to a room within the Temple of the Sun. Francisco ordered that Atahualpa's women and fresh clothes be brought to him and that he be made comfortable.

Inés ran into his arms and held him tightly. "My poor brother, what have they done to you?" she cried.

"Don't worry my dear, I already have an idea," he tried to sooth his sister lovingly. "They're after our gold and silver! Look at their eyes how they lust after it. Do you see? They're just barbarians. Once they have all the gold and silver they can carry, I am sure they'll leave. Relax, my darling."

CHAPTER 16

The next day, Francisco and Atahualpa met face to face for a peaceful conference. Felipillo was there to translate for the two leaders. Atahualpa was ready with an offer.

"I promise to give him," Atahualpa told Felipillo, "a room filled with gold and two rooms filled with silver if he gives me my freedom."

As Felipillo translated for Francisco, Atahualpa looked around the room to survey its size.

"Tell him," continued Atahualpa, "that I'll order my subjects to bring golden idols, statues, jars, pots, and even the dishes from my own royal dining service!"

As Felipillo spoke, Atahualpa walked to the wall and extended his hand high above his head to point to a spot on the wall. He looked at Francisco with a smile and nodded his head to gain agreement.

"He need many months," said Felipillo, "but he give you gold more than you fit on ship. Then you let him go to Quito, to home."

Pizarro agreed. He had not thought of asking for a ransom. Months would give him time to send Diego de Almagro to Panama for supplies, men, and horses. If it took long enough, he could even send men to Spain with samples of the treasure of this advanced civilization to impress the King.

Weeks passed. Gold and silver objects of great beauty and artistic value poured in from all over the empire. Atahualpa continued to rule the Inca Empire from captivity with total authority. On several occasions, he issued orders through his spies for his Quitan army to attack the *White Strangers*. Then, in fear that his captors would kill him, he would issue another order for the army to stay away. Atahualpa, still intent to complete his task of taking Huascar's half of the empire, sent orders to Generals Quizquiz and Chalcuchima to assassinate his brothers who could claim the Inca throne.

Through the use of the Indian interpreters and much pantomime, Pizarro learned that Atahualpa had over 100,000 armed warriors ready to do battle. General Chalcuchima awaited only the signal from Atahualpa to come and invade Cajamarca. General Quizquiz kept order in Cuzco but was also ready to come to the aid of Atahualpa. General Rumiñavi was standing watch with Atahualpa's army from Quito. Grossly outnumbered, the *White Strangers* became more nervous with each day that passed.

Pizarro may have captured the Inca King without losing a single Spanish soul, but he didn't know what to do next with his distinguished prisoner.

"Well," said Francisco to Don Alvarez one day as they walked together across the square to the temple to visit Atahualpa, "whatever is *his* now, will be *ours* once we conquer this country."

When they arrived at the temple, Hernando DeSoto and Hernando Pizarro were playing chess with Atahualpa.

"He's so different when his subjects are not around," smiled DeSoto to Francisco. "He's so happy and convivial. Look, he's beating your brother at chess!"

"*Taptana!*" yelled Atahualpa as he slammed his knight down on the chess board.

"What does that mean?" asked Francisco.

"It means *surprise attack*, damn it!" growled Hernando Pizarro. Hernando looked up at his big brother with genuine disappointment in his eyes. "He did, he beat me. He calls the game *taptana* and he's very good at it. But he very nearly breaks the pieces by slamming them down so hard on the board."

Atahualpa was joyously setting up the chess men for another game.

"Where's Felipillo?" asked Francisco.

"I don't know," answered DeSoto, "but Martinillo is outside, hey you!" DeSoto pointed and addressed one of the black slaves. "Go get Martinillo."

The black man ran outside and returned moments later with Martinillo, a teenaged Indian boy of slight build with angular features. He had very large hands and feet.

"Tell Atahualpa," said Francisco, "that he is most fortunate that he has not been defeated by an army that is as cruel as his own. Tell him that I am known to give pardon and to show mercy to men who are peaceful."

Martinillo translated for Francisco. Atahualpa looked at the aging and thin white man. "You play *Taptana*!" said Atahualpa in a loud voice.

Francisco wasn't sure if he was being judged or being invited to play a game.

"No," said Francisco shaking his head, "no play."

Atahualpa *was* peaceful. He sent his army home and only kept those near that served him. But the longer Francisco Pizarro held him prisoner, the clearer it became that it would be impossible to set him free. Francisco knew that if Atahualpa were released, he would immediately begin a war against them which they would lose.

When Diego de Almagro returned from Panama with an additional ship and many more conquistadors and horses, there was great excitement in the camp. Francisco Pizarro ordered his men to assemble in the main hall of the castle at Cajamarca. "We learned much while you were gone," said Francisco to Diego de Almagro. "We learned that this Inca Empire is three times larger and holds twice the population of Spain."

Francisco turned to face his men and the new men who had arrived with Almagro from Panama. "Much time has passed," he addressed them. "We have gained all we can from our prisoner. We can't keep him here forever."

"Send him to Spain to face the Inquisition," shouted Father Sebastiano. "He's an obstinate heretic, send him to Spain!"

Almagro frowned which caused his eye patch to sink into the flesh of his cheek. "That would be very unwise!" he shouted. "Once the Inca find out that their king is on one of our ships, they'll attack it and kill us all. Give Atahualpa his throne, he'll be obedient, I trust him."

"Well, he doesn't trust us," argued Francisco. "He'll never trust us again, we already tricked him twice. Remember, if he'd kill his own brothers for getting in his way, what will he do to us if he has the chance?"

"At least we ended their Civil War," shouted Juan. "Now they all agree to hate *us*!"

"Find another Inca King, one that will be grateful to us," yelled Hernando. "Inca Huascar has a little brother, a crown prince named Manco. Make him the King. He's only a boy and we could control him easily!"

"Good idea," agreed Almagro. "Let's find this Prince Manco!"

"Fine, but what should we do with Atahualpa?" asked Francisco.

"Burn the heretic at the stake!" yelled Father Sebastiano. "Many natives have accepted our faith, but he won't. Just burn him!"

"You will sacrifice a human being?" asked Father Pedro. "Are you a savage? He has cooperated and has remained peaceful. Why would you want to light him up like a torch?"

"You ask us to save one heretic and thereby cause the death of many Christian men, Father Pedro? I thought the tenet of Christ was that one died to save many," answered Francisco.

Everyone was silent.

"How will the murder of Atahualpa endear you to the Inca people," asked Pedro.

"It won't, but it is tradition, Father. How does any kingdom beget a new king? If we can't find Manco or another suitable replacement, then I'll marry Atahualpa's sister, Princess Inés, and become Inca King myself! Atahualpa offered her to me, you know."

"She could be your granddaughter, Francisco!" rebuked Almagro.

"If it honored Spain, I could marry a five-year-old child. Do you know nothing of royal marriages, Diego?

"Well then, marry Princess Inés and let Atahualpa have his freedom," begged Almagro.

"I will *not* give freedom to Atahualpa," answered Francisco.

In protest, Father Pedro walked out of the room. Don Alvarez followed him. It was decided. Francisco's plan to marry a beautiful young princess would provide him the opportunity to produce a crown prince and become Emperor of the Inca Empire himself.

"We might need this *Prince Manco* for a little while, Hernando. Choose men for a mission to locate him. We'll discuss the future of Atahualpa in the morning."

The room cleared out. Heavy footsteps sounded their way to the open door. As the voices drifted away, Francisco Pizarro still sat in his chair. "Leave me now, Father," he said to Sebastiano who had remained by his side.

"It is the right thing to do, Francisco. You have no other choice."

"He is innocent, Father. He's committed not a single crime. He hasn't so much as injured one of my men since he's been here. He even supplied us a room filled with gold and two rooms filled with silver . . . Father, are you sure?"

"Yes, Francisco, I am sure."

Outside in the sunshine, Father Pedro turned to Alvarez with a severe frown on his face. He placed his hand on his forehead as if to contain his thoughts.

"What bothers me the most," said Father Pedro, "is that the very God they claim to represent, they know nothing of."

CHAPTER 17

The next morning, the men met in the enormous hall of Cajamarca castle. Father Sebastiano acted as the "Defender of Indian Affairs" to make sure that Atahualpa would be treated fairly. Father Pedro did not attend; however, Don Alvarez sat quietly on the front row with the other staff officers. Important natives had been invited to the meeting and Francisco watched them to try to read their mood. The majority of the Inca nobles in attendance were men who had been loyal to Inca Huascar. Even so, there was only respectful concern for Inca Atahualpa. He was the son of the Sun God, a god himself and he was their King.

Atahualpa entered with two guards, his hands in chains. His body was slim but strong. He held his head high and gazed defiantly at Francisco.

"Inca Atahualpa Yupanqui," proclaimed Francisco formally, "is it true that you have continued to conspire and foment rebellion against us since you have been our captive? Is it true that your Quitan forces are on their way right now to attack us and that they bring with them Carib Indians to eat our dead flesh? Do you deny this charge?"

Felipillo translated the accusation for Atahualpa and listened as he answered in Quechua.

"Atahualpa speak," said Felipillo, "This *MY* Empire! It is *White Strangers* who intrude and attack my people. I am son of Sun God, Inti, I am God. I defend Empire against *YOU*. Is that crime? Yet I am in chains. I am prisoner. How can I make plan against you?"

Felipillo became quiet and stared at the floor. It took all his strength and courage to keep his teeth from chattering. He wanted to fall at the feet of Atahualpa and honor his King.

"Is it true," continued Francisco, "that you killed Huascar's general, Atoc, and fashioned his skull into a drinking cup from which you enjoy sipping wine?"

Atahualpa smiled. "The Fox do same to me if he catch *me*," answered Atahualpa through Felipillo. Everyone in the courtroom smiled at Atahualpa's humor.

"Atahualpa, do you deny that you usurped the Inca throne, that you unjustly imprisoned your brother, Huascar, and then had him murdered?" asked Francisco.

Francisco looked at the Inca nobles to see if this charge excited them. He didn't see a single look of approval.

Felipillo translated Atahualpa's retort. "Viracocha choose Inca King. You see I am alive so you see Viracocha choose *me*."

"Atahualpa has repeatedly rejected the Christian faith," yelled Sebastiano.

Everyone in the courtroom voiced their opinion at once. As the noise of conversation and dispute between the soldiers escalated, Francisco hit the table with a loud bang. Momentarily, the room was again silent.

"Atahualpa, I find you guilty of all the accusations brought against you this morning and you are sentenced to burn at the stake," said Francisco.

"Do you have any last wishes?"

Atahualpa spoke with Felipillo. "Inca Atahualpa say last wish to give his little sons in Quito to you, Señor Pizarro."

"We will not provide for a bunch of heathen bastards," grumbled Sebastiano.

Two strong soldiers, obeying Father Sebastiano's orders, grabbed Atahualpa by the arms and took him outside to the city square. A stake had been erected to which Atahualpa was tied. As the brush was scattered at his feet, it became evident to Atahualpa what was happening.

"This *taptana*—surprise attack," said Atahualpa angrily to Hernando DeSoto who stood close by.

DeSoto shrugged his shoulders helplessly and shook his head. As he continued to meet the desperate gaze of Atahualpa, injustice squeezed his chest and tears threatened his eyes. His breath caught in his throat and he finally looked away in anguish.

The crowd of Spanish and Indian onlookers gathered around him. The Indians fell prostrate to the ground in front of their Lord, the Inca King, the Son of the Sun God. Again, Felipillo and Atahualpa talked.

"No burn Atahualpa!" yelled Felipillo on Atahualpa's behalf, "Inca Atahualpa say you be father to his sons and he be *Christian* for you."

Father Pedro, who was watching sadly from the back of the crowd, rushed forward and joyfully baptized Atahualpa in the name of the Father, the Son, and the Holy Ghost. Although he wasn't sure if Atahualpa accepted the Christian faith to save his children or to avoid being burned alive, to him, it didn't matter. He spoke kindly to the soldiers and instructed them that Atahualpa was no longer a heathen and; therefore, would not be burned at the stake. "Untie him, please," he told them.

But Pizarro had not commuted the sentence. All that had changed was the manner in which Atahualpa would be killed.

In the great square where solemn feasts had been held for generations, atop a stone platform where his father had once sat upon his granite throne to survey his troops, Atahualpa was instructed to sit upon a simple wooden chair. Although he wore his Inca fringe, he regretted that he had never made it back to Cuzco for a formal coronation ceremony. He did not hold his golden *champi*.

Lopez roughly placed a loop of rope around Atahualpa's neck that was attached to a stick. The noose rested just below Atahualpa's large, gold ear plugs that were partially concealed by his long black hair. The crowd gathered around him. He was taught to fear nothing, especially not his own death.

"This Check Mate," said Atahualpa in Spanish as he stared into the eyes of his friend, Hernando DeSoto.

"*The Lord is my Shepherd, I shall not want,*" prayed Father Pedro. Lopez began to twist the stick and the rope noose tightened. "*Surely goodness and lovingkindness . . .*" continued Pedro with tears in his eyes. Atahualpa's eyes began to bulge and a vein on his forehead swelled. "*And I will dwell in the House of the Lord . . .*" Atahualpa died tied to a chair in the Cajamarca town square.

"Praise Viracocha," wept one of the holy women from the Temple of the Sun God. "He wasn't burned. Now he will live forever."

When Atahualpa's wives and serving women returned to his room in the Temple of the Sun, they looked for him. Inés walked to a chair where Atahualpa liked to sit, "I don't see him," she wept, "Atahualpa, where are you my love?" She looked in every corner of the room but was unable to find him anywhere.

A few days later, the scouts returned from their reconnaissance to see if Atahualpa's army from Quito was on the way to invade Cajamarca. They reported to Francisco Pizarro that the roads were clear and no Quitan warriors had been seen.

CHAPTER 18

The days which followed Atahualpa's Spanish burial were disturbed by disagreeable incidents. General Quizquiz continually fomented rebellion. One night, his warriors set fire to all of the newly constructed Spanish buildings in Cajamarca. Francisco understood that he would have to act soon. The last of Atahualpa's gold and silver ransom had been melted down in the furnaces and the men were restless.

"It's time for us to move on," said Diego de Almagro to Francisco. "My men are ready to seek their fortunes. I promised them enough gold to sink their ships and cripple their horses! Your men have already obtained wealth beyond their wildest dreams. I say it is time for us to march to Cuzco," declared Almagro, "or perhaps," he said with a hopeful smile, "you will share Atahualpa's ransom with them? I'm sure that would help them settle down."

"You know I can't do that. They played no role in his capture and they'll receive no part of his ransom. The others have been with me for almost three years now. They deserve it all."

"Then let's go," said Diego. "Let's go to Cuzco, the *holy city*. It's full of gold and silver. My new men remain penniless while your men barely have enough llamas to cart their riches. We'll conquer the rest of the Empire on our way to Cuzco! How long have you been here anyway?" asked Diego.

"I've been here for eight months now," answered Francisco in a tired voice.

"What are you going to do with General Chalcuchima? I still can't believe you got one of Atahualpa's Generals to just walk into Cajamarca and give himself up," said Diego with a smirk.

"Well, it wasn't quite that simple," said Francisco, "but don't worry about him, I have plans for him. We'll take him with us. He'll make a good hostage for now. The Indians won't be over anxious to attack us with their General in our midst."

"When do we leave?" asked Diego happily.

"All right, all right, Diego. Just keep in mind that it's no less than 600 miles to Cuzco and we have a lot of people and supplies to move. It's going to take us months to get there. You better put Chalcuchima in chains and appoint your best men to guard him. I don't want him to escape into the mountains. I'm having enough trouble with General Quizquiz and Atahualpa's army from Quito."

"Of course," answered Diego. "I'll appoint a special force to guard Tupac Huallpa as well. I'm sorry you couldn't find Prince Manco, but I suppose Tupac Huallpa will be just as good. But he's so frail. I'll do my best to keep him alive till we reach Cuzco. Don't worry, Francisco. I'll put Rodrigo Orgóñez in charge of your new Inca King. He's a wonderful lad—came all the way from Oropesa with nothing but his good name and his little brother. Seems he got in trouble for brawling with everyone he met." Diego smiled at Francisco as they fancied themselves young again. "He's young and ambitious and I know he'll return trouble for trouble. His love of fighting will serve him well here."

Diego turned to walk toward the door of Francisco's office. He took three steps and turned around to face Francisco once more and asked, "Will Inés, I mean, *Doña Conchita*, travel with you or would you prefer that she travel with the other women?"

"Let her be with the women, Diego. She's very nervous and doesn't understand a word I say to her. She'll be more comfortable with the other women for now."

For the next three months, Pizarro and 300 conquistadors traveled southeast toward Cuzco. General Chalcuchima, chained and heavily guarded, was taken along as a hostage. The new Inca King, Tupac Huallpa, one of Huayna Capac's brothers who had been crowned by Francisco himself, rode in a litter on the shoulders of ten strong *Rucana* Indians. *Rucana* men, specially chosen for their smooth running gait and trained from their early youth, were the preferred litter bearers of the Inca elite.

There was a large entourage of natives. Many Indians chose to follow the *White Strangers* and brought along their women and children. The women cooked meals for the men and the children herded llamas that were loaded with supplies. There were also Indian slaves brought from Panama and black slaves brought from Africa to assist the conquistadors with their weapons, armor, and horses. Some of the conquistadors chose to travel in litters and led their horse by the bridle to let them grow fatter. A colt, born to Gonzalo Pizarro's mare in Cajamarca, was carried on a litter.

As they slowly and carefully ascended the Andes, the Inca Highway narrowed and was replaced by great steps. The air got cold and thin. Glaciers glimmered blue in the noon sunlight. But along the road about every seven miles or so there was a house erected as a resting place for the traveling Inca elite. Also, at a distance of approximately every 70 miles, they came to an important Indian city to which the Inca subjects brought the products of their labor for storage.

There were skirmishes with Indian forces along the way; however, only a few conquistadors were killed. A horse was killed and some of the men were injured by rocks and arrows but the troops moved forward unharmed toward Cuzco. In contrast, thousands of native warriors died: Run down by horses and slashed to pieces by steel Spanish swords.

In Jauja, Francisco ordered the construction of a church and other buildings and proclaimed it as the new capital of Peru. It was in Jauja that he buried Tupac Huallpa who had been ill for some time and had died along the road while lying in his silver-plated litter.

When the conquistadors were only a one-day's march from Cuzco, just past the Inca town of Jaquijahuana, they were approached by a peaceful escort under the command of an interesting young native. It was Manco, the young Inca prince. He had been hiding from Atahualpa in the mountains for the past two years as Atahualpa fought to gain control of the Empire. No one had been able to find him.

Manco was attractive and dignified and wore a simple, white, wool robe fastened by a belt made of the purest gold. The belt buckle was shaped like the paw of a great puma. In spite of being plain, Manco's robe gave the impression of superb elegance. As Manco greeted Francisco Pizarro, he smiled. His graceful movements and air of dignity made his distinguished ancestry obvious to all. Yet he seemed to have nothing of the commanding and overbearing ways of Atahualpa. As soon as he greeted Francisco's officers, a humble smile spread over his face.

Don Alvarez, who had become quite fluent in certain aspects of Quechua conversation, was summoned to translate. "The Viceroy," (for that is the title Francisco Pizarro now preferred) began Don Alvarez cautiously, "say good that you be loyal to him. You are good man and suffer much from Atahualpa cruelty. He say he want to put power in your hands."

Manco smiled but retained his composure. Don Alvarez thought he noticed a flame spark up in Manco's eyes when he said the word *power*.

"What *power* do you mean, Don Alvarez?" asked Manco politely.

"Power Atahualpa take from you—Viceroy give back. You wear Inca crown and we protect you."

Manco did not answer but the light in his eyes glowed more brightly.

"Viceroy Francisco Pizarro make you Inca King," continued Alvarez. "But he want something from you."

As Pizarro spoke to Don Alvarez, Prince Manco raised his eyes to look at him and, for a moment, he looked just as fierce as Atahualpa. Don Alvarez swallowed hard.

"Viracocha will make me Inca King. What does the Viceroy *want*?" asked Manco with a humble voice that did not quite match the look in his eyes.

"You be his son."

Manco felt the bile rise in his throat but he bowed his head in humble consent, "I shall be as his son," he murmured.

"You help him take Cuzco and you stay in Cuzco as Inca King."

Manco breathed deeply, not quite sure to believe what he was hearing. "I will conquer the Holy City for the noble Viceroy," he answered. Manco breathed deeply and looked down as though the deliberations were concluded.

"More," said Alvarez nervously, "you prove loyal to Viceroy and kill Chalcuchima in Cuzco town square."

Prince Manco's face darkened and his lips trembled slightly. General Chalcuchima was *Atahualpa's* general and would have happily killed Manco had he been able to find him in the mountains. Yet his child-like smile disappeared.

"An Inca King will need experienced generals."

"You do this. General make much trouble for Viceroy. Teach lesson to people . . . and to General Quizquiz."

Manco's brows knitted together and his eyes searched the floor. A tension-laden pause followed and Juan felt it necessary to intervene.

"You Viceroy *son*, so small favor for *father*?" asked Juan Pizarro in very badly pronounced Quechua.

"Of course, Señor," Manco answered. He forced the smile to return to his face. "I shall do what the Viceroy requests."

CHAPTER 19

Vira, *Amauta* Kusa Akchi, Cura Ocllo, and Pani trudged through the mountains toward Cuzco. Kusa Akchi led them to the *holy city* where, he hoped, with the assistance of Pani's brother, they might find a safe place to hide. The last news he had was that Cuzco was still in the hands of General Quizquiz. Although Quizquiz was their enemy, Kusa Akchi hoped that the small entourage would not be noticed by Atahualpa's faithful general. Kusa Akchi was very slow and weak. He leaned heavily on Cura Ocllo but never complained. The women complained.

"Will we ever get there?" asked Vira wearily.

"Just a little farther, my dove. We'll rest for a minute," was Pani's routine answer.

One morning after several days on the road, they were startled by the sound of barking and Vira's little pet dog, Cuna, appeared behind them on the road. Vira smiled and stretched out her arms to greet the little fellow who sniffed and rubbed his coarse fur on Vira's bare and bleeding feet. Vira took him up into her arms and he seemed for the moment, shaggy and dirty as he was, to be the most precious creature on earth.

Violent thunderstorms plagued the hikers and Vira finally collapsed from the strain on her nerves and body. She remained unconscious with a fever for two days in a cave. Pani gathered herbs and Cura Ocllo made soup and tea with them to try to feed Vira. In the end, Pani thought it was the constant nudging and licking of little Cuna that gave Vira the strength to continue.

"We must reach Cuzco, maybe we can find Manco there," mumbled Vira weakly.

Amauta Kusa Akchi sighed. He knew that in Vira's imagination, Manco was still the crown prince of the southern empire. But Manco couldn't protect her now. Only *Viracocha* would be able.

For months, the frail entourage walked through rough terrain from one small Indian village to the next. At the *Tambos*, the places where Inca relay messengers would meet to exchange information, the *Amauta* asked for news but news was scarce and the relays had been interrupted by fighting. The Indians helped them along the way by sending llamas to carry supplies for the weary travelers but in their attempt to remain inconspicuous, they refused all offers of litters and guards.

Kusa Akchi tried to estimate their distance from Cuzco. It was twilight and the group was exhausted. It was decided that they would rest for the night and make an early entrance into Cuzco feeling as fresh and rested as possible. As the twilight darkened, he thought he saw something odd. His eyes were weak so he spoke to Cura Ocllo, "Cura Ocllo, look over there, do I see something pink in the sky?"

Cura Ocllo looked in the direction the old man pointed. "I'm not sure, *Amauta*, but it looks a little like the glow from a fire."

Then they all heard the explosions. Terrible noises like thunder, but this time, it was not a storm. The city of Cuzco was on fire.

"It sounds like the weapons of the *White Strangers*," said Kusa Akchi. His heart was breaking.

The four lost souls stood there listening to the explosions and watching the glow of the fire in Cuzco. Finally, the explosions ceased and there was silence.

"Is it over?" asked Vira.

"We'll have to go into the forest and live like wild beasts," said the *Amauta*.

"No, Kusa Akchi, we're not beasts," said Vira, "we'll never be beasts. Let's keep going, maybe we will find Manco or Pani's brother, Turi."

"I am only one, old, unarmed man with three women. Two of them are beautiful virgins," said Kusa Akchi. Vira and Cura Ocllo looked at each other. "We will find terrible misfortune in a conquered Cuzco."

"I have my poisoned dagger," said Vira. "I'm not afraid and I feel much stronger now. Pani and I will go on and send help for you. I would rather die than retreat into the forest like a scared animal."

The *Amauta* recognized the traits of Inca Huayna Capac in Vira. "All right, Princess," he said in a low voice. "My place is with you now. I will come with you and try my best to keep you all safe."

They began immediately toward Cuzco. They left the main road and used hidden footpaths to avoid detection. At first, the smoke made it hard to breathe and they coughed a lot but a night breeze picked up and blew the smoke off to the southwest. When they reached the first houses on the edge of Cuzco, they saw that the damage was not too bad: Only the thatched roofs of a few houses were burning.

In the darkness, a frightened Indian slipped past them now and then but they reached the quarter of the *Puma's Tail* without difficulty. They found the old, gray house built of large stone blocks and surrounded by a thick wall. They stopped before the gate which was decorated with an enormous stone head of a puma.

"Inca Huayna Capac gave this house to his faithful warrior," whispered Pani. "My brother, Turi, saved one of his sons in battle," she boasted. "So he gave him this house as a reward. Did you know that my people are descended from *pumas*?"

Kusa Akchi smiled. "What a wonderful place to hide the Inca's treasure," he remarked with relief.

They went through the gate into a small garden surrounded by massive walls. There were ancient trees and fragrant flowers. Cuna ran around exploring and sniffing under every bush. Vira breathed in the perfume of the flowers and smiled.

They stopped in front of the house and hesitated. Light filtered through a window.

"Wait here," said Pani as she went through the door. "I'll be right back."

When Pani returned, she motioned for the others to follow her. She led them into a room that felt like a cave. There was a huge fireplace with ceramic pots on the floor in front of it. The furniture included a wooden bench, a heavy block of stone used as a table to hold a torch light, and a basket of food in the corner. Cuna hurried toward the basket with excitement. From the dark background emerged an old Indian, clad in a brown wool robe that reached his knees. His hair was white and his features were haggard. His cheeks were hollow but he had incredible dignity. He came forward and his eyes beamed with joy. He threw himself face down on the stone floor to honor his visitors and then rose to his knees to kiss the hems of their ragged and torn robes.

"How far you have traveled! Welcome to my home noble Princesses and *Amauta*," he said with great respect. "Welcome also my dear sister, Pani."

Vira smiled. She was dirty, barefooted, and her gown was in shreds from the long, arduous journey. "Thank you, Turi. I am Vira and this is Cura Ocllo, my sister. We gladly accept your home as our refuge."

The *Amauta* looked around the primitive room searching for something.

"Where is the entrance to the secret cave?" he asked.

Turi nodded. "Certainly, great *Amauta*," he answered. But then guessing the intention of Kusa Akchi he added hesitantly, "it is moldy down there and very dark. It's a place to hide Inca treasure. It is no place to lodge royal princesses!"

"What is needed now is safety, not luxury," said the priest. "There is grave danger. Show me the entrance, take me to the room and let me see it."

The old Indian pushed away the stone block on which the torch was balanced and Kusa Akchi threw back a heavy rug that covered the entrance. A gust of mold and the smell of decay hit him and he shrank back and murmured, "I wonder . . ."

"The place will be fine," said Vira, taking charge of the situation. "This is just what we were searching for. No one will seek a royal princess in that dark hole.

"Turi and I will tidy it up and make it cozy and comfortable for you, my dove," assured Pani.

"Turi, have you any news about my brother, Prince Manco?" asked Vira.

Turi was not prepared for the question. He looked uncomfortable as he answered, "Prince Manco was away for a long time, Princess Vira, but he has returned."

"He's here?" squealed Vira with delight. Cura Ocllo's eyes brightened and the two young women had a small celebration. "Is he all right? You'll have to bring him here so he can hide with us!" As tired as they were, the girls danced with joy.

"Manco needs no protection, Princess Vira. Just today he opened the gates of Cuzco for the *White Strangers* and will become the new Inca King."

Everyone in the room stood at attention and stared at Turi. "What do you mean?" asked Vira in a quiet voice. "What do you mean that he *opened the gates for the White Strangers?*"

"Manco cooperates with the *White Strangers* and they will crown him Inca King tomorrow at Haicapata Square."

"What about General Quizquiz and General Chalcuchima?" asked Kusa Akchi. "Did they fight against Manco?"

"General Quizquiz has retreated to the mountains. Prince Manco delivered Cuzco into the hands of the *White Strangers*. General Chalcuchima was executed in the Square. The *White Strangers* burned him alive."

Kusa Akchi backed away and leaned against the stone wall. He buried his face in his hands and shook his head and moaned. "Has Manco joined the *White Strangers*? Is it possible . . ."

"No!" yelled Vira. Cura Ocllo shook her head in denial. "No, we don't know what happened. Don't say that! What about Atahualpa?"

"Atahualpa was executed in Cajamarca," said Turi.

"And Huascar is dead. My poor, dear brother. He only wished that we would all be happy and well."

"The *White Strangers* crowned your uncle, Tupac Huallpa, as Inca King but he was already terribly ill and died during the march to Cuzco. Many of your brothers were assassinated by Atahualpa's army while he remained a captive in Cajamarca. The eyes of the *White Strangers* fell upon Prince Manco."

"No, we don't know what the *White Strangers* might have said or done to Manco. My Manco would never abandon his people and turn away from everything we hold true. Manco is afraid of nothing!"

"Either way, Manco is in danger. The *White Strangers* cannot be trusted," declared Kusa Akchi.

"Perhaps Manco has a plan to save us all," suggested Vira. "Perhaps he is only playing their game until he is ready to take over," she hoped with all her heart.

"You told us what you saw at Prince Coca's palace, Vira, do you really believe that Manco could cooperate with such men and keep his honor intact?" asked the *Amauta*.

Cura Ocllo felt sick. She was not afraid to die. In fact, for most of her life, she had been instructed on how to do it properly in a way to please Inti, the Sun God. She couldn't believe that Manco would rather cooperate with the *White Strangers* than die an honorable death in battle.

She didn't know what to think and she felt a deep disappointment in her heart.

Vira glared at the *Amauta*. "Don't judge my brother hastily, Kusa Akchi," she cautioned. "You have not heard his side of the story."

"Enough," said Kusa Akchi. "We are weary and uninformed and I still have work to do. Turi, would you please bring me a llama?" asked Kusa Akchi. "We should make a sacrifice to thank Viracocha for guiding us safely through the mountains to this safe refuge."

"The only animal around here is that little dog," answered Turi as he pointed at Cuna.

Vira quickly swept Cuna up from the floor and clutched him to her heart. "You'll not touch my little pet," she hissed. "If Manco is to be the Inca King, then I am *still* a princess and this little dog is mine!"

"We are starving here," said Turi.

"Well, if it is as Turi says, then pray Viracocha will forgive us that we have nothing to sacrifice," said Kusa Akchi.

"Viracocha should have saved our empire from the *White Strangers!*" shouted Vira bitterly.

"We cannot know the ways of the Creator," reproached Kusa Akchi. "To criticize him is blasphemy, Princess."

"You are right," answered Vira. "I'm sorry. Anyway, tomorrow Manco will be crowned and, perhaps, our empire is not lost after all." She tried to be cheerful but she was extremely tired.

Kusa Akchi looked closely at Vira and saw how weak and vulnerable she truly was. "Turi, how can we guard her? Do you have any servants?"

"Sometimes in the evenings my friends come and we make music together. There are at least 15 of them who are fine, young, strong warriors. They will gladly guard the princess. Truth is, they would be eager to hide with her to avoid being dragged away as slaves by the *White Strangers*. They will fight to the death for her."

"Then it is settled," pronounced Kusa Akchi. "I have to go now. Come Cura Ocllo, we must go to the temple and assess the situation. There is no time to rest."

Cura Ocllo looked at Vira with tears in her eyes. The long, strenuous journey through the mountains had forged a bond between the two young women of mutual admiration.

"What will I do without you?" asked Vira as she went to embrace Cura Ocllo. The emotional young women hugged and cried.

"For so many days, I woke up with you and went to sleep with you," said Cura Ocllo. "Together we have ached with hunger, fallen to the ground with weariness, and tried to maintain our dignity. I've grown so accustomed to be near you, Vira."

Kusa Akchi, not one to approve of demonstrations of affection, touched Cura Ocllo on the shoulder to summon her to leave. As the girls let go of each other and the tears continued to flow, Kusa Akchi and Cura Ocllo walked out into the darkness.

Kusa Akchi turned back to wave, "I will come to check on you, Princess. *Qamña allinlla*, now you be good. Goodbye Pani, Farewell Turi. Viracocha's blessings and protection be on you all."

And they were gone.

"Come, little dove," spoke Pani gently. "Let's wash off the dust of our journey."

Vira watched as Turi, armed with a broom and a hatchet, disappeared through the hole leading down to the secret chamber. She shuddered at the thought of living in that dark, windowless cave.

Pani took a kettle of boiling water from the fire and poured it into a large pot of cool water to warm it up. "What a shame," she moaned, "I never thought I would have to wash you with plain water, my dove. If only I had some perfumed oils for you." Pani wept as she wiped Vira's face with a warm, wet cloth.

Vira smiled and embraced Pani. "Please Pani, don't grieve. The morning will come and Manco will be King. Anyway, water is fine."

Cuna jumped up onto Vira's lap and licked the droplets of water that ran down her face and neck.

"See," laughed Vira, "Cuna *prefers* water!"

From behind tears of weariness and apprehension, the women smiled lovingly at each other.

"You know, my dove, you'll have to hide until *Amauta* Kusa Akchi returns with the truth of what has really transpired between Manco and the *White Strangers*. If they're using him, if he is actually their slave in disguise, then you will not be safe among them. You're so beautiful, my dove, they will devour you."

"Don't worry, Pani. I know. I saw them with my own eyes. But, there was that one man, *Don Alvarez de la Vega* . . ." Vira pronounced the words as though they were the most lyrical and sacred sounds she had ever spoken.

Pani's loving smile turned into a scowl. "Oh, my dear, after all you have suffered, you still dream of *him*. If only I could wash those feelings away with this warm water. My poor, little princess . . . My poor, little princess . . ."

Vira's right hand rose to her mouth to gently touch her lips with her fingertips.

CHAPTER 20

I n Cañaracay, the Cuzco palace of Inca Huascar, exciting preparations were underway. Manco was being dressed for his coronation. His *mamaconas*, the holy women who attended to all of Manco's needs, had already draped the coronation gown, woven from fine *vicuña* wool, strands of pure gold, and hummingbird feathers, across his shoulders. A *borla*, a sacred headpiece decorated with feathers and jewels was placed upon his head.

An attendant approached him formally and announced, "You have a visitor, my Lord, a holy Amauta."

Prince Manco looked at the attendant cynically. "Does he look like an assassin?" he asked trying to make light of his dire situation.

"No, my Lord. He is old and says his name is Kusa Akchi and that he was your tutor when you were young."

Manco's mask-like smile disappeared at the sound of Kusa Akchi's name. Memories awoke in his heart like forgotten songs.

"Is he alone?" asked Manco.

"No, my Lord, there is a woman at his side."

"Please, bring them in!"

Amauta Kusa Akchi entered leaning on Cura Ocllo's shoulder. Cura Ocllo wore a thick veil; however, Manco's memory of her beauty had not faded. His heart beat fast as he welcomed his visitors.

"Glory to you, Manco Inca Yupanqui," said the *Amauta* formally with a bow. Manco was shocked to see how frail Kusa Akchi had become in the two years since he had seen him. But when their eyes met, Manco saw clearly that the fire still burned brightly in his eyes.

"It is so good to see you both," said Manco honestly. "Cura Ocllo, you are like a beautiful mountain blossom, my heart sings to see you again."

Cura Ocllo curtsied shyly and looked down.

"I will bow to you," said Kusa Akchi sternly in his dark, gruff voice, "but I tell you Manco, it is an insincere gesture at best. My warning; however, is completely sincere—beware of the *White Strangers*."

"Well, my noble friend," he answered with the smile he used so often on the Spaniards, "from you I accept even reproaches willingly. I must confess that usually only praise is able to reach my heights."

Manco motioned for his attendants to leave. The holy women pulled back their hands and scuttled reluctantly away from him but they did not wish to cease their preparations. Again, he motioned for them to move away to the edges of the large room.

"Is it true? Did you deliver Cuzco into the hands of the *White Strangers* and execute General Chalcuchima in the great square as I have heard?"

"Don't dare to accuse me, *Amauta*," warned Manco like an angry child. "You don't know my heart and you are not privy to my plans. I prevented innumerable cruelties and the desecration of holy temples by cooperating with Viceroy Pizarro. I know what you think—but *try* to understand. The *Viracochas* will conquer Atahualpa's forces. They are the law for now. General Rumiñavi and General Quizquiz are still fighting them. They will be glad to kill me too if they get the chance. Our ancestors welcomed cooperative Indian tribes into the Empire. The *White Strangers* have welcomed us. I only capitulated out of necessity. For my cooperation, they have rewarded me richly."

"But you have to realize, Prince Manco, that you cannot trust them," chided the Amauta. "Look what they did to Atahualpa and Chalcuchima. Have you heard what they did to Prince Coca and Sapaca?"

Manco lowered his eyes from the hard glare of the priest. When news of the intrusion of Spanish forces into Prince Coca's castle had reached him, he immediately dispatched scouts to search for Vira and Sapaca. Although he cared very deeply for the safety of his relatives, he had done nothing more for them. Still, he desperately longed for Kusa Akchi's approval and Cura Ocllo's admiration.

"It pains me," he stated flatly, "that you and I disagree about what is best for the people."

"With every step you take, Manco, you build a larger tomb for your people. Don't you see that the *White Strangers' peace* means slavery for us?"

Consumed with righteous indignation, *Amauta* Kusa Akchi turned away from Prince Manco, leaned on Cura Ocllo for balance, and began to walk out of the large room.

"Please don't leave me," begged Manco. He was like a lost child reaching out for a friend. "Please, even if you don't approve of what I'm doing, you have to try to trust me. Stay here with me and be my Advisor."

Kusa Akchi halted his steps and turned back around to look at Manco. But he said nothing.

"Be my advisor," Manco repeated. "And let Cura Ocllo be my wife. I have room for you here. There is nothing you will lack."

Kusa Akchi and Cura Ocllo exchanged glances. Manco had been right about one thing: Kusa Akchi did not know Manco's heart. His mind raced with possible scenarios. If he walked out for his principles, he would disobey an Inca Prince, a prince to be crowned by an occupying power as King. If he stayed, he sacrificed all for which he stood. And there was Cura Ocllo to consider. The old *Amauta* was in a terrible bind.

"I should marry you?" asked Cura Ocllo breaking the tense silence in the room. "You do nothing to help your people and now you would keep me from fulfilling my sacred duty to Inti and Viracocha? I don't understand, Prince Manco. But I will obey the request of my King."

As Manco gazed at Cura Ocllo in confusion, not exactly sure of what she was saying, he smiled hopefully. "You accept then?" he asked for clarification.

Cura Ocllo looked at Kusa Akchi, her eyebrows raised in question. "If *Amauta* Kusa Akchi stays as your Advisor, then I will stay as your wife."

"Good, then it is decided." Manco indicated for his holy women to tend to Cura Ocllo's needs. Ten of them whisked Cura Ocllo off to another room to bathe and dress her for the coronation. She would have the best of everything.

Kusa Akchi watched in awe as Cura Ocllo was taken away from him with such rapidity. He stood alone looking at Manco. Another attendant approached Manco and said, "My Lord, you have another visitor."

"Does *this* one look like an assassin?" he asked with a smile, but he was serious.

"No, my Lord, it is your sister, Princess Vira!"

"Vira!" exclaimed Manco with unbridled joy. "Bring her in! Bring her in!"

Kusa Akchi limped forward abruptly, "You cannot keep her here. You must send her into hiding. She's not safe here among the *White Strangers*."

"Advising me already, Kusa Akchi? Good, then you accept the position?"

As Vira entered the room, Manco was transported back in time once more. "My beautiful little sister!" he shouted and ran to embrace her warmly. "How are you? Look at you, you've changed! You're even more beautiful than before!"

Vira ran to meet his embrace and was shouting joyous words of reunion with her brother even as he spoke. As Manco held her, he felt like himself again. He remembered the lessons they had learned together, the games they had played as children, the memories they shared . . . Manco's pride surged up in his chest and he was overwhelmed with a sense of what is right and honorable.

"My sweet, little sister! You can't be here. Two of Pizarro's men have already asked for you. You can't stay with me. Even if I marry you and make you my *Coya*, my Queen, they will take you from me. They only let me keep what they don't want. And they *want* you."

"What do you mean, Manco?" asked Vira. "What two men? Is it possible that one of them is Don Alvarez de la Vega? If so then please know that I accept!"

Manco kept a hand on each one of Vira's shoulders and gazed deeply in her dark eyes. They were mirrors of his soul.

"Yes, he answered, "Don Alvarez de la Vega has asked for you. But Hernando Pizarro outranks him and has asked for you as well. I would have no choice but to give you to the brother of our Spanish Viceroy. I don't like him, Vira. I don't want to give you to him. He's cruel and hard."

"I have seen him, Manco. You're right, I don't want him. Did you hear what happened to Sapaca and Coca? They killed Sapaca's son—our little nephew! It was horrible, Manco."

"I know, Vira. I sent men to look for you and Sapaca. Here *you* are, but I have had no news of Sapaca's fate. I wish you had arrived earlier. I have to go now. It is almost noon and my coronation will begin soon. When can I see you again? Where will you hide? No, don't tell me. I don't want to know. *Amauta* Kusa Akchi, take her away and see to her safety. Be cautious! Please, go quickly."

As Vira and *Amauta* Kusa Akchi left the room hastily, the holy women swarmed around Manco like bees and quickly completed their preparations.

Kusa Akchi and Vira left the palace. They practically ran to meet Turi who was waiting in an alley. He wrapped a dark brown cloak around Vira and led her off along the back roads to the safety of his house.

CHAPTER 21

T he coronation ceremony of the new, teenage puppet Inca King, Manco Yupanqui, took place in the traditional manner in Cuzco's main plaza. Commander and Viceroy Francisco Pizarro attended with Doña Conchita at his side. Seated near Pizarro with his court, were Alvarez; Diego de Almagro; Hernando, Juan, and Gonzalo Pizarro; Father Sebastiano, Father Pedro, Hernando DeSoto, and many other officers. They sat in seats of honor atop a high platform that had been erected for that purpose. They were not there to interfere with the festival, merely as spectators.

According to custom, the holy *Amautas* set up the holy idols from the temples along the path that led to the palace gates. The royal throne hewn from granite was still located at the end of the path and it was decorated with golden, silver, and ceramic idols. Next to the granite throne, under pavilions and seated on low wooden stools, sat the forefathers. Manco had ordered that they be delivered from their tombs on royal litters carried by uniformed bearers with great veneration and respect. A large crowd of Indians stood behind the nobles wearing checked government-issued tunics.

"What are those *things* seated beside the throne?" asked Father Sebastiano. "Is it possible? Are those shriveled corpses? This is the work of the Devil! Are they *real*?"

"They can't be," argued Francisco. "Juan, after the coronation, find out what those things are," he ordered.

"Of course, Francisco, I will. Do you think the Indians will accept Prince Manco as their new King? Do they really think he is a *god*?" asked Juan.

"We'll see," answered Hernando. "And yes, he is a *god*; can't you see his *halo and his wings?*"

When Manco mounted his throne and stood there surveying the large audience surrounding him, there was a hush of astonishment. He was certainly kingly and carried himself in the manner expected of an Inca King. He was wearing the *llautu* and held a golden *champi* in his right hand. Even Francisco Pizarro and Father Sebastiano were stunned that this was the same boy they had met previously.

"Look at that," muttered Hernando. "Francisco, does the expression on his face look conquered and submissive to you?"

"It certainly does *not*," interjected Sebastiano. "I knew this was a bad idea."

"Stop whining," growled Francisco, "for all we know he's a marvelous actor. Now be quiet."

"He looks just like Atahualpa," remarked Juan, greatly impressed.

Hernando DeSoto leaned over to Father Pedro and whispered, "He does look rather savage and imperial, Father. Could becoming Inca King have changed him so drastically?"

Father Pedro shrugged.

"Well, he's gloriously handsome!" declared Diego de Almagro. "He'll have no trouble subduing all the Indian *women* of the kingdom looking like *that.*"

"I said be quiet," grumbled Francisco. He turned to Father Sebastiano and said, "I like the boy. He's humble and simple. He's just acting. He has to convince the crowd that he is an Inca King."

When the sacred ceremony was completed, Manco descended the steps to his throne with graceful elegance and walked toward the Viceroy and his entourage. He shifted his golden *champi* to his left hand and extended his empty right hand to Viceroy Pizarro after the European style. Francisco grasped his hand in a firm handshake.

"Hail Inca Manco Yupanqui!" declared Francisco. "We are honored to witness this grand occasion. Congratulations to you and your people!"

Manco went down the line to shake hands with Pizarro's men. "Thank you for attending my coronation. Please stay and celebrate with my people. We will sing, dance, and drink *chicha* and later tonight you can come to my wedding!"

Standing again on level ground and eye to eye with Pizarro, Manco seemed once again his usual boyish self. Francisco embraced him and kissed him on both cheeks. "Of course, my son, we will stay and celebrate with you!"

Father Sebastiano grimaced at the insincere show of affection.

Don Alvarez looked at Manco who was smiling and laughing good-naturedly, and he wondered, could Manco be that talented of an actor?

CHAPTER 22

According to ancient rituals, *Amauta* Kusa Akchi placed Cura Ocllo's hand in Manco's and chanted prayers and blessings over them. They were both so young and beautiful. Cura Ocllo did not wear a veil so that the Spanish guests were able to delight in her exquisite beauty. While Manco held the hand of his young bride, his eyes were fixed upon her with genuine enchantment. She wore a splendid gown and a crown of snow-white feathers. Sparkling gems adorned her hair. Manco felt cold resistance in her hand and she would not let her eyes meet his for even a moment.

After the new King was joined with his new wife, they turned around to greet their guests in the reception hall after which everyone worked their way to the banquet hall for the feast. Food had been scarce in Cuzco, but the Spaniards provided supplies plundered from Inca storehouses on their journey from Jauja to Cuzco.

The walls of the banquet hall were covered with beautiful woven rugs and ornately decorated golden discs. The Inca did not use tables but had arrayed the dishes on the floor and placed beautifully embroidered cushions to sit on. The royal castle had not been plundered and General Quizquiz had not permitted his warriors to take very much of Cuzco's gold to ransom Atahualpa from Cajamarca. It was the first time Pizarro and his men saw the unveiled opulence and artistry of the lifestyle of the Inca nobility. Greedy Spanish eyes even coveted the golden place settings.

"Poor Inés," whispered Diego to Don Alvarez. "Remember how she used to look when she was with Atahualpa in Cajamarca? She was a blossom, so radiant and lovely. Just look at her now, she knows everyone hates her."

Inés was sitting on the floor next to her husband Francisco. She looked uncomfortable dressed in a purple, silk gown that had recently been brought to her from Spain. She also wore a black lace Spanish mantilla adorned with emeralds that was the latest fashion at the Court of Madrid. The lace veil was draped over a large comb on the top of her head and fell to her knees, but it did not cover her lovely face.

"She certainly does look sad and detached," answered Don Alvarez. He knew in his heart that this was an understatement, for her young eyes looked haunted.

"What do you suppose she's thinking right now?" asked Almagro, making conversation. "*Por Dios*, I'd kill for a glass of good Spanish wine! I'm tired of *chicha*!"

"I don't know," answered Alvarez in a manner that implied it was none of Almagro's concern. But Alvarez also wondered what thoughts troubled the young girl. He wondered if Inés was still angry that Francisco wouldn't permit her be buried with Atahualpa as she had requested. He wondered if an Inca female could really love a man and how Inés could have married her own brother. Alvarez shook his head. All he knew is that the girl looked miserable next to Francisco.

"I bet she's wondering who hates her the most: Atahualpa's family for her betrayal, Huascar's family for belonging to Atahualpa, or *us*, for distracting our commander." Almagro laughed at his own cleverness.

Francisco rose to propose a toast to the royal couple. Manco rose also. Through Felipillo, who was becoming more confident as the Viceroy's preferred interpreter, Francisco commended and praised Manco and his new bride. With humble words, Manco thanked Francisco for his blessings.

Inés had to rise to praise and compliment the bride. The glances of the two women crossed like swords. Cura Ocllo granted her nothing more than a stiff nod of her head. There was such rich contempt reflected in Cura Ocllo's dark eyes that Inés lowered her gaze and did not again dare to look up from her plate.

Don Alvarez had recognized *Amauta* Kusa Akchi and Cura Ocllo immediately upon arriving at the coronation earlier in the day. During the wedding which followed, he watched them closely and wondered if Francisco and the other men also recognized the former captives. But not a word was said about them.

A loud voice dominated the conversation in the room and Don Alvarez looked up to see Hernando speaking to Manco with Felipillo's assistance.

"*Por Dios*," exclaimed Almagro. "I pray it isn't another toast, I'll soon have to pee again!" Almagro was getting drunk on the *chicha*. Fortunately, it was not another toast.

"I will soon make another voyage to Spain to visit the King," announced Hernando as if to remind Manco that he was *not* Hernando's king. "I do hope you will provide golden treasure and the finest Inca art to satisfy the needs and good taste of King Charles."

"I will do my best," answered Manco. "I have been informed that many of my *Amautas* have gone to extreme efforts to hide sacred idols from the temples since you began to collect Atahualpa's ransom. They fear that if you take them all, they will have nothing left to worship. It is their responsibility to keep our sacred idols safe. But they are made of pure gold and will be of great value to you. My warriors will do what they can to find them."

Wishing to change the subject from gold, Cura Ocllo turned to Don Alvarez and asked, "Kind Sir, I wonder if you have a wife in Spain?"

"Ha," laughed Hernando. "Our Don Alvarez is a real woman-hater! I don't think he'll *ever* take a wife!"

Manco and Cura Ocllo looked at each other with confusion. They both knew how Vira felt about him. They wondered if this could be the same man."

Just then, hand maidens and Manco's other wives and concubines arrived to usher Cura Ocllo away to prepare her for her wedding night. She feigned feminine excitement and waved gracefully to the wedding party. The men stood as she left the room. There was hearty laughter heard among the Spaniards as Cura Ocllo disappeared around the corner.

Gonzalo Pizarro watched Cura Ocllo's graceful exit and decided that one day he would take her for himself.

"By the way, Juan," asked Francisco leaning over toward his little brother. What were those things sitting on the stools beside Manco's throne?"

"They are mummies, Francisco. *Real* mummies! The Indians think they're still alive!"

"Burn them," ordered Francisco.

CHAPTER 23

Cura Ocllo's handmaidens removed her wedding gown and feathered crown. As she sat before a large mirror, one of the women began to brush her jet black hair and gently remove the precious gems. Cura Ocllo looked angrily at her reflection. She couldn't believe this was happening.

The handmaidens pulled a long sleeveless gown over her head that covered her slippered feet. It was beautiful and soft and embroidered with delicate blossoms. Cura Ocllo began to weep and fled from the room. She ran down the corridor and burst into the room where Kusa Akchi was staying. The old man was there getting ready for bed. But he welcomed Cura Ocllo warmly for he had been missing her company.

Manco excused himself from the wedding feast. After many long farewells, he walked excitedly to his new rooms. But his bride was not there. "Where is she?" he yelled at the handmaidens. They shrugged and looked at him in bewilderment.

Manco ran to Kusa Akchi's apartment and barged in. As Manco rushed toward Cura Ocllo, she scooted behind Kusa Akchi like a scared little girl.

"Don't touch me!" she shouted at him. I'm a Sun Virgin, you can't touch me!"

"Yes I can," retorted Manco, "I'm the Inca King now. Remember? You were there when I received the *llautu* and the golden *champi!*"

"No, you're not the real King; you're only a *puppet* king. I want Kusa Akchi to take me to the mountain temple so I can marry Viracocha instead!"

Manco looked at the *Amauta*. "What should I do?" he asked pitifully. "I have the right to take her."

"She is small and fragile and you are strong and tall, yes, Manco, you can take her," answered Kusa Akchi. Cura Ocllo stayed crouched behind the old man. "You can send your guards and take her away in chains if you wish. You can even torture her like your friends the *White Strangers* like to do when people don't cooperate with them. Go ahead, Manco, it is your choice to make."

"No," said Manco with despair, "you give me no *choice*."

Manco looked at Cura Ocllo. "This is not what I want. Why do you treat me this way? Don't you know that I've loved you since the first time I saw you?"

Manco gasped and stepped away. He couldn't believe he actually spoke of his true feelings. Cura Ocllo was defiant, obstinate, proud, and cold: Why should he love her? He turned and walked out of Kusa Akchi's room. As he walked alone through the dark stone corridors he thought to himself, "I'll have her body once I possess her heart. When she sees that I do not present an affront to her fanatic patriotism, she will learn to love me. She will see that I am the true Inca King. I thought I saw love in her eyes once when she smiled at me," thought Manco, "and I will see it again."

CHAPTER 24

Manco assumed his role as Inca King and resumed the administration of *Pizarro's* new empire. Francisco doled out estates to his soldiers who wished to remain in Peru. Many of the conquistadors decided to take their gold and silver and return to Spain. When business was settled, Francisco and Hernando departed for the west coast.

"Our only connection to Spain," he explained to Almagro, "is over the ocean. If we are to establish lucrative trade with Europe, we need port cities and safe harbors. I don't want anyone to come to my New World and see nothing but natives and mountains."

Hernando Pizarro sailed to Spain with letters and a ship filled with Inca treasure and slaves to please the King. Diego de Almagro was left to govern Cuzco under the constant watch of Juan and Gonzalo Pizarro.

Time passed. As more Spanish conquistadors arrived in Peru to seek their fortunes, the balance between Spanish and Inca power tipped. Respect for the Inca throne diminished. Although Manco was having some success organizing the Indians in their agricultural and mining activities and collecting the results of their work for the store houses, he was constantly pestered by the Spaniards.

No matter how much gold and silver Manco gave them, they demanded more. "If I could turn the mountain snows to silver, it would still not satisfy their lust," he complained. "The more I give them, the *more* they demand!"

Old Diego de Almagro was not taking his task of running Cuzco very seriously. He was glad to rest for a while and merely endeavored to enjoy each day as much as possible. He moved into a luxurious palace on Cuzco's square built by Atahualpa's father, Huayna Capac. He was joined by Juan and Gonzalo as well as Don Alvarez de la Vega and a few other officers.

Tension began to build between the newcomers and the conquistadors who were present at the capture of Atahualpa. The new conquistadors had spent all their money on passage to the New World. Now they were poor and looked hopefully toward Almagro to guide them to their coveted riches. In contrast, the conquistadors who fought at Pizarro's side when Atahualpa was captured were now fabulously wealthy and extremely grateful to Francisco for their surprising success.

Their success in Peru was truly a miracle. Francisco Pizarro, low-born and illiterate, was now rich and powerful and living in luxury. Such a miracle could not have occurred in Spain.

Gonzalo Pizarro was more interested in Manco's wives than his gold or silver. He was particularly interested in Cura Ocllo whose beauty he observed during the wedding feast. His mind had seized upon her and he constantly pestered and harassed Manco to give her to him. Manco refused to deliver Cura Ocllo to Gonzalo and tried to placate him with other women from his household. But Gonzalo, only 23 years old at the time, would not be satisfied with any other woman.

Gonzalo was tall, graceful, black-bearded, ruggedly handsome, and a renowned womanizer. It was only his excellent horsemanship and precise aim with Spanish weaponry that gained him the respect and admiration of the men. Although the Pizarro family was not known for their generosity and benevolence, it was obvious to everyone that Gonzalo was the stingiest of them all.

Time passed and tensions grew. Juan and Gonzalo harassed Manco without mercy. After an absence of nearly two years, Hernando Pizarro returned from his voyage to Spain. Francisco greeted his brother in Lima, his new port city recently declared the new capital of Peru. Jauja was located too far inland to serve his purposes any longer. Francisco built a splendid palace where he lodged like a king surrounded by courtiers and his young mistress, Inés.

"King Charles has granted you the title of *Marquis*," reported Hernando happily. "But don't get too excited big brother," warned Hernando, "King Charles was so impressed by the Inca gold and silver I gave him, that he wants more, much more. It seems he's been *over-using* his resources lately, or, um, how shall I phrase it? He's broke. Oh, and there's one more thing," hesitated Hernando uncomfortably. "He decided to divide the

Inca Empire in half: You have received Governorship of the north half and he granted Diego de Almagro Governorship of the southern half. I'm sorry, Francisco. I just hope Diego doesn't think he gets to keep Cuzco."

"Damn it," yelled Francisco as he beat his fists on the wooden table. "How could King Charles do this to me? I *begged* him in my letter *not* to grant a title to Diego. What am I supposed to do *now*? Does he think *he* is the new Inca King? Does he think he can do to me what Huayna Capac did to his *sons*?"

"Where is Diego?" asked Hernando.

"I left him in Cuzco. I never thought this would happen. I told Juan and Gonzalo to keep an eye on him. Our little brothers are millionaires now. I actually advised them to relax and enjoy the spoils of war. Stupid!"

"It's all right, Francisco, you couldn't have known that King Charles would do this."

"Well, you have to go immediately and tell Almagro. I don't have a choice," declared Pizarro angrily.

"What if you use this news to your advantage, Francisco? What if you offer money and men to Almagro to go and explore and conquer his new lands to the south? Alvaredo brought fresh men and horses with him on his ship. I know it would be hard to sacrifice troops, but you have more money than you could possibly ever spend. You could get him out of Cuzco and out of your hair for a while."

"Yes," agreed Francisco. "Who knows, maybe an angry Indian will take care of him for me," said Francisco as he smiled with one side of his face.

"Can you believe it, little brother? King Charles has done to me exactly what Huayna Capac did to Atahualpa . . ."

CHAPTER 25

Late one evening, Diego de Almagro, Don Alvarez de la Vega, Hernando DeSoto, Gonzalo Pizarro, Juan Pizarro, Lopez, and a few other Spanish officers were sitting in a large room decorated in rich Inca fashion. The men had long since put away their scratched and dented battle armor and were dressed in black velvet tunics and wide puffed short trousers. Their legs were covered by long black silk stockings. Instead of helmets, they now wore hats with long feather plumes. Although they were millionaires and lived the life of leisure, unrest had settled over them like a fog.

"What's the matter, Almagro?" asked Don Alvarez. "Why are you sulking over there in that dark corner with that faraway look in *your eye?*"

"Very funny," Almagro smirked.

"Really, Diego, what thoughts are marking your face with such a sad expression?"

Almagro was already deep in his cups. "I miss my son," he answered like a pouting child. "He's the only family I have left." As Almagro emptied another bottle of Spanish wine, he sighed dramatically.

Alvarez walked over to him, rather unsteady on his feet from the wine bottles he had emptied, to cheer up his old friend. "Now Diego, you know that every soldier has his duties. Young Diego will come back soon. He'll be covered with glory and medallions for his bravery!"

"You're right," sighed Almagro again. "I know he'll return when he completes his military training. I just wish there were more I could do to ease his way through this world. What will I leave for him when I die—I, the Mayor of *Tumbez*? I had hoped he wouldn't have to struggle through life the way I did. I love him so much."

Everyone in the room nodded in sad emotion.

"Hey, Alvarez," continued Almagro in a steady slur. "Do you know the difference between being fair and really loving someone?"

"Ah . . . philosophy . . . how I love to ponder the philosophy of drunk, old men," teased Juan.

"Shut up, Juan," barked DeSoto. "Do you have respect for *no one*? You should watch out. King Charles is very sensitive regarding the sanctity and divine right of *kings*. He would not approve of the manner in which you treat Manco. You can't even muster respect for a man with direct authority over you. Your pride and greed make me sick!"

"I would have *killed* you already," yelled Juan as he rose to his feet, "if it weren't for your *pitiful* friends, Soto! Too bad your horse was so fast. But don't you worry, my friend, I have a faster horse now!"

"Shut up, all of you," slurred Almagro. Slowly and angrily, Juan sat down as Hernando DeSoto stormed out of the room and left the palace.

"Now listen, Alvarez, all of you, listen here! The difference between being *fair* and *really* loving someone is this: You see, *fair* is when you make sure that no one suffers *more* than you. *Love* is when you make sure that no one suffers *as much*!

"Hey, that's pretty good old man," said Alvarez.

"Francisco gave a larger share of treasure to his *horse* than he gave *me*," complained Almagro. "I'm his *partner*! I thought he *cared* about me!"

"You shut up, old man. You got more than you deserve. Stop complaining," chided Gonzalo.

"What are you talking about?" asked Lopez. "You've got the whole city of Cuzco in your lap. Aren't you in charge here? Why should Francisco get fat all alone? He never sacrificed an eye like you did! *You're* the one who lives in the *holy city*!"

Almagro sighed again. Lopez's words seemed to caress his spirit. But he knew it wasn't fair. Francisco received all the glory and Diego got a gracious pat on the back.

"Yes Diego, you're looking at the situation out of the wrong *eye*!" teased Gonzalo.

The men roared with laughter. Juan fell out of his chair and rolled around laughing on the flagstone floor. Alvarez patted Diego on the back to comfort him but couldn't keep from laughing himself. Almagro slapped Alvarez's hand away and swigged deeply from yet another bottle of wine.

"I'll just get what I can get out of King Manco," he said. "He's my ticket! Francisco doesn't have to know . . . Hell, he *wants* me to get along with Manco!"

"Manco likes you, old man!" shouted Juan. "You've got everything under control here!"

Again, the room burst with drunken laughter.

Almagro thrust the wine bottle over to Alvarez who grabbed it and filled his glass. "Drink, Alvarez, drink to my son! Drink to *love*! Who knows what tomorrow may bring? Take what you can from life. Grab at it, my boy. All you have is *now*."

Don Alvarez drank deeply. If he drank enough, maybe he could black-out the past. But he was drowning in a dark mood. He was angry and agitated. The wine only seemed to intensify his bitterness. He missed Father Pedro. Why did he have to go to Lima with Francisco? Well, he thought, at least he had orders to travel there next week. His thoughts turned back to Doña Elvira . . . Damn *women*, damn *Cuzco*, damn *everything*!

Abruptly, Don Alvarez rose to his feet and, with all his drunken adrenaline, threw his glass at the stone wall.

"I'm going for a walk," he announced when everyone stared up at him.

"What is it?" asked Almagro. "Are you thinking about that woman who broke your heart again? That's what *I'm* doing!" laughed Almagro sadly. "Why did she have to die giving life to little Diego? He was such a small baby."

"God did you a favor, Diego, to take away your woman. Those creatures don't have souls," grumbled Don Alvarez. For a moment he recalled a woman's face that was sweet and innocent with dark slanted eyes. He shook his head to rid himself of the useless memory.

"My woman was noble and kind-hearted. If only I could have her back. I would be nicer to her now . . ." Diego dropped his head upon the table. He sobbed and moaned for a short while and then fell fast asleep.

"Anyone interested in a little amusement tonight?" asked Lopez to everyone in the room with a wink. Lopez did not want to go to sleep yet. In his lively state of inebriation he had far more colorful plans than to wrap his face in pillows.

"We've sent all the male Indians away to labor in the gold and silver mines. There's no one to prevent us from having a little fun with their wives and daughters!" stated Lopez.

Everyone laughed aloud.

"Count me out," answered Gonzalo getting to his feet. "I'm going to be busy getting what I want from Inca Manco."

"Well leave him a few women to enjoy," teased Lopez. "You've taken all of the prettiest ones already."

"No," said Gonzalo, "I didn't get the prettiest one yet. But I'll get her tonight." Gonzalo headed out and made his way toward the Temple of the Sun. He was determined to get Cura Ocllo for himself.

"I'm too tired for any crazy adventures tonight," said Juan. "I'm going to bed . . . alone."

"Well, you'll all be sorry when you miss out on the opportunity *I* offer you! I found something and I want to show you!" bragged Lopez mysteriously. "It's something for your brother Hernando, you know, to welcome him *home!*" It's someone, I mean *something*, he has wanted for a long time." Lopez let out a lusty laugh. "We can have a little fun with her until Hernando gets back."

"Then you better hurry," warned Juan.

With complete indifference to the woes of his new world, Don Alvarez followed Lopez out into the night. When the cold air touched his burning cheeks, he felt a slight sense of relief. "Why shouldn't I have some fun," he asked Lopez. "I'm not a monk. Everyone else does it, and Father Pedro's not here, is he?"

"That's right," said Lopez with a malicious grin, "You're no better than *me*, are you?"

Upon the dark sheet of sky, small stars twinkled. The night air was filled with the strange, seductive fragrance of exotic flowers. Don Alvarez followed Lopez through empty streets toward a quarter of the city called the *Puma's Tail*. He was lost deep in his own troubling thoughts when Lopez stopped in front of a small, ancient, stone house surrounded by a high and impenetrable wall. Lopez pressed his index finger over his lips. His fingernails were long and dirty.

"Where are we?" whispered Alvarez.

Again, Lopez pressed his finger to his lips.

Lopez looked around for a way to enter. He pushed the gate and, to his surprise, it wasn't locked. "Hernando's girl lives here," whispered Lopez, hoarse with excitement. "Are you coming or are you too scared?"

Alvarez was too drunk to pass up a dare. As he passed through the unlocked gate, he noticed the head of a puma carved in stone that decorated the entrance. Suddenly, the men were startled by loud barking from a small dog that flew toward them in the dark garden. Cuna attacked Lopez's ankle ferociously but Lopez kicked him away and hit him with the back of his spear. Cuna laid flat in the grass and didn't make another sound.

With nothing but the moon to illuminate the path, the men walked toward the door of the house. Lopez pushed it open and, with Alvarez close at his heels, pressed in.

Don Alvarez, looking over Lopez's shoulder, found himself in a room only dimly illuminated by a single torch. He saw the vague silhouette of an old Indian man and woman, who both screamed and flung their hands in the air in despair and shock. But all these figures faded when he caught sight of a maiden standing only a few steps away. She was illuminated faintly by the pale light, yet he recognized her immediately. It was Princess Vira! At this discovery his heart began to throb violently. Was this a vision? Had he passed out? He was trying to understand what was happening when Lopez ran forward and grabbed Vira roughly by the arms.

In a flash, the room was packed with wild and angry Indian warriors. They seemed to have come streaming forth from a hole like fire ants as if the earth had opened. They flung themselves on Lopez first. A spear penetrated his stomach and another pierced his chest as he fell to the ground.

Don Alvarez just stood there. He felt a spear pierce his shoulder and another spear pierce his leg. Something struck hard against his head and he swayed dizzily. Through the mist of approaching unconsciousness, Alvarez saw Vira run toward him. She placed herself between him and his attackers and defended him with her own body.

"Don't touch *this* one! Stop! He saved my life!" shouted Vira in agony.

Her clear voice rang through the murderous shouts and growls and immediately, the Indians put down their weapons and obeyed her order. Alvarez felt far away as in a dream and then there was nothing.

CHAPTER 26

onzalo failed in every attempt to obtain Cura Ocllo. With his entire being, he yearned to merely have a glimpse of her beauty again. He pestered and harassed Manco incessantly. Every day he visited the royal palace and demanded that Cura Ocllo be handed over to his possession like so much gold. He made terrible threats and behaved rudely and violently toward Manco.

Manco resisted. In his limited Spanish, he told Gonzalo, "Of my women and of my treasure, you can take all. But you will never touch my *Coya*, my Cura Ocllo."

Gonzalo offered bribes to Manco's Indian servants to deliver Cura Ocllo to him, but none were taken. He offered horses, Spanish armor, weapons, and anything he thought they might covet—but nothing could purchase their cooperation.

Gonzalo thought about storming the palace and taking Cura Ocllo for himself by force. But he knew his face and form were too recognizable. He didn't know where in the palace Cura Ocllo dwelt. It was an enormous building and he feared he would not locate her. He would never be able to penetrate the inner workings of the Inca King's royal palace.

He understood why Manco refused to hand her over. Of all the women he had seen in this New World, she was the most beautiful. He remembered the first time he saw her in the dimly lit temple in Tumbez. How had she and the old man escaped? He remembered how she wept and tried to conceal her beauty with her veil. That was years ago. They were just *children*.

Then he saw her again in Cuzco when she married Manco. He was surprised that Francisco did not recognize her and the old priest. He hoped no one else recognized her. Gonzalo was convinced that Cura Ocllo was meant for him alone since his path had met hers once again in this crazy world. He was a man now and had proved his valor in battle. He had to have her. And, of course, she would be *lucky* to have *him*.

Gonzalo's anxiety was greatly heightened by the knowledge that he had to accomplish his mission before Hernando returned to Cuzco. Hernando didn't like to be troubled with non-military issues. He was always trying to please King Charles from afar. Gonzalo knew his older brother well enough . . . Hernando would not approve of such an unfriendly act against the puppet Inca King.

Gonzalo had not seen Cura Ocllo since her handmaidens summoned her away from her wedding feast. It was his memory of her that haunted and tormented him. Many nights he awoke from a deep sleep during which he dreamt that she was kissing him with her full lips and caressing his face. He could see into her dark exotic eyes. When he woke up and invariably discovered that it was *not* Cura Ocllo who lay by his side in the bed but some other nameless female, his disappointment was crushing. His dreams ruined the possibility of finding contentment with any other woman.

He had seen the old *Amauta* who was with her in Tumbez. He worked for Manco now as some sort of advisor. Gonzalo watched him closely but never observed Cura Ocllo in his company. How could a person live for so long in one place and never venture anywhere? When did she see the sunlight and enjoy the passing of the seasons? Was she able to gaze upon the moon when it was full?

Because he was so young, Gonzalo struggled to receive good assignments from his officers. It was with chagrin and frustration that he finally agreed to take charge of converting the Cuzco Temple of the Sun into a chapel in which to hold the required daily masses. In hindsight, considering his reputation, Gonzalo wondered why they wanted *his* assistance at all. For within the Temple of the Sun lived the *mamaconas* and the *mamacunas*: The beautiful women who served as temple attendants and temple virgins. These were the women who made the Inca King's clothing and accessories: The clothes he *never* wore twice.

"But the temple attendants and the sun virgins live within the Temple of the Sun," explained Father Pedro. "They cannot be thrown out onto the street. They are holy and dedicated to the worship and service of their gods. Their role is similar to our nuns!"

"Nuns?" scoffed Francisco, "You would compare our Sisters of the Holy Roman Catholic Church to native pagan temple prostitutes?"

"No, Francisco," he capitulated. "But these women are not accustomed to mainstream society. They are reclusive and live merely to serve the Inca King and their gods. If they are not permitted to remain in the temples, you need to give them a safe and acceptable alternative."

"I'll *give* them to Manco. They are *his* concern," answered Francisco dryly.

But Diego de Almagro was of a different mind than Francisco Pizarro. Although he received orders to convert the Cuzco Temple of the Sun into a chapel, he decided to maintain a portion of the temple as a permanent residence for the *mamaconas* and the *mamacunas*.

"I want to keep Inca Manco happy and comfortable," explained Diego. "It is his tradition to use the Temple of the Sun as a place of worship and a residence for the holy women. The temple is big enough for us all. We will install a grand bronze bell on the top and renovate the front chambers for masses. There will be room for all to sit comfortably!"

In a half-hearted effort to perform his assigned duties, Gonzalo explored the Cuzco Temple of the Sun. There was nothing left inside except stones and some wooden furnishings. The gold idols, gold-plated altar, and gold wall coverings had sailed years ago on ships to Spain. But the stones themselves were glorious. Gonzalo spent long hours walking the perimeter of the building's terraces marveling at how the enormous stones had been fitted together so carefully that mortar was not necessary. In fact, there was not room between the stones to insert even a leaf of parchment.

The clever design of interlocking stones made the foundation of the structure practically earthquake-proof. Had Gonzalo not spent the last couple of years living in Cuzco and had not personally experienced the tremors, he might not have understood the value of such massive architectural foundational design.

As he walked the interior perimeter of the lower levels of the temple, Gonzalo discovered a hole. Once concealed by a heavy woven carpet, the hole was the opening to a secret tunnel. With nothing but a candle for light, Gonzalo lowered himself into the hole to discover a very narrow spiral stairway that led straight down into the earth.

Hopeful that he had found a secret hiding place for Inca treasure, Gonzalo was deeply disappointed when he realized that all he had found was a crude passageway. At the bottom of the spiral stairway, he found himself within a tunnel that gently sloped upward. It was dark and dank, and the thick musk of wet earth filled his lungs.

The tunnel continued for a distance of only about 35 yards and then ended abruptly. Crouching so that he would not hit his head, Gonzalo looked up and saw pinpoints of light filtering in from above. With his hands over his head, he pushed with all his strength and a great disk broke free. He pushed it up and out of the tunnel. When he emerged from the ground, Gonzalo was looking at a small grove of trees at the top of a small hillock near the Huatanay River.

Convinced that his discovery was not noteworthy, Gonzalo continued with his assessment of the temple.

"Show me where the temple women live," said Gonzalo to *Amauta* Kusa Akchi in Spanish.

"Follow me," answered *Amauta* Kusa Akchi. "But only Inca King and *Amautas* may enter."

"Haven't you realized by now, old *ñawpa*, that I out-rank your Inca King?" taunted Gonzalo.

Reluctantly and with much trepidation, Kusa Akchi led Gonzalo down a long corridor. In his bare feet, the *Amauta* made no sound at all. In total contrast, the noise from Gonzalo's hard boot heels ricocheted between the rock walls and rock floor. At last, the men reached the entrance to the wing used as residence for the *mamaconas* and sun virgins. They lived their lives in seclusion and served only their gods and their Inca King. They cared for the temple and the needs of the priests during the required sacrifices, festivals, and daily rituals.

The old *Amauta* made a loud sound by clearing his throat. There was a flutter of white as the women moved about within the chamber in preparation of Kusa Akchi's entrance. He spoke to them in Quechua and told them to cover their faces with their veils for a *white stranger* was present.

Gonzalo peered in around Kusa Akchi's shoulder and saw a vision he didn't expect. It was Cura Ocllo. He watched her reach over her shoulder and lightly drape a lace veil across her beautiful face. What was *she* doing here? Gonzalo's breath caught in his throat. His heart raced and he felt confused. He needed air. It was too dark in this place.

"It is enough," said Gonzalo, "get me out of here *Amauta*. I need air."

Kusa Akchi was startled but greatly pleased and relieved that Gonzalo had not demanded to see more. He knew the reputation of this Pizarro brother. He was the worst womanizer among the conquistadors. To lead Gonzalo Pizarro into the *mamaconas* residence was like releasing a puma in a children's nursery. With deep relief, he led Gonzalo quickly to the front entrance of the temple and out into the sunshine. Gonzalo stumbled as though drunk until his eyes grew accustomed to the glare. He looked at the old *Amauta* and backed away without a word. He needed time to think.

Within hours, Gonzalo had devised a plan. It was simple. All he needed was a dark hooded poncho and bare feet. He would take her. As soon as the sun went down, Gonzalo would take Cura Ocllo.

After waiting for darkness and drinking a few glasses of wine with the men to stabilize his nerves, Gonzalo entered the Cuzco Temple of the Sun through the tunnel he had discovered. He wrapped himself in the large poncho and removed his boots. Quietly, he retraced the path to the quarters of the *mamaconas*. The women were busy embroidering and weaving. The silence was pure. Gonzalo saw Cura Ocllo seated in a corner upon a wooden stool working on a piece of white material. Gonzalo watched and waited. One by one, the women put down their handiwork and retreated from the room.

After an eternity had passed, Gonzalo could wait no longer. He cleared his throat loudly. As the few women who remained in the room looked around in surprise and reached for their veils, Gonzalo walked in, grabbed Cura Ocllo by the arm and commenced to drag her from the room. She gasped and involuntarily resisted by stepping backward. When Gonzalo turned his head to look at her, she recognized his face.

She screamed. It was the most horrifying and shrill sound Gonzalo had ever heard. His blood curdled in his veins and he panicked. As white-robed holy women ran toward him to rescue their little sister, he picked up Cura Ocllo and ran from the room at full speed.

Cura Ocllo kicked her legs and flailed her arms. She tried to claw his face with her finger nails but he held her backwards over his shoulder. She beat his back with her fists and tried to twist away from him. Where was *Amauta* Kusa Akchi?

Gonzalo ran. The howling women chased him down the corridor. Some of them detoured to seek assistance from the priests.

"I know who you are," screamed Cura Ocllo as Gonzalo's shoulder pounded her abdomen. "You are Gonzalo Pizarro. You were at my wedding. Release me! I am a Sun Virgin! You can't touch me!"

Gonzalo didn't even slow down. Was he laughing? When he reached the hole to the spiral stairway, he put her down and shoved her down in front of him. She turned around to resist descending the steps. He faced her and placed his index finger over her lips, "Shhh," he smiled at her. He could hear the *mamaconas* scuttling down the corridor in pursuit.

Cura Ocllo stared at him with eyes wild with shock and fear.

"Don't worry, my Lady," teased Gonzalo in Spanish, "I'm the handsomest man you'll ever see and now I'm all yours."

For this very occasion, Gonzalo had bothered himself to memorize a new Quechua word and he whispered it now in Cura Ocllo's ear, "*Añallaw.*" One word that meant so much, one word that summed up the feelings he had for his prize: How wonderful, how beautiful, and how sweet. Gonzalo was thrilled.

The expression in his eyes made her soul sick and her flesh creep. Cura Ocllo wailed. She lunged at Gonzalo's face and bit down on his nose. She clawed at his eyes with her fingers and shoved her elbows in his chest. As he fought her off, she scratched his face and spat at him. She grabbed handfuls of his hair and beard and ripped them away. Gonzalo slapped her and pushed her down the steps. What was wrong with her? Was she crazy?

With adrenaline lending him great strength, Gonzalo grabbed Cura Ocllo by the hair and dragged her through the black tunnel as she twisted and struggled against him. When he pulled her out into the starlit night, she fell on him again and attacked him viciously. It took every bit of his strength, but he hoisted her over his shoulder again and ran. When the *mamaconas* and *Amautas* emerged from the tunnel in pursuit, Cura Ocllo was already gone.

By the time Gonzalo got home with his prize, he was filthy, bruised, and bleeding. Cura Ocllo was filthy, bruised, and bleeding as well. But she wouldn't give up. Gonzalo's servants came to his assistance. There were numerous casualties, but Cura Ocllo was finally tied to a chair with rope. She was furious and dangerous.

"Just leave her there for now," gasped Gonzalo as he struggled to catch his breath. "She'll settle down. Put something in her mouth to shut her up—but don't hurt her. Heat some water for me, I need a bath. And get some bandages, I think I'm hurt."

There was a wild scurry of activity as the servants dealt with the unusual situation. Gonzalo sat down heavily in an arm chair and stared at Cura Ocllo in wonder. Cura Ocllo glared at him with hatred and struggled against her bonds.

Gonzalo didn't know what to say. Almost as if to comfort himself, he muttered, "Don't worry, everything will be all right."

When his servants came to prepare his bath, Cura Ocllo closed her eyes tightly and wept.

Gonzalo limped to the bath chamber and wondered if he had made a mistake.

CHAPTER 27

L ate the next morning, an anxious and hung-over Almagro visited Manco's palace and expressed his wish for an audience in regard to very important matters. Within a few minutes he was admitted into a spacious but only dimly lit room where the young ruler sat upon a comfortable armchair. He motioned to a chair but Almagro would not sit. He remained standing, nervously fumbling with the plume of his velvet hat.

"Where is my *Coya*, my wife?" demanded Manco in Spanish.

"Surely I don't know the whereabouts of your wives, my Lord. What do you mean?" asked Almagro.

"Someone take Cura Ocllo from Temple! Where is she? Gonzalo take her! I want her back now!" screamed Manco.

"I don't know anything about this occurrence," answered Almagro nervously. He wouldn't put it past Gonzalo to kidnap the *Coya*. He had been desperate to have her. "I will send my scouts to find her for you, my Lord."

"Well," answered Manco, "if you not here for *Coya*, then why you come?"

"Hernando Pizarro has returned from his voyage to Spain, my Lord," reported Almagro. "He arrived early this morning and has given me orders from Francisco to travel south for an extended military campaign to explore the southern lands of the Empire."

Manco looked at his interpreter for assistance.

"Another campaign already?" asked Manco with an obvious frown.

"King Charles appointed me *Governor* of the southern half of the empire," stated Almagro proudly with a weak smile. "I now possess the same lands Huayna Capac granted Huascar. I must go and occupy the country and establish peace."

"You go away now?" asked Manco. "I like better when you stay in Cuzco. I will miss you, Almagro," said Manco sincerely.

"General Quizquiz is still ambushing and assaulting our Spanish forces, Manco. I am told he is currently organizing his troops for yet another strike against us. Can I trust you to cooperate with Hernando? He will need your support while he is here."

Manco conferred with his interpreter.

"When my *Coya* come home, then I will cooperate for you," offered Manco. "General Quizquiz like to kill me too," said Manco with a frown.

"There is one more matter about which I am extremely worried, my Lord," stammered Almagro. "Last night, two Spanish officers went out for an evening stroll and did not return. This morning we found the body of the one we call *Lopez*. He was murdered with spears.

Manco bit his lip. "I sorry, Señor," he said, "I say to Viceroy that your army be *your* business."

Almagro cleared his throat. "My Lord," he said, "I do not seek reparations for the death of Lopez, but I must find the other officer. It is a friend of mine named Don Alvarez de la Vega."

Manco sprang to his feet. "This serious, Almagro. I say you, *I* find Señor Alvarez if *you* find Cura Ocllo."

"Don Alvarez has orders to report to Lima next week. Francisco will be furious to learn that he is missing. But I must go now." Almagro rushed toward Manco and grasped the young man in a rugged hug. "I have so much in common with Huascar now. You are truly like a son to me."

"Go with peace, Diego. My brother, Paullu, go with you. He very popular with my southern people. I send porters to carry your supplies. Take what you need. You my friend. Come soon to me again."

"Thank you so much, Inca Manco. It will be a glad day when I see you again. Don't let the Pizarros treat you too badly. You don't deserve that. God bless you!"

As Almagro turned to leave, Manco yelled to him in Quechua. Almagro looked at the interpreter and shrugged.

"The Pizarros give gold to their friends. But all Inca Manco has received from them is their steel. If you stay away too long, he does not guarantee that he will still be alive upon your return. He says goodbye."

"Goodbye," responded Almagro with sadness in his eyes. He knew in his heart that Manco was right.

CHAPTER 28

As Manco slouched miserably upon his throne in his royal palace in Cuzco, *Amauta* Kusa Akchi appeared and announced, "Important Cañari messengers have come, my Lord. They wait below in the garden to speak with you."

"What do we have to do with the Cañari? You know I'm not supposed to receive secret messengers," complained Manco dryly. "Anyway, everyone knows that they are loyal to the *White Strangers*. It's probably just a trap to catch me breaking my word to the Pizarros. Send them away."

"But King Chincha is with them," insisted Kusa Akchi. "I beg you to receive him."

"King Chincha!" laughed Manco instantly recalling the incident with the cantuta blossom and the love song. It seemed like a lifetime ago. Old memories stirred in his heart of long-ago beautiful days when he was still a prince, a *REAL* Inca prince, instead of a wretched shadow king. "Of course, please bring him in."

A young Indian walked proudly toward Manco.

"You are not King Chincha," declared Manco. "What is going on here?"

"I am his son," responded the visitor. "My father died in Cajamarca with Atahualpa. I also am called King Chincha."

Manco recalled how angry Chincha had been when he left the royal court after Huascar denied him Vira's hand in marriage. So he *had* joined with Atahualpa after all. Manco turned to his visitor and welcomed him with a nod of his head. Kusa Akchi stayed in the background watching anxiously.

"Manco Capac," began the new King Chincha in a gentle tone, "I did not attend your coronation and my people have fought against you. But

130

I have seen the cruelty of the *White Murderers* with my own eyes. I wish, on behalf of the Cañari, to accept you now as my King. And I bring you an offering."

Manco gasped. Two strong Cañari warriors entered the hall and between them was Cura Ocllo. The Cañari, well known for their cooperation and loyalty with the Spaniards since the beginning of the conquest of Peru, had been accepted into Gonzalo's inner circle. When they saw that Gonzalo had kidnapped Cura Ocllo from the Temple, Inca Manco's *Coya* who had once been a Sun Virgin, their pride could not accept the trespass over sacred ground. They spirited Cura Ocllo away while Gonzalo slept and were now returning her to Manco.

"I hope to reestablish union with you, Inca Manco," stated the young King Chincha hopefully.

There was silence in the room as Manco stared at Cura Ocllo in astonishment. She was scratched and had a black eye. Her eyes were swimming in tears. A gentle smile graced her pretty face. She looked so different from the defiant and obstinate creature that had refused him on his wedding night so long ago.

As in a dream, he watched her come toward him with light, noiseless steps. Bending low, she touched the edge of his robe to her lips. "Allow me, please, my Lord, to pay homage to the Great Inca," she whispered as he lifted her gently. Her face beamed with a warm glow and there was love in her eyes.

Manco led Cura Ocllo to his throne and made her sit. "Are you all right, my love?" he asked her with sincere concern. "Did he hit you?"

"Don't worry, Manco," answered Cura Ocllo. "He is far worse than I. I am afraid I caused him serious injury."

"I beg you, my Lord," continued King Chincha, "to break your alliance with the *White Monsters*! They are not *Viracochas* like we hoped. They may look like Viracocha, but they are *nothing* like him! They are not *liberators*, but *occupiers*! Dare to stand at the head of your people and defy those who drive us into slavery, humiliation, and death!"

Manco bit his lip again and frowned deeply. He looked at Cura Ocllo and then turned to face King Chincha.

"We know your intentions are noble," continued Chincha, "but we are young and inexperienced. Ask yourself if the path you have chosen is good." Manco looked thoughtfully around the room.

131

"Look at me, Manco *Capac*," said Kusa Akchi. "I have been with you as your tutor and your spiritual counselor since you were weaned. I know your soul better that I know the palm of my own hand. You believe that serving the Spaniards will bring peace. You still think that Spanish greed can be satiated. Time proves that you were mistaken. Your people die by the thousands. They labor till death in the mines or hide in damp cellars in agonizing fear. The *White Strangers* rape and dishonor our women, even the descendants of the royal house. They are blood thirsty conquerors."

Kusa Akchi stopped to catch his breath. When he spoke again, his tone was softer, "I beg you, Manco, understand at last that the moment has come. We have one last chance for freedom. Let us begin the great battle and either win or die."

Manco trembled and groped for words or a good argument. When he finally spoke his voice was shaky and defensive.

"How can I make war against the Spaniards who have put their faith and trust in me?"

"You trust *them*," the *Amauta* replied heatedly, "while they help themselves to *your* women, *your* treasure, *your* food, *your* land, and *your* power. They are brutal and merciless!"

Manco stood stiffly, as though his feet were part of the stone floor. He threw a pleading glance at his old tutor then raised his eyes to his vassal. Did they think he never had doubts? Was he so good at concealing his emotions that Kusa Akchi didn't detect the torment in his soul? Now Kusa Akchi spoke his fears into his very face. Manco doubted that an opportunity to revive his kingdom would come. Perhaps it was time to test the saying: *One glorious death is worth hundreds of shameful lives.*

Manco had one last concern. General Quizquiz would never accept him as Inca King. Quizquiz served Atahualpa loyally and still fought for revenge against the *White Strangers*. Manco commanded the public execution of his friend, General Chalcuchima. An abyss of hatred separated the two men. When Manco finally spoke, it was with hesitation.

"What about General Quizquiz," he asked, "who participated in Huascar's humiliation and in the massacre of my family? Which one of us could put aside our personal differences?"

King Chincha advanced a step toward the Inca, his eyes burning with fanatical fire. "Why don't you ask him yourself?" he asked.

Kusa Akchi drew back the curtains and, in the dark background, appeared General Quizquiz. He wore a simple cloak and stood without a weapon. He bowed to Inca Manco. He dared to come although he knew the Viceroy had ordered Manco to arrest him.

Manco was deeply moved. His heart, rigid and stiff during the past weeks, was suddenly overcome by deep emotion. He opened his arms and pressed King Chincha to his breast in a firm embrace. He approached Quizquiz and, for a long moment, they stood facing each other.

"We have a common enemy now," said Quizquiz, "and he doesn't fight like we do. He is fierce and cruel. It would be better for us to unite and face this enemy together than to continue fighting against each other."

Manco extended his right hand to Quizquiz in the fashion of the Spaniards. Instead, Quizquiz bowed and kissed the hem of Manco's robe.

"Oh, Creator Viracocha," prayed Kusa Akchi with his hands raised high, "please grant success to your people in light of the great sacrifice our Inca offers for his nation."

"Time forces us!" warned King Chincha. "We are not safe here. We must leave at once and return to our armies. Inca Manco, will you join us?"

"It is too dangerous," said Quizquiz. "It is enough that we have his alliance. The Spaniards watch his every move. We cannot put his life at risk."

After a short silence, Kusa Akchi suggested, "When the rains cease, let Manco be carried on a litter as though he would make a casual trip to a mountain temple. His bearers can carry him instead along a secret route to a safe place where Quizquiz and Chincha will wait to meet with him."

Manco nodded. King Chincha and General Quizquiz bowed deeply and took turns to place a kiss on Manco's cheek with deep reverence as was done in the old times. Manco embraced them both affectionately.

Before King Chincha and General Quizquiz departed, *Amauta* Kusa Akchi voiced the following prayer:

"Oh Viracocha," he prayed, "my father, who said *Let there be Cuzco!* and by your will it was made and is preserved with such grandeur! Let these sons of yours, the Inca, be conquerors and despoilers of all mankind. We adore you and offer our sacrifices to you so that you will grant us what we beg of you. Let us be prosperous and happy and do not allow us to be conquered by anyone, but let us always be conquerors, since you made us for that purpose."

When they were gone, Manco turned to Cura Ocllo who was now standing at his side. Her eyes held the glow of one who had witnessed a miracle.

"Cura Ocllo," Manco said with a voice heavy with sorrow, "you finally see me for who I really am but it is too late. Our days are numbered. Kusa Akchi is used to taking care of you. You will have to hide with Vira now."

Cura Ocllo looked up at Manco and smiled. "You talk, my Lord, as though you would say farewell to me right now."

"It *is* farewell, my Cura Ocllo. I have to go and this is probably the last time I'll ever talk to you."

Cura Ocllo's eyes filled again with tears and a look of infinite tenderness softened her proud features. "Well, my Lord. I can stay with you while you wait for the rains to cease—if it is your wish. We can spend the nights together." She tenderly laid her hand on his breast.

Manco could not answer. He was overcome with joy as he lifted her into his arms and carried her to the royal chamber that had been prepared for them on their wedding day. He had not entered the room since then. He placed Cura Ocllo gently upon her bridal bed and she let him undo the gem-clasps that held her gown together. They kissed passionately and Manco learned with gratitude that his young wife could love just as hotly as she could hate.

CHAPTER 29

Time passed and the Andean rainy season came to an end. The Inca governors and Indian Chiefs fanned out into the countryside to recruit warriors and spread the news for everyone to prepare for rebellion. Already the Inca chain of command had functioned effectively and the people knew that the time had come to wage war against the *white strangers*. General Tiso, Manco's uncle, had begun a successful campaign to attack Spaniards. His strategy was to ambush them when they traveled to their *encomiendas*, or estates granted to them by Pizarro, to collect their tributes. Indian warriors began to learn that, when the conquistadors were alone and isolated, they were much easier to kill.

Dawn arrived like the wings of death to claim Cura Ocllo's new lover. Manco heard Kusa Akchi's light knock at the door, the signal for departure. He held his bride and kissed her soft skin. Kusa Akchi knocked again.

Reluctantly, Manco dressed. Instead of his attendants, the affectionate hands of Cura Ocllo fastened his tunic. He bent for one more kiss. A sob escaped him as he turned away from her. She clung to him passionately.

"My love," she said, "now that I'm really your wife, my place is at your side. Wrap this cloak around my shoulders. I'll cover my face with a mask like an Oracle. No one will guess who I am. Then I can go with you into the mountains and die by your side if the battle is lost."

Manco was moved by her offer but didn't know how to respond. He wanted her with all his soul but he wanted her to be safe. As he wrapped the warm cloak over her shoulders he hoped that she would fare better with him than with Vira in her dark cavern. Together, they hurried through the corridor to an entrance where *Amauta* Kusa Akchi was waiting.

At the door of the reception hall they stopped in horror. The clatter of Spanish weapons froze them in their tracks as the door flew open and

Hernando Pizarro stood before them. He was dressed in full battle armor and faced them with sarcastic contempt.

"Going somewhere, my Lord?" asked Hernando as he bowed ironically. "Taking a little, secret excursion into the darkness with your lovely wife?"

Manco did not answer but stared stiffly at Hernando.

"Well," said Hernando with sharp hostility, "you'll just have to stay here with me. Perhaps you miss the feel of chains around your neck and ankles."

Manco felt the blood turn cold in his veins. Never again would he let a Pizarro put chains on him as Juan and Gonzalo had done for a time prior to Hernando's return. With a flash of brilliance, Manco twisted his face into the familiar boyish smile that always appeased the Spaniards.

Manco put his index finger on his mouth and said, "Not so loud, Señor, it's a secret, I don't want your officers to hear."

"What do you mean," stammered Hernando. The look of malicious contempt faded slightly from his face.

"It's the gold statue of my father that the *Amautas* hid near Quito. My spies found it and I want to get it for you! Why else would I sneak off into the mountains?"

"You mean that your secret outing is to acquire gold for me?" asked Hernando with surprise and happiness.

"That's right," said Manco. "I wanted to surprise you but you returned to Spain sooner than I expected. Then the rains were upon us. But if the *Amautas* find out that I have learned their secret, they'll hide the statue somewhere else. If your officers find out, they might try to steal the statue from me before I can give it to you. It is a life-sized statue of Huayna Capac, Señor! It is solid gold!"

"So what is your plan?" asked Hernando.

"I'll go in front with the Queen and my most trustworthy litter bearers. Order four or five of your armed guards to follow us at a distance, that way you can be sure that we won't try to escape."

"All right," said Hernando appreciatively. "I'm sorry I insulted you. I'll send four soldiers to follow and protect you. They can help you carry the statue home. I'm sure it must be very heavy."

"Thank you, Hernando," said Manco. "You are wise to consider the great weight of the gold statue I will give you. Thank you for your generous kindness."

Hernando accompanied Cura Ocllo and Manco politely to their litter and ordered four armed soldiers to accompany them. As he watched them disappear into the rising sun, he thought about the number of gold bars that could be made from a statue as big as a man.

As soon as Kusa Akchi saw Hernando interfere, he dispatched a messenger to find King Chincha and General Quizquiz to tell them that Manco's secret escape had been discovered by Hernando's spies.

Hernando Pizarro waited impatiently for the return of the Inca and his new treasure. Days passed and then a week. But there was no news of the sovereign or of the Spanish soldiers who had accompanied them. Alpaca herders found the dead bodies of the guards, mortally wounded by Indian spears. It became obvious to the Spaniards that Manco had escaped into the mountains to set in motion a long-overdue retaliatory campaign against his oppressors.

CHAPTER 30

General Quizquiz travelled north from Cuzco with his army to enlist new warriors for the great rebellion. Inspired by his new allegiance to Inca Manco and driven by his new mission, Quizquiz and his men were making progress. As they traveled north, many new warriors joined their forces. When they marched back to Cuzco to begin the great rebellion, Quizquiz was confident that he would bring with him many fresh warriors to join Manco's army.

Suddenly and unexpectedly, Quizquiz's army met a large army of conquistadors headed south. Pedro de Alvarado had been second-in-command to Hernando Cortés during the conquest of the Aztec Indians to the north. Alvarado had recently arrived in Ecuador with 550 conquistadors and a burning desire to carve out his own governorship in the New World. After a series of unexpected bloody battles in which only a few Spanish soldiers were killed, Quizquiz's forces were completely discouraged.

"Make peace with them, they are invincible," urged Huaypalcon, one of Quizquiz's top commanders. "From where did these *white strangers* come? They get stronger and we get weaker."

"I haven't been home for over two years!" shouted a warrior.

"We're tired! We can't fight any longer!" yelled other warriors in the group.

"Tired?" mocked General Quizquiz. "You're tired? You want to go home? And what do you think you'll find *there*? Peace and happiness? It's more likely that you'll find your homes burned and your families in slavery.

Quizquiz reached inside his tunic to hold the little amulet he still wore around his neck. He thought about his mother. He wished he could have seen her once more before she died. He thought about Inca Atahualpa. Why had he trusted the *white strangers?*

"The army is our life now. We have no homes anymore. We live to kill the *white strangers.*"

"No, no more," insisted Huaypalcon. "They are impossible to kill. You continue fighting if you wish, but we're leaving."

"Treason!" he shouted to his troops. "This is insubordination! You'll all be executed for this! How can you bring such shame upon your Inca King?"

"Are you sure he is *our* Inca King? Don't you think it is more likely that he is the Inca King of the *white strangers?*" asked Huaypalcon ironically.

As General Quizquiz filled his lungs to continue heaping scorn upon his warriors, Huaypalcon threw a lance that struck him in the chest.

In utter disbelief and shock, Quizquiz stared at him with his grave black eyes. Had it come to this? How would Manco take Cuzco without his assistance? He *failed?* After all this work, he really *failed?*

With the point of the lance sticking out of his back and blood staining his worn tunic, Quizquiz fell to his knees. He looked his men squarely in their treasonous eyes and held the tiny amulet that contained the tooth of a llama and a lock of his mother's hair. By what trick of Viracocha could he be killed by the hands of his own warriors?

As the well-trained unit that they were, the warriors of General Quizquiz ran forward in unison with their clubs and battle axes to kill their leader. His last thoughts were of his King and companion, Atahualpa, and of his mother.

CHAPTER 31

When Alvarez opened his eyes, he didn't know where he was. He was lying on a small narrow mattress in a strange room that felt like a dungeon. The walls were dark stone and there were no windows. It was stuffy and the cool air smelled like mold. Next to his bed was a small table on which was spread a tablecloth embroidered with bright colored flowers. On the tablecloth sat a bright, blue, ceramic jug. On the floor next to his bed was a low, four-legged stool topped with a small cushion. His heart sank as he considered the unfamiliar surroundings.

He concentrated with great effort to remember what had happened and how he came to be in this dismal chamber. Did he drink so much that he blacked out? Deep in his feverish mind, memories began to stir. Lopez, where was Lopez? Vira . . . did he see Vira? Was she here? Had it been a dream?

He closed his eyes and tried to move. The pain in his right shoulder and left leg was tremendous. Vira . . . Lopez wanted to take her to Hernando . . . He was going to take her for himself first. God, I was with Lopez . . . What must Vira think of me now?

Alvarez lay in the small bed in agony, not just from the pain of his wounds, but also from the pain of knowing the reason he saw Vira. Vira, she threw herself between him and her own protectors . . . did she save his life . . . did she live in this dismal dungeon? Is it possible that she moved from a cheerful, royal palace to this subterranean dungeon void of sunshine, beauty, and luxury? Alvarez was deeply shocked at the possibility.

Slowly his memory cleared. He passed weary fingers over his face and felt his beard. It was longer than he remembered. How long had he been here? His forehead was oily and he had bandages on his arm and leg.

He heard the sound of approaching steps and closed his eyes. He heard the rustle of clothing and felt the touch of a cool hand on his forehead.

"Come, Pani, he's much cooler now." It was a young woman's voice speaking in Quechua. "Will you help me change the bandages again?"

Alvarez heard another set of footsteps approach. He kept his eyes closed as the two women removed the bandage on his upper arm. The pain was so intense that he pressed his lips together tightly in order not to moan. After the women carefully rewrapped his arm, the pain eased and he heard someone walk away.

Someone sat down on the stool next to his bed. A strange sense of feverish happiness spread over him like a wave. Was Vira sitting beside him now? He was afraid to open his eyes and dispel the delirium.

With immense effort and unimaginable hope, Alvarez finally opened his eyes. He turned his head slightly to look and what he saw inundated his soul with relief: It was Vira. She sat on the stool embroidering. Her dark head was bowed low to see her fine stitches in the meager light. Her hair was braided. She wore a simple, short-sleeved dress cinched at her waist with a scarlet braided cord. Her arms were bare. Alvarez watched her silently with his eyes only half open. She was beautiful. He watched her fingers move. Alvarez remembered a flower he saw once in the mountains. The Indian interpreter told him to *never* pick one of those flowers.

As he fell asleep, Alvarez thought about Vira in Prince Coca's palace. He could feel her hands touch his face as she kissed him goodbye.

When he opened his eyes, he didn't know where he was. What day was it? Vira . . . he was with Vira. He looked and saw that she was sitting on the stool sewing. He heard the voice of Father Pedro: *There are many beautiful and good women in this world, Don Alvarez.*

Why would he follow *Lopez? You're a Christian knight . . . a solemn oath Father Pedro . . .* I was drunk . . . I wasn't *that* drunk. I would never let Lopez touch Vira, never! I didn't even let *myself* touch her when I had the opportunity. Why would this uneducated pagan girl nurse her enemy back to health? Why would she save my life? Deep shame and remorse consumed him as he fell asleep.

When he opened his eyes, he knew where he was. As he lay in the bed with his eyes half closed, a vow framed in his heart, more strong and adamant than any vow he had ever made. He would live to protect Vira.

Vira stirred as though she sensed that he was awake. She rose and bent over him as she had done a thousand times before. He felt her breath on his face and smelled a sweet perfume which seemed familiar. She touched her fingers lightly to his forehead. An overwhelming joy surged through him and he opened his eyes.

Vira gasped, emitted a sound similar to that of a startled bird, and drew away her hand. She stared at him with her lightly slanted dark eyes. "It's you, you're here . . . you're awake! You found me . . . how did you ever find me? Please forgive my servants for hurting you, my Lord, they were ordered to protect me."

Alvarez smiled. "Princess Vira," he murmured, "I am ordered to protect you now also, ordered by my own heart!"

"The man that grabbed me, I remember him. He is the one who killed little Maita at Prince Coca's castle. What was he doing here? He *never* should have touched me. Please don't be angry at us."

"Princess, I could never be angry at you."

Alvarez tried to raise himself upon his uninjured elbow to get a better look into Vira's eyes. "You act more like a Christian than anyone I know except for Father Pedro," said Don Alvarez.

"What is *Christian*, is it something good? Does that make you happy?" asked Vira.

She lifted her eyes and he saw that her lovely face was thin and bore signs of suffering and sorrow. Yet her voice was calm and firm when she spoke.

"Princess Vira," smiled Alvarez, "I'm so glad to see you again. I knew you were beautiful, but I didn't realize you were also kind and generous." Alvarez looked around the room, "Vira," he asked, "where are we?"

"This is where I live," she answered quietly.

"You live here?" he tried to hide his pity.

"Yes, my Lord, I sleep over there with Pani, my nurse." She pointed at the far corner. This house belongs to Pani's brother."

"Oh, Vira, why does life have to be this way? Why must we be at the wrong place at the wrong time?"

Alvarez gently took Vira's hand in his and kissed it lightly.

Shuffling steps were heard approaching and Vira quickly drew away from the bed.

"This is Pani, my nurse. My mother died when I was born so Pani raised me and has cared for me ever since. Look Pani, he's awake and he speaks Quechua!"

"The *white stranger* should eat," said Pani dryly, "here's soup."

"Are you strong enough to feed yourself?" asked Vira.

"I don't' think so," answered Alvarez weakly, "can you help me?"

Pani rolled her eyes. Vira pulled the stool closer to his bed. She took the bowl from Pani and moved the spoon toward his mouth. Her hand trembled. Alvarez felt the warm fluid travel all the way down to his empty belly."

She can see in my eyes that I love her, he thought.

She could.

Instinctively, Vira moved away from him. "That's enough soup for now. I'll bring you a drink for the pain. It's our holy drink, I'll be right back."

As Alvarez awaited Vira's return, he met the gaze of the old woman, Pani. She stood in the dimly lit background observing him from a distance with suspicion. He was tired of always being mistrusted.

"Are you angry or afraid?" asked Alvarez.

"Yes," answered Pani curtly. "A skunk's scent can be perceived for very long distances."

"I won't hurt you," comforted Alvarez.

"I know that," said Pani, "but you hurt my little dove. You have her heart, can you not see?"

"Don't fear for her," he said softly. I will never harm Vira. I will protect her."

"You will not harm her on purpose."

Pani threw him a searching glance. He had heard that Indians always wore a mask upon their faces to conceal their feelings. They were known to not flinch even during the vilest torture. Now he understood. She bowed and left him with his doubts.

Vira returned with a ceramic jug and it seemed to Alvarez as though she was a ray of sunshine that penetrated the cave's gloom.

"This is *chicha*, our holy drink," she told him. "It will refresh you and ease your pain. But we have no cups. You must drink from the jug."

She raised the heavy container to his mouth. Alvarez grabbed it to help her with the weight and drank in long gulps.

When he was finished, Vira peered into the jug and laughed. "Well, I can see you like it!" She placed the nearly empty jug on the floor and sat down on the stool.

"Princess," he started.

"Call me Vira."

"Vira, will you stay with me."

"Where would I go? But you need to sleep."

"When I sleep I have nightmares."

"Last night, in your dreams, you were talking to me. Not all your dreams are dark, my Lord," assured Vira with a sly smile.

"I was so happy to wake up and see you beside me."

"I'll be close by when you wake up."

"You are a sweet girl, Vira."

"I'm not a girl, I'm 18 years old. Had my father lived," Vira paused, "I would have married some awful Indian chief long ago."

"You do not wish to marry?" teased Alvarez.

"No! Marry a stranger that smells of llamas and is too old to chew his meat? No, thank you! Anyway, it doesn't matter, that world is gone now."

"I'm so sorry, Vira. I'm sorry about your brother and your niece."

"And my little nephew," sighed Vira.

"I thought we were coming here to bring prosperity and salvation to you, not *destruction*."

"We already had prosperity," stated Vira. "What is *salvation*?"

Alvarez looked at Vira. "You shouldn't be so good to me. You're far more worthy than I."

"You use too many Spanish words, my lord, what is *worthy*?"

Cuna ran down the stairs to the dark room. His long nails clicked on the stone floor. He ran to Vira and scratched on one of the legs of the stool.

"What's that noise?" asked Don Alvarez nervously.

"Oh, it's just Cuna, my little dog." Vira lifted Cuna up so Alvarez could see him.

"Oh, your little dog, is he hurt? Lopez kicked him and hit him with his spear."

"He's all right. He's very clever, *aren't you Cuna?*" Cuna wriggled in her arms and licked her face. "Cuna talks at night to the moon goddess. Pani thinks she healed him."

"Moon goddess? I thought you believed in *Viracocha?*"

"I do, Viracocha is the Creator. But there is no life without Inti, the Sun God. And the old people, the Indians who lived here before us, also believe in the moon goddess. She is a beautiful woman. Dogs are sacred because when they bark at night they are talking to her. There are many gods."

144

"Do you believe in the moon goddess?"

"I don't know, I suppose it's just a story. But sometimes, when Cuna howls a lot at night, something terrible happens the next day. Cuna howled all night in the garden the night before your men arrived at Prince Coca's palace."

Alvarez cringed. No matter what subject they discussed, the topic always returned to the cruelty of his men.

"I like Cuna because he is so loyal to me," explained Vira. "He followed me that night when we fled Prince Coca's castle in the dark."

"Cuna! Cuna!" a man's voice was calling for the dog.

"That's Turi. Turi, come quickly, he has awakened at last!"

An old Indian man emerged from the darkness. He wore a gray sleeveless poncho. His face was lean and his tiny eyes were suspicious. For a moment he hesitated but when Vira nodded to him, he bowed to honor the *white stranger*.

"Thank you, Turi, for helping me. When I am able, I will reward you for it," assured Alvarez.

"I need no reward," answered Turi harshly. "I obey my mistress." He bowed again, picked up Cuna, and backed out of the room as noiselessly as he had entered.

"That was pleasant," said Alvarez sarcastically.

Vira smiled and shrugged her shoulders.

"Vira," asked Alvarez, "have you thought about me since the last time I saw you?"

"Often," she whispered, "and I prayed that I would see you again."

He closed his eyes, he was so tired. But he didn't want to fall asleep and leave Vira. What if this had all been a dream?

CHAPTER 32

When Alvarez woke up, he heard music. He discerned the sound of a flute and a drum mixed with many voices. The exotic and extremely sad melody filtered down to his bed. A man sang in a deep warm voice:

We weep and mourn
Tears fall and clothes are torn
Our Inca is slain
How deep our despair
The pain of our loss
Our hearts cannot bear
The Sun's light is gone
Black darkness leaves us cold
The foe bares his legs
What voice will lift our soul?
How will his glorious eyes
Watch over his people
Oh Inca, your land cries

The music ended in a long diminuendo. Alvarez sat up and asked Vira, "What kind of music is that? It's so sad and sweet."

"It's traditional Indian music," she explained. "They're the men who attacked you. I asked them to come and play for you. Do you like it? Is it all right that they're here?"

"I like it, I'm glad they're here," Alvarez assured her. "Can I see their instruments?"

Vira rose and started toward the stairs. She stopped and looked back, "Are you sure it is all right with you if they enter your room?"

"As long as they bring instruments and not weapons!" smiled Alvarez.

Vira hurried up the stairs and returned in a few moments with a few young Indian musicians. Like all the other Indians he had seen, the young men wore knee-length wool tunics. They lined up in front of Alvarez's couch and, at Vira's signal, knelt down on the stone floor to pay homage to the *white stranger* they had wounded.

Alvarez nodded and motioned for them to arise and come closer.

"This is a *queña*," said Vira.

A young man handed him his flute. It was a long, hard reed tube, about an inch in diameter, with no mouth piece. It had five finger holes to change notes.

Small drums covered with llama skin called the *tam-tams* were hit with reeds to keep rhythm.

Alvarez examined the simple toy-like instruments. He was amazed that such simple pieces had been so effective in revealing the mood of these primitive and mysterious men.

"Are you from Cuzco?" asked Alvarez.

The young warrior who played the *queña* looked anxiously at Vira. She nodded her encouragement so he answered, "No, I am from the mountains. My father and mother are dead, for they would not go with the *white strangers* who came to our village. My little brothers and sisters were taken in chains by the *white strangers*. I was with General Rumiñavi's army. My older brother was with me but the *white strangers* captured him and cut off one of his hands. They let him go and he found me and begged me to walk to Cuzco to search for our siblings. But my brother was too weak and the journey killed him. Now I am alone. I have not yet found my little brothers and sisters. I play my *queña* and sing for them and pray that they hear me and remember me.

Alvarez sighed. Every word the youth uttered grieved him. Vira sensed his anguish and quickly dismissed the musicians. As they ascended the stairs, she turned to Alvarez. "Please forgive them, my Lord. They didn't mean to make you sad."

"His story and his song are sad, Vira. It is right that I am sad."

That night, Alvarez dreamt that he was sitting in a gilded arm chair. There was a long line of young Indian warriors, so long, that Alvarez could not see the end of it. One by one, an Indian warrior stepped forward and laid his right arm on a stone block, palm up. With his sword, Alvarez chopped off the hand with one blow. Each time Alvarez raised his sword, another Indian warrior presented his hand to be cut off. As the sword sliced through the flesh, it struck the stone with a loud clash and sparks would fly. There was a large mound of hands next to him and they were moving. Each hand found a partner and they put themselves together to pray. Alvarez woke up drenched in sweat. Vira was at his side wiping his forehead and urging him to wake up. He pressed his head to her chest and he let her hold him as he cried.

The next morning, Vira fretted with concern for Alvarez. She knew he was not accustomed to the constant darkness of the subterranean chamber. She wished she could take him out into the garden. She worried that the tediousness of his long recuperation would discourage him.

"Why don't you tell me about your gods?" asked Vira. She hoped to distract Alvarez from his pain and discomfort.

Alvarez hesitated. He had never talked about God before, not to anyone. He took a deep breath and wished Father Pedro was there.

"Well Vira, I only have one God."

Vira smiled at Alvarez and waited for him to continue. Alvarez fidgeted uncomfortably.

"God made everything—everything we can see and everything we can't see, like air and wind. He made you and me."

"Go on," encouraged Vira. But Alvarez didn't want to go on. He wanted Father Pedro to tell Vira about God. That was *his* job! But Vira was like a child awaiting a story. He felt compelled to continue.

"When God made the first man and the first woman, the devil tricked them into eating a forbidden fruit called an apple. You've never seen one because they don't grow here, but they're delicious and have a red peel."

"What is *devil?*" asked Vira.

"The devil is a bad angel," answered Alvarez.

"What is *angel?*" asked Vira.

Alvarez used Spanish words when he didn't know the Quechua equivalent. He wondered how he was going to be able to tell Vira about Jesus with his limited Quechua vocabulary. He wondered if the words he needed even *existed* in Quechua. What if Vira was a stranger to the concepts of angels and the devil?

Alvarez shrugged his shoulders and made it clear to Vira that he couldn't explain the word *angel*. Vira shrugged her shoulders also. "Oh well," she said, "just go on. It's all right."

"When they ate the apple, they could suddenly understand the difference between right and wrong and good and bad. God was upset that they ate the apple when he told them not to, so he sent out of his garden. They went into the world but he still watched over them. The man and woman had children and their children had children. There are many stories about all of these children. Some of them were good but most of them were very bad. After many seasons passed, God felt sorry because everyone was unhappy. Many of his people were liars, cheats, and thieves. So God sent his son, Jesus, to save us and teach everyone to be kind and good and to share and to tell the truth."

"I was taught to tell the truth and to do what is right and good."

"Anyway," continued Alvarez, he was getting the hang of this now, "some people loved Jesus but some people thought Jesus wanted to be the king. But he didn't. The men who were in charge of the city took him captive and tortured him and killed him. To kill him, they nailed his hands and feet to a wooden cross and left him to hang until he died."

"How can people be so cruel?" asked Vira cringing. "One time my great uncle killed one of his enemies. He hung his body upside down, cut him open, and removed all his bones. He turned him into a big kettle drum! His head, hands, and feet were still attached and they played him like a drum, can you believe it—a drum!"

"I've never heard of such a thing," answered Alvarez. "That's very unusual!"

"I'll just stick with the *tam-tam*!" giggled Vira. "The story of your god is very sad. Maybe you can believe in Viracocha instead. He's very strong and good."

"But I'm not finished," said Alvarez excitedly. "After three days, Jesus' mother and his friend, Mary, went to the cave where he was buried and Jesus was gone! An angel told them that Jesus was alive again."

"He was alive again? You mean like our old Inca Kings? How did he become a mummy in just three days?"

"No, he was really alive, not a mummy. He could eat, talk, walk, and everything!"

"That is very strange, Alvarez. Our Inca Kings cannot eat and walk and they are only able to talk through their Oracles. You mean, Jesus could move?"

"Yes, it was just like nothing had happened to him except that he had holes in his hands and feet from the nails. He went up to Heaven to be with God, his father. But he promised to come back one day."

"When will he come back?"

"Nobody knows. It could be tomorrow or it could be in a thousand years."

Alvarez wished again for Father Pedro. "It's complicated, I'm tired, Vira." He touched one of Vira's long, black braids with the fingers of his good arm. He let his fingers slowly slide down along her braid to where it was cinched at the end with a silver clip.

"Vira, what happened to Lopez?"

Vira grew pale and covered her face with her hands. "He's dead, my Lord. My Indians were so scared. They carried his body away and left it somewhere outside of the city. I'm sorry, my Lord. I recognized him. I try to feel sorry but I am angry that he murdered little Maita. What will happen?"

Alvarez locked her hand safely in his firm grasp. "Don't worry. What about your brother Manco: Do you have contact with him?"

"No, he doesn't even know where I am. I saw him once, just before his coronation. He warned me that Hernando Pizarro, your leader's brother, had asked for me. I don't dare to go into the streets. Once in a while, at night, I go into our garden to breathe the fragrant air."

In spite of the incredibly sad situation that surrounded him, Alvarez had never felt so happy in all his life. To be near Vira is what he wanted.

After many more recuperative days had passed, Alvarez began to feel a little better. He was growing confident that soon he would be strong again. He started to think about reality again: How would he travel 400 miles through the mountains to Lima to report to Francisco? Had Hernando Pizarro arrived in Cuzco as planned? How was he going to explain his absence?

"Vira," asked Alvarez, "are any of your Indians messengers or runners?"

"Only Turi. He is old, but he is the one I trust."

"Do you think he could take a message for me to Lima, the new city Francisco Pizarro is building on the coast? He would have to cross the mountains. It is quite far."

"Turi is incredibly strong and capable," assured Vira.

"Do you think I could ask him to find Father Pedro and bring him here to us? He's one of our holy *Amautas*. He is good and kind. He's a real Christian man."

"Again, what is *Christian*?" asked Vira.

"I'm a Christian," answered Alvarez. "I believe in Jesus *Christ,* so I'm a *Christian*."

"When you first came to our land, we all called you *Viracochas* because you looked so much like Viracocha with your beards and light colored skin." Vira smiled at Alvarez but her heart was breaking. She didn't want him to leave her, not *ever*.

"Turi won't have to return to Cuzco alone, Vira. Some good men, friends of mine, will come back with him to get me. I don't think I can ride my horse yet but I have to go to Lima as soon as possible."

Vira's head dropped and the wind was sucked from her lungs. She hid her face so that he would not see her tears. She had known this day would come.

CHAPTER 33

A few days later, Don Alvarez was able to get out of his bed and walk. The wound in his shoulder was healing well in spite of the fact that it was the second time he had been stabbed through it. His leg; however, still caused him intense pain.

"Do you think you could climb the stairs, my Lord? The sun went down long ago and there is only a sliver of a moon. Perhaps we could all go outside and sit in the garden."

Alvarez wasn't sure, but he wanted Vira to be happy. Limping badly, he managed to follow Vira to the stairs. Very slowly they made their way up, crossed the little kitchen, and went out into the garden. It was night. Vira was right, the moon was nothing more than a thumbnail and the darkness was pervasive. But the fragrant flowers and fresh night air filled their lungs with renewing energy. Cuna sprinted around the perimeter of the wall and returned to lick Alvarez on the hand. Vira petted Cuna gently on his little head.

His leg was killing him. Sweat ran down his forehead and the sides of his face. "I have to sit down," stated Alvarez with alarm.

"Come sit on the bench," comforted Vira. She led him around the corner of the small house to a stone bench.

As Alvarez tried to get comfortable, Vira thought about asking him not to go away to Lima, but she changed her mind. She looked up at him with eyes in which he could see infinite devotion. She was smiling at him.

After they rested together for a few minutes, Vira teased him, "When you were unconscious and your forehead burned with fever, you called my name. Well, here I am!" She desperately yearned for the handsome man she loved to kiss her. She was young and healthy and had dreamed about him for so long. Her mind was befuddled.

Alvarez laughed and tried to relax beside her on the bench. But his body didn't feel like his own. Emotions, desires, and pain overwhelmed him in such a strange mixture. He put his good arm around Vira's shoulders and pulled her close. He raised her chin and looked into her luminous dark eyes. He kissed her lips. He placed soft kisses around her mouth and on her cheeks. He kissed her again on her mouth and she broke away. To his surprise, her eyes brimmed with tears.

"When I die, said Vira, as long as my body is not burned, I will live with Viracocha where the air is always warm and food is plentiful."

"What's wrong?"

"If you take me completely, which is what I want, I will have to kill myself."

Alvarez smiled dumbly, "What are you saying? Did I understand you correctly?"

"Yes, I could use my poisoned dagger on myself, I still have it."

"No, you *won't* use your poisoned dagger! I'll take it away from you! Why do you saying such a thing?"

"You don't understand. I'm an Inca princess. You are not permitted to have me."

"You're wrong! I *do* understand—I just don't agree! Don't you see that *everything* has changed? Anyway, you don't have to kill yourself because I can't *take* you right now! I'm in so much pain that I'm afraid I'm going to be ill! I'm going inside!" Alvarez was livid. How ridiculous! What a silly woman!

Alvarez left the dark garden as fast as he could hobble. Vira and Cuna followed him inside and down the stairs. He muttered a cold good night and turned toward the wall. He was soon fast asleep.

Vira watched Alvarez as the days passed. As he got stronger, she became weaker. As he was able to get up and move around with greater ease, she took to sleeping long hours in her bed. She knew he would leave soon and she might never see him again.

Alvarez peered over the wall to see into the dark street. "Are you so anxious to leave?"

"No, I'm anxious for Father Pedro to arrive." His eyes were soft and warm as she gazed into them. He made her smile.

The next day, early in the morning, Turi led Father Pedro to his small stone house in the quarter of Cuzco called the Puma's Tail. They were alone. With much excitement, Turi led Father Pedro down the stairs to

Vira's subterranean refuge. They were followed by Pani and Cuna, who was barking at Father Pedro as loudly as he could.

Vira stared at the man Alvarez embraced with delight. He wore a shabby brown robe tied in the middle with rope. He looked humble and unimportant. But when her eyes met his, she suddenly understood. His brown eyes were warm and tender yet commanding and powerful. Involuntarily, she lowered her gaze from his. She felt shy yet strongly drawn to him. Vira thought he must possess a strange power over people.

"Come here, Father," said Alvarez cheerfully in Quechua with a radiant smile. "Meet my true love!" Then, in Spanish, Alvarez quietly confessed to his friend, "This is the woman who has freed me from the bondage of my anger and hatred against women."

Father Pedro approached Vira and extended his right hand. "I have seen you somewhere before," said Father Pedro.

"Yes, Father," answered Alvarez on Vira's behalf, "that night at Prince Coca's palace . . . it's her . . . Princess Vira, Inca Manco's sister!"

Father Pedro gasped but quickly recovered his composure. He moved toward Vira as though he approached the King himself. He bowed his head to her and took her hand in his.

"Thank you, my daughter, for saving the life of my dear Alvarez. And thank you for healing the wounds that cut so deep into his heart." Father Pedro turned to Alvarez and continued in Spanish, "We have to go immediately. There's trouble in the mountains. Do you have your things ready? Where's your horse?"

Vira panicked at the discussion of secret plans in a language she couldn't understand. She pressed her hands to her heart in dismay. But quickly Alvarez strode to her side and put his arm around her shoulders.

"I have only one more thing to get ready, Father," said Alvarez. He looked deep into Vira's desperate eyes and said in Quechua, "Vira, will you marry me?"

Vira's mouth dropped open and her hands flew to her cheeks. Did she hear right? Did these sounds mean something entirely different in his language?

Alvarez spoke to her softly. "Vira, my love, will you marry me? Will you be my wife?"

"You will marry me and leave me here?" asked Vira in shock.

"No, you will come with me! You will stay with me forever!"

Pani gasped. Turi laughed and grabbed Cuna up into his arms to pet him. Everyone was looking at each other with silly smiles in the torch light in the dark cave. It was surreal.

Vira was overcome with happiness. She threw her arms around Alvarez's neck and hugged him tightly. "Yes, yes, I will marry you. I will be yours forever!"

"There's just one matter that must be resolved," he said to Vira seriously.

"What is it? I'll do anything, my Lord, anything!"

"Do you remember what I told you about Jesus?"

"Yes, I think I remember most of it."

"Will you become a *Christian* so you can marry me, Vira?"

Vira trembled like a leaf in the wind. The man of her dreams would be hers! She was ecstatic. But, Jesus? She had just heard about him! She didn't *know* Jesus. She believed in *Viracocha*!

"Oh Viracocha, can you please forgive me? I will speak the words they need to hear, but I will always believe in *you*! No matter how many new gods they give to me, I will always love you the most."

"Yes, I will do what you say," announced Vira with confidence.

Father Pedro directed her to kneel down. He sprinkled some drops of water upon her head from a tiny bottle he held. "Vira, you will now be renamed *Veronica*, I baptize you in the name of the *Father, of the Son, and of the Holy Ghost. Amen.*"

Vira didn't understand what happened but the gentle voice of Father Pedro reassured her. Alvarez knelt down at her side just as humble and reverent as a slave. He held her hand and repeated words spoken by Father Pedro. He turned to Vira and said in Quechua, "I take you, Vira, to be my wife, so help me God."

Then it was Vira's turn. "I take you, Alvarez, to be my husband, so help me God." But in her heart she apologized to Viracocha: *Oh, Viracocha and Inti, God of the Sun, hear me now; I will be faithful to you until I die!*

Alvarez drew her to his heart and tenderly kissed her. There was no wine that had ever made him feel so intoxicated. His heart soared.

Pani approached the young couple. Tears streamed down her face. She bent low and humbly kissed the hem of the Indian tunic Alvarez was wearing.

As quickly as possible, supplies and essentials were loaded on the backs of llamas. Twenty of the young musicians assembled to carry a simple wooden litter. The sun was still high in the sky when they left Cuzco. The curtains were closed, sheltering the happiest couple in the world. Vira, now Doña Veronica de la Vega, sat comfortably on soft cushions. She rested her head on the shoulder of her Spanish husband. He held her hand in his and watched her with such devotion that he was aware of nothing else. Opposite them sat Father Pedro and Pani. Pedro fell asleep and Pani held Cuna on her lap. The litter, led by Turi, was carried at a fast pace. Turi knew that the worst dangers were not rivers and mountain passes, not precipices and rope bridges, but angry Indians that could approach from any direction.

"Do you love me, Vira?" asked Alvarez.

"I love you more than my own life, my Lord," she answered.

"Don't call me *Lord*," he asked gently, "I'm your husband, not your *Lord*. Call me Alvarez."

"Alvarez," Vira tried out the new sound on her lips, "how many other wives do you have?"

Alvarez laughed so loudly that he woke up Father Pedro and made Cuna whimper. "None, Vira! Christians only marry one wife! You'll always be my only wife!"

Vira closed her eyes in delight and thanked Viracocha for her good fortune. But this time she remembered to thank Jesus too.

Once Father Pedro was fully awake, he spoke to Alvarez in Quechua. His Quechua wasn't as good as Alvarez's but it was fluent, "An old friend of yours has come to Lima."

"Who?"

"Galez, Baron of Sevilla"

"Carlos? That's wonderful! We've known each other since childhood. He's a brave soldier. The Viceroy will be served well by Carlos!"

"Good, good, I'm glad you're pleased," continued Pedro. "Now, I don't want to shock any of you, but I must tell you some important news."

Everyone, even Pani, looked expectantly at Pedro.

"Inca Manco has left Cuzco."

"Oh that doesn't mean anything," comforted Vira. "Inca kings often go to mountain temples to worship Inti and sometimes they go hunting for *guanaco*."

"No," Pedro shook his head slowly, "rumor has it that he joined with rebel Indians in the mountains and is organizing a rebellion with General Quizquiz."

Vira gasped. "Quizquiz will *kill* Manco. It's a trick!"

Alvarez held Vira's hand. "Manco deserted? But what about Almagro?" asked Alvarez.

"Francisco gave money and men to Almagro to explore the southern territories. King Charles granted governorship of the southern Inca lands to Almagro. Almagro is long gone."

"What? That's crazy, Francisco must be furious! He would *never* share the spoils of *his* conquest with Diego!"

Vira fretted anxiously. "Quizquiz *hates* Manco." Pani patted her knee uselessly.

Alvarez continued, "Well, who is in Cuzco? Who's in charge of the city?"

"Don't worry, my son, Cuzco is in capable hands. Hernando, Gonzalo, and Juan Pizarro are in control of the city. It seems as though it was Hernando who let Manco escape. He was duped by the promise of a golden statue."

"That sounds plausible," agreed Alvarez. "Hernando has been away for a long time and needs to refill his coffers!"

"Anyway," continued Pedro in Spanish. "That is all I can tell you for now. Let's not upset your bride any more than necessary."

"I think my bride will be more upset if she can't understand what you say," answered Alvarez in Quechua. He wondered if Pedro suspected that Vira might share Spanish secrets with her missing brother.

Suddenly the litter came to a halt. Father Pedro drew the curtains apart and was immediately filled with dread. Cuzco was on fire. From their mountain overlook, Pedro, Alvarez, Vira, and Pani could see that the city below them was burning. The emerald and ruby steeples and golden roofs were tinted with a red light. It seemed as though Manco's revenge had begun.

Turi ran over to the litter. "We escaped Cuzco just in time! Praise Viracocha for saving our Princess!"

Pedro opened his arms toward Cuzco as if to embrace all who suffered there. He made the sign of the cross in the air and bowed his head to pray.

"Do you know if Francisco is sending men to Cuzco to help?" interrupted Alvarez.

"No," answered Pedro. "Francisco has only 200 men to protect Lima. He will keep them there."

"What will happen if Cuzco falls to the Indians?" asked Alvarez in Spanish.

"We need to go," urged Turi. "Pray to Viracocha that we are not attacked."

They closed the curtains. The Indians ran as fast as possible bearing their burden toward Lima. Sweat poured down their brown chests in rivulets. They breathlessly hurried up curved and steep mountain passes. No whip drove them: It was love and devotion to save their Princess. Alvarez was amazed by the Indians' dedication to Vira.

"If we were to speak gently to them about God instead of whipping and punishing them, so many Indians could be saved," said Father Pedro. "Gratitude is what changes a man's heart."

Hours passed in silence. Alvarez was stunned by the endurance of the Indians. It pained him in many ways to have to ride in a litter. His wounds hurt his body, but riding in a litter hurt his pride.

Suddenly, the litter stopped so abruptly that Vira and Alvarez slid forward off of their seats and bumped against Pani and Pedro. Cuna yelped as Alvarez reached to part the curtains to see what happened. Instinctively, Vira grabbed his arm and pressed her finger to her lips motioning to them all to be silent. They could hear men arguing.

"How dare you stop us? We are in a hurry. You must let us pass!" shouted Turi.

"Why should we let you pass, old man?" answered an angry male Indian voice. "Who are you hiding in that litter? We're not letting any *white monsters* pass! Give us something for the tips of our spears!"

"I have nothing to do with *monsters* of any color," answered Turi in a dignified tone. "We're taking Princess Vira Yupanqui to safety. Cuzco has been attacked. Make way for the Inca King's sister!"

At once the din ceased. After a pause, the voice of the Indian, much less menacing now, was heard again, "Prove that you are telling the truth!"

The curtains opened and Vira showed herself in the moonlight. Suddenly the blood-thirsty assailants went face down to the ground. Their leader beat his chest and pleaded, "Royal Princess, forgive us for delaying you."

Vira nodded graciously and told them that they were forgiven. Turi led them away as fast as they could move.

"The Indians are so devoted to you and your family, Vira. I've never seen such loyalty before," whispered Don Alvarez visibly shaken.

"My people are capable of great love . . . and also great hatred."

Alvarez shuddered. He wondered if Vira would be able to adapt to the Spanish way of life. He worried that she would not be able to understand his people and their customs.

"Vira," said Alvarez gently, "when we get to Lima, I will take you to visit Inés. Her Christian name is Conchita and she lives with Francisco Pizarro in his palace."

"Inés? The same Inés who was with Atahualpa?" asked Vira. "Inés is living with *your* Pizarro? Isn't he the man who *killed* Atahualpa?"

Alvarez tried to read her secret thoughts but found her face to be strangely without expression.

"She seems content with him, Vira," answered Alvarez hopefully. "I heard she has already given him two children and that he dotes on her. You and Inés can be friends now."

Vira leaned back into the cushions and said nothing.

Each day, the mountains rose higher behind them until finally they could see the plain to which they were descending. They rested in a small village called Morococha for several days while two of the litter bearers ran swiftly down to Lima with a letter to Francisco to inform him that Alvarez was coming with his new wife and needed a house in which to live.

It was in Morococha that Vira and Alvarez were finally able to consummate their marriage. Vira's Inca pride was affirmed when she was convinced, without doubt, that her love for Alvarez was worth dying for. She was being absorbed by him, like water by dry sand.

The Indians delivered the letter and brought a response from Francisco back with them. The letter informed Alvarez that suitable lodging was available since a high-ranking officer recently departed for Spain.

Lima, *the City of Kings*! The new Spanish capital looked like a town transplanted from Spain. Francisco's new palace towered above the new city of Spanish houses, churches, and shops. Instead of thatch, the roofs were made of earth-colored clay tiles.

"Is it real?" asked Vira, "Do people live in those houses? They look so delicate."

Unlike the earthquake-proof stones used to build in Cuzco, the Spanish homes were built of brick and wood.

Alvarez led his wife into a lovely white house with wood trim. "Is this the house or the garden?" asked Vira in surprise.

"This is our house, my love, see, you can sit here and sew or take a nap. Over here you can sit and read once I teach you how. This is your new home. The best room of all is over here!"

Alvarez led Vira into a spacious bedroom decorated in Spanish style with a large comfortable bed covered with colorful silk blankets. Vira laughed. She was impressed by the velvet drapes and thick carpet. It was all too good to be true. How different it was from the dark cave in Cuzco where she hid in seclusion for so long.

"Will you be happy here, my love?" asked Alvarez as he held Vira close and kissed her cheeks.

Vira nodded and smiled. She walked as in a dream through the luxuriously furnished and artistically decorated rooms. She knew in her heart that, what the rooms lacked in gold and silver would be compensated for by the presence of Alvarez. As long as he was with her, she could live anywhere.

Her first formal Spanish meal was served on a large table covered with a white table cloth. Vira was accustomed to eating while lounging on the floor on cushions. A Spanish cook sent by Francisco prepared spiced peppers in cream sauce, chicken and rice, and spaghetti with marinara sauce. Vira hardly tasted the strange food for her happiness was overwhelming.

"Pedro will give you Spanish lessons," announced Alvarez.

"Of course, my love," answered Vira. "Are you *sure* you don't want me to feed you?"

"I'm sure," answered Alvarez with a smile.

When Vira and Alvarez finally went to bed, they lay quietly in each other's arms. Their bodies molded together like the magnificent stones that interlocked without mortar to form the earthquake-proof Inca walls. For Alvarez, it had been a lifetime of suffering and bitterness followed by a waterfall of redemptive goodness. For Vira, it had been a lifetime of hopes and impossible dreams followed by a reality in which she lost everything but found a love that exceeded her greatest expectations.

As Alvarez held Vira and listened to her breathe, he wondered how she would adjust to this new world. "She'll be uncomfortable at first," he thought. "She'll feel different . . . as though she doesn't belong here. But then, God will give us a child. Our baby will make us as one. She'll be content for now, for *my* sake. But when she follows our son into our Spanish ways, she'll find true joy.

CHAPTER 34

The mood in Viceroy Francisco Pizarro's palace was somber. Small groups of Spanish knights assembled to discuss the dreadful news filtering in from Cuzco. No official messengers had arrived for nearly a week and, other than the report from Don Alvarez de la Vega, no one in Lima knew the fate that befell those left in the city. It was rumored that the revenge of the Inca and the Indians would be merciless considering the way they had been treated.

"I heard the Indians are no longer afraid of our horses," commented a knight.

"I heard that Inca Manco *rides* a horse now and even wears armor he stole from us!" said another.

When Alvarez arrived, he hurried into the reception hall where the Viceroy was waiting.

"Isn't that Don Alvarez de la Vega?" asked one of the knights.

"Yes, have you seen his new *wife*? No wonder he sides with the Indians now!"

The knights laughed maliciously.

"Now aren't you all ashamed, gossiping like old hell hags," rebuked Carlos de Galez in defense of his friend. "Your comrades suffer in Cuzco while you poke your noses in other people's personal affairs. At least he *married* her."

"*Por Dios*! She's an *Indian wench*!"

"She's an *Inca Princess*: An Inca Princess, in fact, from the same family as Doña Conchita, the mother of Viceroy Pizarro's children," said Carlos wisely.

Carlos walked away whistling a happy tune. "He's lucky I don't let him have it right here," said one of the knights.

"I know he's a newcomer, but watch out; I heard he's an artist with the sword. You better leave him alone," answered another.

Carlos knew that they would change the subject.

Don Alvarez knocked on the door of Francisco's study. It seemed a lifetime ago when he knocked on the cabin door of his ship's Captain.

"*Adelante,*" *h*e heard Francisco's voice, less masterful than he remembered, invite him to enter.

Francisco stood before a window, his face was drawn and pale in the light. There was a look of helplessness in his stance and he seemed to have aged ten years in the last few days. He approached Alvarez with sincere affection and extended his hand. Father Sebastiano sat in an arm chair not far from Francisco's desk. He did not get up.

"Is there news from Cuzco?" asked Alvarez as he sat in a chair.

"No, no news this morning," answered Francisco shaking his head sadly.

Alvarez sighed. He knew how deeply attached Francisco was to his brothers, especially Juan.

Just then, the door opened and a servant announced that a messenger had arrived from Cuzco. "Send him in immediately!" exclaimed Francisco as he walked back to his desk and sat down.

Alvarez got up to leave but Pizarro motioned for him to stay. After a few minutes passed, a soldier entered. He wore no armor, only a torn and dirty wool cloak. His face was dark with dust and soot and he was stained with blood.

"Do we still hold Cuzco?" asked Pizarro desperately.

"Yes, Viceroy," stammered the soldier. "Hernando wants you to know that there won't be any more messengers for a while because he isn't able to spare the men. There are fewer than 200 of us in Cuzco now. The earth around Cuzco has changed color, my Lord," reported the messenger dramatically, "it is the color of Inca tunics. It is a massive Indian army. The Indians are so numerous that, at night, their campfires resemble a cloudless black sky filled with countless bright stars. It is only a guess, but we estimate there are 200,000 Indians that fight against us."

"How is Hernando, is he well?"

"Your brother, Hernando, fights with great courage."

"What about Gonzalo?"

"Gonzalo was wounded but is recovering now. He was injured while defending a storehouse set on fire by the Indians. He was able to save some of the food, but we are practically starving. Everything else in there burned."

"And Juan?" Francisco's lips trembled as he spoke the name of his favorite little brother.

"Forgive me, Señor, to report that your brother, Juan, is dead."

Francisco audibly sucked in a quantity of air. He shifted in his chair and then rose to his feet. As he walked toward the window, he ordered, "Go on."

"Your brother, Juan, led our attack on the fortress of Saqsaywaman that overlooks Cuzco. Our only hope was to take the fortress. Our natives helped us maneuver through the hoof-traps and wicker barricades but we were out-numbered. It took us all day to reach the fortress. We were able to break through the gateway but the Indians dropped large rocks and stones on us from above. Juan was not wearing a helmet."

"What is the purpose of providing expensive armor if they don't wear it?!" said Francisco in exasperation. He paced the floor and clasped his hands behind his back.

"Well, you see, Viceroy Pizarro, the day before, Juan was hit in the jaw with a large rock from an Indian sling. His face had become so swollen from the injury that he was unable to fit into his helmet. I yelled to him to use his shield, but he didn't hear me. A large stone hit him on the head so hard that I heard his skull crack. But he didn't stop fighting. We almost took the fortress entrance but, at the end of daylight, as darkness fell, we were forced to retreat and Juan fell from his horse and collapsed. His Indians carried him back to Cuzco and, for the next few days, he drifted in and out of consciousness. Hernando and Gonzalo made sure that he received the best medical care possible. He lived for twelve days, Señor. We buried him in Suntur Huasi, but he requested, whenever it would be possible, that his body be taken back to Trujillo for a proper burial."

Francisco stared at the soldier in disbelief. His eyes widened and he leaned against his desk. He pressed a hand to his forehead, "No, don't tell me this, not Juan."

"He was in the front of every skirmish, Viceroy. He could not be held back. The Indians screamed and made terrible noises, there was such confusion . . ."

Francisco sank into his chair and buried his face in his hands. Minutes passed and he remained motionless. The two soldiers watched sympathetically as their commander grieved. They did not dare to comfort him. Sebastiano squirmed nervously.

When Pizarro lifted his head, his eyes were dry. He had mastered his grief. He turned to the messenger and asked, "What about *our* Indians, have they deserted?"

"At first, they fought well with us, Señor. But then they started slipping away from us to join Inca Manco. It is hard to trust the Indians that remain. We sleep in our armor with our swords in our hands."

"Go get cleaned up and rest. Return this evening and be prepared to give me all the details," ordered Pizarro. With a motion of his hand he dismissed the exhausted soldier.

"Well, I almost forgot why I asked you to come, Alvarez," said Francisco with a forced smile on his tired face. He brushed his hand across his forehead. "Sunday we'll celebrate High Mass in the new chapel to pray for our men in Cuzco. It will be the first time we ring the new bell. I'd like you to join me and sit with me and Doña Conchita." There was a pause, "I suppose we'll have a requiem for Juan . . ."

Francisco looked at Father Sebastiano who received the instruction silently with a nod.

"My wife and I gladly accept your invitation to sit with you," answered Alvarez. Father Sebastiano released a deep sigh and shifted in his chair.

"No Alvarez, just you. Your wife can come another time."

Alvarez rose stiffly. "I'm terribly sorry but I cannot attend without my wife."

Francisco felt too tired to argue.

"Very well, if that is how you feel, you may bring her. But you are warned that this is not the most opportune time for you to display your new Indian wife. Tensions are high," warned Pizarro. "I know, I have Conchita, but it's different, she's been with me for years now, and anyway, I out rank everyone here. But now with Manco's rebellion in Cuzco, anger flares against the natives."

Alvarez turned to leave. "I'll send some dresses over for your wife. Make sure she wears one to the mass. She must *not* show up wearing her native clothing."

"Thank you, Señor," muttered Alvarez as he left the study with a bitter taste in his mouth.

"Father Sebastiano," said Francisco in a voice barely louder than a whisper, "I can't bear the suspense. I must receive more news from Cuzco."

"You know there is no way for a messenger to penetrate the circle of Indians that surrounds the city," answered Sebastiano. "You would be sending the messengers to their certain death."

"Is it better that I remain uninformed?" asked Francisco incredulously.

"Do what you must, my son. Do what you must do to save your brothers."

CHAPTER 35

P ani and Vira bolted the door. Only Cuna, comfortably lounging in a basket, was allowed into the dressing room.

"Let's try the black one first," said Vira excitedly.

Pani helped her slip into the silky black dress sent to her by Viceroy Pizarro himself. She stood before the tall Venetian mirror and cried out in surprise. Was it her? Was the image she admired hers? The elegant long dress flowed to the floor accentuating each of her delicate round curves.

"But what about this?" asked Vira with concern as she covered her cleavage with her hands. "There is a part missing."

Pani looked around the bed heaped with dresses and trimmings. In spite of the fun she was having with her mistress, she wondered at the excess of having so many dresses from which to choose. "Here," she exclaimed as she lifted a large red velvet flower. "Try this!"

Pani fastened the flower to the décolletage and clapped her hands together proudly. Everything was covered satisfactorily. The brilliant red color of the flower accentuated the beauty of Vira's young and happy face. She was stunning. She twirled around like a child admiring her own loveliness.

"Now the hair," said Pani with concern. The servants had washed Vira's hair in an unusual perfumed liquid from Spain. Vira's glossy black hair was no longer straight and shiny. Instead, her black hair was fluffy and soft. Pani pulled and wrapped and tucked to her best ability, but the hair had a mind of its own. After much time and effort, she was able to wrap the fluffy waves together on the top of Vira's head with a large Spanish comb.

"And to finish," exclaimed Pani, "it's called a *mantilla*!" Pani draped a long black veil over the high comb on Vira's head.

Vira looked in the mirror and laughed. "Who thought of such a thing?" she asked giggling at her image.

There was a light knock at the door. "It's me, my love, may I enter?" asked Alvarez.

Pani opened the door and Vira modeled her new outfit for her husband. "You're the most beautiful woman I have ever seen," he said appreciatively.

"You have such a sweet mouth," said Vira as she rushed toward him and he caught her laughing in his arms.

"Stop!" yelled Pani, "It will all fall apart! I'll never get her back together again!"

Vira and Alvarez laughed at poor Pani as she groaned. "Don't worry, Pani, no damage done, see? She's still beautiful to behold!" assured Alvarez as he patted Vira's *mantilla* back into place. Pani sighed, she was exhausted. Alvarez wrapped a warm velvet cloak around Vira's shoulders and led her to a litter waiting to carry them to the new chapel.

CHAPTER 36

Small clusters of Spanish knights with a few noble women, fresh from Spain and other Spanish strongholds within the region, crowded the yard and steps to the chapel before Mass. Francisco watched and listened proudly as the new bronze bell clanged the call to worship. He felt true satisfaction knowing that he had personally handled the bellows at the forge to construct the bell. The sound of it echoed in his bones.

People chatted into each other's ears when Alvarez and Vira arrived in their litter. Everyone watched and greeted the couple coldly but with respect. As they passed, all eyes followed them curiously.

"She's beautiful," declared Carlos de Galez.

"She is lovely," answered a knight close to him, "but he'll soon tire of her. What could she possibly have to offer a man of culture?"

"You're the one that tires easily," snarled Carlos. "Is it now five children you have from six different women or six children from five different women, hmm, I have trouble keeping it straight. Not all men behave like rabbits!"

Everyone laughed heartily but the offended knight put his hand on the hilt of his sword. "Later, my friend, we'll take this up later," assured Carlos.

Alvarez and Vira joined Francisco and Conchita and entered the chapel in silence. Vira was surprised by the coldness in Inés' eyes as they greeted one another. Had life with Francisco hardened her heart to her own relative? Vira imagined that Inés was in a difficult position and was probably doing her best.

The new chapel was beautiful. The altar and walls were lined with gold-plated moldings and large oil paintings of the saints. Incense burned in gold censers and filled the chapel with a strange perfume. Vira looked at the large cross hanging on the wall. She tried to relax and listen to the voice of the priest but he spoke in yet another language unfamiliar to her.

Suddenly, everyone stood. Vira quickly stood beside her husband. Then all the people bent down on their knees. Vira looked at Inés and saw that her attendant gracefully arranged the folds of her wide silk skirt as she knelt upon a thick purple cushion. Vira did not have a cushion or an attendant to help her. She hesitated and Alvarez noticed. He folded his coat and placed it on the floor for her to kneel upon. He cinched her gown and helped her to her knees lovingly.

When the Mass ended, Vira and Alvarez followed Francisco and Inés outside. As Francisco spoke with Alvarez, Inés turned to Vira and asked, "For whom do you pray in Cuzco: The Spanish or their attackers?"

"I pray for peace," answered Vira diplomatically.

"And how do you like the gown my husband sent you? It seems to fit you rather well," snarled Inés.

"I'm sorry I haven't been able yet to thank you properly for the gift. I love the gown; it is truly a thing of beauty." Vira felt as though she had been punched in the stomach.

"It's nothing," stated Inés. "Your husband serves my husband well. He deserves our kindness now and then."

Vira was recovering from the initial offense. With the pride due an Inca Princess, she recovered her wits and returned the insult, "Did you know, Inés, that my husband was a knight of the Queen of Spain and that his father was a nobleman and that he can *read and write?*"

Inés, knowing that her husband was a bastard herdsman who *could not* read and write, gritted her teeth in anger.

As Francisco and Alvarez approached them, Vira watched Inés. Inés looked at Alvarez with obvious admiration and longing in her eyes. Instead of anger, Vira suddenly felt a stirring of pity for Inés. She was so young and lovely and her husband was a stern and angry old man.

As Alvarez, young and handsome, took Vira's hand and tucked it into his elbow to escort her away, Vira understood. A wave of gratitude rushed through her and she squeezed her husband's firm arm. With a wise and sympathetic smile on her face, she nodded farewell to Inés and Francisco.

CHAPTER 37

Vira sat on the patio one morning while Alvarez attended a conference with the Viceroy. She was surrounded by flowers. Brightly colored macaws flaunted their royal plumage as they flitted from shrub to shrub. Vira gazed pensively at the roses, the peonies, and the fragrant flowers imported from Spain. She regarded them with admiration and pity and wondered how they would fare transplanted in foreign soil.

Was she ungrateful? Alvarez provided for her every need. Even Pani, Cuna, and Turi were comfortable in their new home in Lima. She thanked Viracocha for her good fortune and wondered how she was supposed to thank her new god, *Jesus*. How could she be grateful for the luxury and comfort she enjoyed when her very life was stained with the blood of her people?

Pani came out of the house to shake her dust rags. She stood by the door unnoticed and tenderly watched Vira for a while. She approached slowly. "My darling little dove," she spoke with great affection, "why are you so sad? What thoughts cause you to wear that faraway look?"

"I was thinking about Manco struggling in the mountains. He gave up his throne to fight for us. While I . . ."

"Manco wants you to be safe and happy," interrupted Pani. "He would have kept you with him if he thought he could protect you."

"Had he kept me with him then I'd be with him now to encourage and help him to be brave," said Vira.

"No, my dove. You'd most assuredly be suffering greatly from the abuses of a Pizarro by now. Don Alvarez de la Vega is your fate. He was meant for you and your destiny can only be fulfilled at his side. Do not despair."

"Manco must worry about me," said Vira.

"You know he will organize *chaski* runners to bring messages to him wherever he goes. The roads will be dangerous, but Manco will find you. And he will find Sapaca also. His warriors and runners will report to him that we are safe in Lima," assured Pani.

"I suppose you're right," sighed Vira.

Later that morning, Vira and Pani were sewing a gown in the new Spanish design from some soft material Vira wove from *vicuña* wool. Vira had worked dyed strands of red and blue into the material to form a repetitive geometric pattern that resembled trees and flowers.

"I always smile for you, Princess, but inside my heart breaks," said Pani choking back a sob. "You worry for Manco . . . I worry for *you*."

"What's the matter Pani?" asked Vira with genuine concern.

"You struggle to learn this new way of living. You are torn between two very different worlds and neither one accepts you."

"It's all right, Pani, I have what I truly desired. You know I have always longed to be the only wife of a man I could love. My dreams have come true! I got my wish! It's what I wanted more than life itself." Vira sighed and put down her handiwork. "*My* dream came true, but Manco's dream did *not*."

"I too have grown to love Don Alvarez," assured Pani. "But his world is cruel and dangerous. The *White Strangers hate* our people. Why can't they treat us as human beings? I understand you, my dove, for it troubles my soul to rest well fed and comfortable amidst such intense suffering."

Just then, the excited voice of Alvarez was heard from the front yard. "Vira! Come here Vira, I have something to show you!" he shouted.

"Go on," encouraged Pani, "I'll finish up here."

Vira smiled at her sadly and ran to meet her husband. He was outside the front door holding a horse. It was the finest horse Vira had ever seen. She was brown and glossy with a long black mane and tail.

"She's Andalusian, Vira. Don't be afraid—pet her," coaxed Alvarez with immense pride. "She just arrived from Spain. I requested her a long time ago."

Vira took a step toward the horse to pet it and it whinnied and stamped a front hoof. Vira jumped back and yelped at the unexpected greeting. Alvarez laughed and came around to hold her arm. "Look, pet her like this," he instructed.

Vira copied her husband and reached out to scratch the mare under her chin. Just as she started to feel comfortable touching her, Vira swayed and fell back into her husband's arms. Alvarez was alarmed. He gathered Vira into his arms and carried her to the bench under a shady tree. "What's the matter? Should I send for the doctor?"

Vira brushed her hair away from her face and failed to restrain a happy smile. Her eyes shone as though they held a divine secret. "Nothing's *wrong*, no, don't send for the doctor. I'm just a little dizzy," assured Vira.

"What? Why are you smiling like that? What is it?" asked Alvarez. He raised her chin to look into her eyes, "Are you?" he asked hopefully.

Vira nodded, "I think so. I think we're going to have a baby!"

Alvarez felt aglow with triumph as he pulled Vira to his heart. He wanted to tell her of his joy and gratitude, but he was beyond words. Instead, he kissed her as though his kiss would convey the message of his heart to her that all his hopes and dreams had come true.

"How long have you known?"

"I have suspected for about a month now."

The horse shook her head and demanded attention. Alvarez ignored her.

"How could you keep this news to yourself?"

"I just wanted to be sure."

Alvarez wondered at the nature of his young wife. He tried so hard to anticipate her needs and wants and yet, she was capable of hiding such significant thoughts and feelings as a suspected pregnancy from his detection. He wished that he were able to divine her every thought. Yet here was proof that he was unable to discern even the greatest of events.

The next morning sunshine illuminated the garden. Vira leaned lazily upon the shoulder of her husband as they sat together on a bench under a lilac bush from Spain. It was in bloom now and its perfume wafted throughout the garden.

Father Pedro sat with them and related colorful stories in which he always made his own part seem insignificant. In reality, the stories were episodes that revealed the sublimity of his life.

Vira waited patiently until he was finished. She looked up at him and he saw that her eyes were filled with sorrow.

"Why is it, Father," she asked quietly, "that you speak always of love and peace, yet everywhere I look I see blood, death, and suffering? Must blood flow to allow your teachings to spread?"

"That seems to be the pattern, my dear girl," answered Pedro sadly. "And I am afraid it is also the nature of war. That the battles of this conquest have continued this long was never Pizarro's intention. Mankind will be consumed by cruel ambition: An ambition that is fueled from the fires of greed and pride. Human beings—Inca, Indian, *and* white, are inclined to evil. Man's inhumanity to man is a perplexing certainty in this world."

"I am so confused, Father Pedro," confessed Vira. "I am accustomed to praying to Viracocha and Inti. Sometimes I even pray to the moon goddess! Now I am supposed to pray to the god of the Christians who, you tell me, is the *only* god. It's hard to know what to believe," complained Vira.

"How do you know that *Viracocha* and the Christian god are not one and the same?" asked Pedro. "Viracocha is the Creator. He created man and woman. He baptized the first Inca King. He told you of a great flood. There are many similarities."

"But it is all so complicated," said Vira as she shook her head. "How will I ever teach my child about the gods?"

Vira looked at Father Pedro and her sad expression was replaced with a radiant smile.

"I wondered how long it would take you!" teased Pedro. "Well, congratulations to you both. I am so happy. Our dismal city needs more children to liven things up. God bless you both!"

"Thank you, Pedro," said Alvarez. "We hope you will agree to be the child's Godfather. As you can see, we certainly need your help raising him!" laughed Alvarez.

"Her," corrected Vira.

"Yes," Pedro gushed, "I would be honored to be *her* Godfather," said Pedro with a smile as he winked at Vira. Pedro knew he would be needed. His friends would soon introduce an innocent child to this world of Indians and madmen.

CHAPTER 38

Winter arrived in Lima, the City of Kings, which was now a year-and-a-half old. Inés had turned seventeen years old and had already given Francisco a daughter and a son he adored. There were 100 Spanish soldiers with 80 horses in Lima to defend the new and glorious Peruvian capital from any and all potential danger.

While Francisco impatiently awaited his requested weapons, soldiers, and supplies to arrive from Spain, bad news from within his empire filtered in with brutal regularity. The arrival of a messenger caused an instinctive spasm deep in the pit of Francisco's belly.

During a surprise nighttime attack, Hernando and Gonzalo Pizarro were finally successful at conquering the fortress of Saqsaywaman which overlooks Cuzco. It took many days and nights of ferocious fighting, and especially heroic efforts on the part of Hernán Sánchez, but finally the Indians retreated. The good news of a small victory was bittersweet to Francisco since the endeavor had cost the life of his favorite little brother, Juan. Now Hernando and Gonzalo, his two remaining brothers, were trapped in a ruined city that was running low on food and water. It was hardly encouraging. Although it was estimated that more than 3,000 natives had been killed, the conquistadors had failed to put a dent in Manco's army.

Francisco sent a relief force of 70 men under the command of Gonzalo de Tapia to Cuzco to lift the siege and free his brothers. While crossing the Andes, the men were crushed by boulders that were pushed down upon them from above by Inca Manco's new and powerful General Quizo. When it was reported to Francisco that Tapia's relief force had failed to reach Cuzco, he dispatched a second relief force of 60 foot soldiers. General Quizo crushed them also with an avalanche of boulders.

Encouraged by his success in the mountains, General Quizo decided to attack the city of Jauja. When the news reached Francisco that the city of Jauja had been taken by General Quizo, Francisco decided not to send any more men to Cuzco. In all, not to mention the wine, swords, armor, weapons, food, and other supplies, the tally of losses endured by the conquistadors totaled four Spanish columns that included over 200 men and 100 horses.

Inca Manco was so greatly encouraged by General Quizo's victories that he issued an order for him to attack Lima. Since Quizo had defeated Pizarro's Cuzco relief forces and had killed so many Spaniards in Jauja, Manco felt the time had come to attack Lima and kill Francisco Pizarro.

Quizo; however, had misgivings.

"My victories," he told Manco, "are due to the mountains. Their horses and weapons are useless when we attack them on steep topography. They can't charge at us as they crawl, one-by-one and out of breath, through the passes. I hesitate, Inca Manco, to meet them on the flat terrain that surrounds Lima."

Although General Quizo was not afraid and would never question the command of his King, he knew in his heart that to attack Lima was a mission that would end in defeat. But Manco did not understand.

"You can do this, General Quizo," shouted Manco. "What victories you have won! No other general can match your bravery and wits. Just promise me that you will try to take Francisco Pizarro alive if you can and bring him to me," he ordered. "You must spare Vira and her household, but kill everyone else and destroy the city. Don't leave a single house standing!"

In complete obedience to his King, General Quizo and his army approached Lima. Francisco's scouts returned to report that a huge native army was headed toward Lima. As rumors spread that a hostile Indian army was approaching the city, Lima's citizens were crippled with fear and anxiety. Don Alvarez de la Vega nervously went home to prepare his household for potential trouble.

"They're only *seven* miles away?" asked Vira incredulously. "What will we do? We must try to escape! We must hide!"

Alvarez held Vira tightly and tried to comfort her.

"I was told there are about 50,000 Indian warriors assembled," said Alvarez. "I don't know that there is anything we can do now. The roads are too dangerous. But don't worry, Vira, God is with us. He will protect us. Father Pedro says so."

"Turi," said Alvarez in dire seriousness. "You will have to protect Vira and Pani. Prepare supplies and get everyone into travel clothes. Take this," said Alvarez as he placed a large dagger in Turi's hand. "You might need it."

"Yes, my Lord. Do not be troubled. I will take care of the women."

"When and if Quizo's warriors make it into the city, you'll have to run. I'll send a messenger to you with orders when to leave. I mean, *instructions*," corrected Alvarez with a sad smile. Out of respect for Turi, Alvarez treated him as a dear friend. He knew that he could never give Turi an order.

"If Manco knows that Vira is living in Lima, then he may have issued an order to spare her. But we can't depend on his warriors to recognize her. You'll just have to run and find a good place to hide in the hills. I'll find you when this is all over. I have to go now. God bless you, Turi, and thank you."

While Vira wept in protest, Alvarez headed to the city square to assemble with the troops to defend Lima. Vira cried and shouted out to him in misery as he rode away on his beautiful new horse.

General Quizo attacked Lima from three sides and advanced across the plain through the cold mist. Many of his warriors blew on conch shells and clay trumpets to create a din. Others beat drums and screamed blood curdling battle cries.

Pizarro hid 80 of his men on horseback within the city. When General Quizo's men reached the outskirts of Lima, he gave the signal to attack. The harquebusiers fired the three-legged guns while the cavalry charged with their lances and swords drawn and smashed into the Indians slashing and spearing great multitudes of them. The fighting was fierce and both sides battled bravely all afternoon. As the twilight darkened, General Quizo and his warriors retreated to the hills that surrounded the city.

For the next five days, Manco's finest general laid siege to Lima. But time was of the essence and General Quizo knew that he was needed in Cuzco to help Manco's army fight for the Holy City. It would not do for two Inca armies to lay siege on two cities at the same time. On the sixth day, General Quizo decided to end the stalemate.

"Today we will take Lima," declared General Quizo to his warriors. "We will capture Francisco Pizarro and all of his Spanish women. Imagine! What strong warriors we can produce with women who birthed men such as these false *Viracochas* from across the sea! There will be no one who can defeat us!"

With this final call to battle, General Quizo launched his assault on Lima. He was carried by his litter bearers in the front line where all his warriors could see him and receive inspiration. The Inca general and his field commanders led the charge. In the din created by the savage yells of native warriors, the harquebuses thundered and shot their invisible arrows.

General Quizo felt a sting in his chest. "No," he assured himself, "it is nothing. I must sit tall and let them see me." But the stinging in his chest became more intense with each step of his litter bearers as they ran. Quizo felt himself start to slump forward.

"I cannot fall. I must sit up straight." The pain became intolerable and Quizo felt darkness move in around him. "I thought this would happen," he assured himself. "Oh, Great Viracocha, you will have to win this battle without my assistance. Please forgive me."

As General Quizo quietly passed into silence, he hoped that victory would be theirs. But the Inca army was routed immediately on the flat ground and General Quizo died in his litter along with forty of his commanders and chiefs. When defeat was realized and the warriors were aware that their leader was dead, they quickly disappeared into the Andes.

CHAPTER 39

Inca Manco grieved deeply for his finest general and the disappearance of the army he depended on to help him take Cuzco. At this point, he was merely waiting for the Spaniards to starve. Although Manco's warriors were too strong to allow Hernando and his men to escape from Cuzco, they were not strong enough to stop the trickle of supplies that made their way into the city.

Thus the siege continued for nine months.

"They have reached Arequipa," reported a *Chaski* messenger to Manco. "Paullu is with them and he rides on a royal litter. It is *Don Diego de Almagro*, my Lord! Your friend! He has at least 400 men with him and many horses!"

"When he sees what I have done to Cuzco, I'm afraid he will no longer call himself my friend," said Manco. This changes everything."

Manco rose from his chair and picked up his *champi* with his right hand. "With all the warriors we have, we are unable to defeat the 100 *white strangers* left in Cuzco. How will we contend with 400 more?"

Manco retreated to his sleeping chamber and summoned Cura Ocllo.

"What am I supposed to do now?" he asked in desperation. "Finally you are with child. My joy is as bright as the sun on the first morning of the first day and my heart flutters like the wings of a thousand birds taking flight. I love you my *Coya*. What I desire more than victory is to live my life with you in happiness and peace. I cannot wait to meet our child."

Cura Ocllo approached Manco and put her arms around his shoulders. He looked down at her pregnant stomach and gently caressed her. For a long silent moment they stood and held each other.

"Manco," soothed Cura Ocllo with a voice like honey, "trust in Viracocha. I know that I carry your son. We will be happy and peace will come. Be brave, my King."

Manco smiled. He had tried every way he knew to handle the situation of the invasion of the *white strangers*. Every time it seemed as though he made a little progress or gained an important victory, the Spaniards came back for more, stronger and more vicious. He was tired. And he needed to assure that Cura Ocllo and his unborn child would remain safe. He promised himself that he would never let anything bad happen to Cura Ocllo again. Her life was his life. Her breath was his breath. If her heart ceased to beat, he feared his heart would also cease to beat.

"The *aqaruway*, the locust, covers the sun and destroys everything in its path," said Manco. He looked at Cura Ocllo and there were tears in his dark eyes. "But then they *leave*. They finally fly away. Why do the *white strangers* not leave and let us repair the damage they have inflicted upon us?"

So he waited and did nothing. After a few days passed uneventfully, the messages began to arrive. Messengers from Diego de Almagro, who had been gone for over twenty months, arrived with a heartfelt request to negotiate a truce. Almagro begged Manco to join with him and help him take Cuzco from the Pizarros. He promised to make Manco Inca King again and restore him to his childhood home in peace. Almagro even suggested that, if properly explained to King Charles, the Pizarro brothers could be blamed for the rebellion. What beautiful promises he made. He called Manco his *son*.

But Manco already knew how Cura Ocllo felt about his previous stint as a puppet king for the Spaniards. Would she dare to leave him again? How would she react when even the lowest-born Spanish soldiers treated Manco with disrespect and cruelty? He vowed to himself that he would never do anything again to put her love and respect for him at risk.

A messenger later arrived from Hernando Pizarro. Hernando and Gonzalo Pizarro were also willing to make a deal with him. Their offer was to *forgive and forget*.

"*Forgive and forget?*" stammered Manco in angry sarcasm. "As if a Pizarro heart would be capable of such feats! Why should I believe a word spoken by a Pizarro? It has been nothing but lies from the beginning. Call a meeting of the governors and administrators," said Manco to Kusa

Akchi. "I will address my subjects on a very important decision I have just made."

Kusa Akchi dispatched messengers to all the loyal Indian chiefs within the Inca Empire. Many of them were already with Manco while others were near Cuzco with their warriors laying siege to the Holy City. But some traveled great distances to see their King. After waiting several weeks for their arrival, a large gathering was assembled in Ollantaytambo to hear Manco's speech.

"My dearly loved sons and brothers," began Manco. "I believe those of you who are present here and who have remained with me through all my trials and tribulations don't know why you have been asked to gather here before me. Remember that necessity often compels men to do what they don't want to do."

Manco continued to speak to his faithful followers of their recent victories and losses. He reminded them of the good lives they shared before the arrival of the *white strangers*.

"Finally," said Manco, "It now seems to me that it is time for me to depart for the land of the *Antis*."

The *Antis*, were people from the rain forest. They had brown-skin and, when clothed, wore white cotton tunics. Many of them preferred to walk around naked with their bodies painted with white paint in swirling intricate designs. They were expert archers and fierce warriors who would lead Manco and his people to a dense, moist cloud forest that clings to the upper edge of the eastern Andes. The place they would take the Inca King was a warm valley between two rivers that is almost perpetually bathed in fog.

With tears in his eyes, Manco said goodbye to his people. It was clear to all those present that Inca Manco Yupanqui, Son of the Sun God, was abdicating control of the Inca Empire. He was retreating to a small area in the far east of his kingdom. He was abandoning the empire of his forefathers and departing for an area within the Amazon rain forest where he was confident that no harm would ever come to Cura Ocllo.

His greatest sadness was that his followers, millions upon millions of them, would have to submit to the grisly will of the Spanish invaders. He could not protect them any longer.

"Remember that the *white strangers* are liars," warned Manco. "If they force you to worship their god," he advised, "pretend that you agree. Do what you must do to appease their wicked demands. And remember me and my ancestors. Remember how we loved you and provided for your needs."

After Manco spoke with his people, many of the chiefs also gave speeches. There were many tears and much sorrow. Idols were brought out and everyone prayed to Inti and the moon goddess for protection and courage. Many llamas were sacrificed to Viracocha and the feasting and ceremonial drinking of *chicha* lasted for many days.

And then they left.

It was a large procession. Among those in the crowd of travelers were the royal family and nobles. The mummified bodies of Manco's ancestors that had not been destroyed by the Pizarros were among them riding in royal litters. Everyone else walked under the protection of the *Anti* archers. There were astrologers, weavers, stone masons, and *quipu* readers. Loyal subjects followed along and took care of cooking and herding llamas. They carried seeds and plants to cultivate when they arrived in their new home. Everyone Manco needed to begin a new life in a new land was with him. There were also five Spanish prisoners, the last of the survivors from Francisco Pizarro's various Cuzco relief forces. They were bound with rope and were guarded by *Anti* warriors.

First, the expedition headed north and climbed the banks of the Patacancha River. After many hours of climbing, they reached and crossed the Panticalla Pass and began a long descent into the *Antisuyu*.

Manco eyed his little son as they reclined in one of the royal litters. He was only the son of one of his concubines but Manco loved him deeply. "Titu Cusi," said Manco to gain the little boy's attention. "What weapon aims for the heels and hits the nose?"

Cura Ocllo elbowed Manco in the side playfully. "He's too young for that sort of humor, Manco," she chided.

"What?" asked Titu Cusi with a look of intense curiosity, "What is it?"

"A fart!" shouted Manco laughing loudly at his own joke.

"Oh Taytay, that's a good joke!" agreed Titu Cusi with admiration for his father.

"I wonder how Pachacuti and Tupac Inca feel to enter the lands again that they conquered so long ago," said Manco to Cura Ocllo in a more serious tone.

"Their eyes do not see and their hearts do not feel anymore, Manco," answered Cura Ocllo cynically.

181

"But they do, my Love," argued Manco. "Their eyes see even that to which our own eyes are blind."

Manco winked at his eldest son. Titu Cusi giggled.

"And just what do you think my *blindness* keeps me from seeing, my wise husband?" asked Cura Ocllo with a smile.

"Your eyes cannot see how much I love you, my dear, nor how pure is my heart. Actually, your eyes are perfect and are the most beautiful wells of treasure in my possession." Manco hugged Cura Ocllo playfully.

"Oh Manco, you are so silly," chided Cura Ocllo.

"Will I get to kill a puma, Father?" asked Titu Cusi.

"Many pumas," answered Manco. "You'll kill so many pumas that I'll order the *mamaconas* to fashion a puma-skin poncho for you to wear. How would you like that? You'll scare the other children like the thunder!"

"Yes, I want a puma-skin poncho!" yelled Titu Cusi with an enormous toothy smile. "Where will we live," asked Titu Cusi. "Will you build my mother and me a big room?"

"I will build your mother and you a magnificent room with a bath and gardens filled with exotic flesh-eating forest flowers," answered Manco.

Titu Cusi clasped his hands and wriggled with pleasure at his father's answer. He became quiet to consider what he would feed his flesh-eating plants.

"And what about *me*," asked Cura Ocllo with feigned envy.

"You, my dove, will have the finest room of all: The room I am in!"

Quietly and uneventfully, the procession continued toward their new home in the Amazon rain forest. They were totally unaware that Almagro and his conquistadors attacked the City of Cuzco, the sacred Inca capital, that very night.

Under the leadership of Rodrigo Orgóñez, Almagro's army caught the Pizarros asleep and completely unprepared. With very little effort and bloodshed, Rodrigo was able to fill the recently renovated Temple of the Sun with prisoners: Prisoners that included Hernando and Gonzalo Pizarro. After nearly a year, the siege of Cuzco had ended.

CHAPTER 40

A lmagro was more determined than ever to keep the city of Cuzco for himself. The intense hardship and physical suffering he endured during the fruitless exploration of his lands to the south had convinced him that Cuzco was his only hope for wealth and power.

"I have learned many lessons from the Inca, Rodrigo," said Almagro one afternoon as they shared a bottle of good Spanish wine. Almagro had moved back into his old home in Huayna Capac's palace on the Cuzco town square. He was content to resume the day-to-day administration of the city. Cuzco was the treasure he most coveted.

"If a man wants power, wealth, and fame," said Almagro, "and most men *do*," he smiled, "he has to control the land and the peasants like a *crop*. The harvest is *taxes*! A city can only be plundered once, my boy, but if you *own* the city and the *citizens*, you'll have a source of income that is virtually inexhaustible!"

"I like the way you think, Diego," agreed Rodrigo, "it is why I stay with you."

"Like you have anywhere else to go!" yelled Almagro as he clapped Rodrigo hard on the back.

"No, Diego, really, thank you for choosing me over Hernando DeSoto. Someone told me that he actually offered you money if you would name him as your second-in-command."

Diego shook his head. "Soto is a good man, Rodrigo. I wish him well in his pursuits. But you were the man for me. I knew it the moment I met you."

"Well," continued Rodrigo, "I just want you to know that I am proud to command your troops. But do you mind if I tell you a secret, Diego?"

"Go ahead, my boy, I may have only one eye, but my two ears are good!"

Rodrigo smiled weakly. "*Orgóñez* is not my real name," he confessed meekly. "I changed my name so I could become a Knight of the Order of Santiago. It has been my greatest wish since I was a boy. The aristocratic name I use is not truly my own."

"Names are not important here, Rodrigo," assured Almagro before he drank deeply from his cup.

"It is not so much *wealth* that I desire," continued Rodrigo, "but, more than anything, I'd like to be a Governor like you. I like what you are doing here in Cuzco."

"Well," answered Almagro, "it is like I said, names don't matter here. Take my name for example. Did you know that I never knew my father? I never even met him!"

Rodrigo shook his head sadly and listened to Almagro with great interest.

"My mother didn't want me," continued Almagro. "She left me with my uncle and disappeared. But he didn't want me either!"

Almagro rose from his chair to get another bottle of wine. After he had uncorked it and refilled their cups, he continued his story.

"Somehow I survived. My uncle didn't want to be concerned with me so he chained my feet together to keep me from running away. If you ask me now, I wonder why he wanted to keep me there!" Almagro shifted in his chair as he recalled his past.

"One time he got so angry at me that he put me in a cage! I don't even remember why. Ah, well, that is so far away in the past. Look at me now! I'm Governor of half of Peru! I assure you, Rodrigo, in this New World, *anything* is possible!"

Rodrigo was glad for the optimism but sad for his friend.

"I'm sure your mother would be proud of you now, Diego. To see what a great man you have become."

"No, Rodrigo, I would venture to bet that she barely remembers me. There is only one person who is proud of me and that is my son. I hope you will continue to mentor him in military strategy, Rodrigo. He looks up to you, you know."

The two rugged men clapped each other on their backs in a genuine show of masculine affection.

"Do you mind if I change the subject, Diego?" asked Rodrigo in a caring tone.

"Please do!" encouraged Diego. He had thought too long on the past already.

"With all respect, Diego, I think Hernando and Gonzalo Pizarro should be executed immediately," suggested Rodrigo. "As long as we hold them captive in the Temple of the Sun, we will have no peace. Francisco will never leave us alone."

Almagro put down his cup and sat up straight in his chair. He shook his head and exhaled loudly.

"Do you think that if I *kill* Hernando and Gonzalo that their big brother will remain peaceful?" asked Diego incredulously. "No my son, there is no way to emerge from this situation peacefully. I am afraid that there will be no peace during our lifetime."

"Then let me attack Lima," suggested Rodrigo. "I'll kill Francisco Pizarro myself! Peru will be *ours*!" he shouted. "I'm not afraid of the Pizarro brothers and their brutality! Let me go, send me to Lima tomorrow!"

"And I should sit here without your protection so Inca Manco can barbeque me? How far away do you think he is? No, Rodrigo, you will not leave me here alone. If you must go somewhere, Rodrigo, go instead to find Manco. Talk to him if you can." Almagro took a long drink of wine and wiped his mouth with his arm, "and kill him if you cannot."

CHAPTER 41

In July, Rodrigo left Cuzco in search of Manco. He headed north with 300 soldiers and enough supplies to last for months. Although his primary goal was to find Manco, Rodrigo hoped even more fervently that he would find silver and gold to plunder. He also hoped to gain the enviable status of *hero* if he could successfully free Manco's Spanish captives. He prayed that his success would bring him a handsome reward and a prestigious title from King Charles. Unlike the King's blurry edicts, Rodrigo's ambition had sharp, clear edges.

Unfortunately for Rodrigo, Manco's warriors demolished the Inca roadway that led to his forest retreat in Vitcos as they made their way toward the Amazon. Rodrigo was continually forced to seek alternative paths into the forest due to fallen trees and huge boulders that blocked his forward progress.

When Rodrigo finally reached Vitcos, his mission was a complete success except for one thing: Manco and Cura Ocllo got away. As pandemonium broke out in the town, runners from the Lucana tribe, the fastest runners Manco had in his service, picked up Manco and Cura Ocllo and carried them away running at full speed into the forest. Although Rodrigo had men on horses chase them throughout the night, they were unable to catch them and eventually returned alone. Manco and Cura Ocllo disappeared without a trace.

Rodrigo returned to Cuzco with plenty of plundered silver and gold, many native prisoners, and even the Spanish captives who were the sole survivors of the Cuzco relief forces sent by Francisco to help his brothers. In addition to his anticipated booty, Rodrigo also captured unexpected valuables: A stash of bloody Spanish armor and clothes. Rodrigo also confiscated the mummies of Manco's ancestors and took them back to Cuzco.

The armor and clothing was actually worth more than gold to Rodrigo. After trekking through the mountains of Chilé for two years with Almagro, many of his men were wearing rags.

Among the native prisoners was Titu Cusi, Manco's eldest son. When his royal identity was revealed to Almagro, Titu Cusi was brought to his palace and was treated as Almagro's own son. Titu Cusi was sent to the military school at Yachahuasi College in Cuzco where he was taught to speak Spanish as well as how to read and write. It was the same school from which his father, Manco, had graduated. Almagro bestowed upon the lad every luxury and entitlement due an Inca prince. But it didn't change Titu Cusi's status as a captive. The boy missed his father terribly.

While Rodrigo was away, Almagro crowned Paullu as the new Inca King to replace Manco. Paullu had spent the last two years in Chilé with Almagro and convinced *old one-eye* that he and his men would never have survived the long journey had it not been for Paullu' s influence and assistance.

Almagro was wise and had learned much about royal Inca families. By crowning Paullu as Inca King, he split loyalties among the people between the two brothers. Almagro saw how, when two royal brothers wore the *llautu*, the strength of each was diminished. This happened with Atahualpa and Huascar and Almagro felt confident that it would happen again with Manco and Paullu. Like Atahualpa and Huascar before them, Manco and Paullu each had their own group of ardent supporters.

Manco tried many times to get Paullu to join him in Vitcos. He knew that when Paullu went with Almagro to explore the southern lands, Paullu was merely following Manco's orders. But Paullu was ambitious and was certain that the Spaniards would win this war.

"Haven't you served them long enough?" asked Manco. "You should come live here in my little Vilcabamba mouse house in Vitcos."

"Almagro's men are my friends," answered Paullu. "They are so brave. Whatever they attempt they always emerge victorious. Your 200,000 warriors were unable to defeat just 200 of them. How could 200 *normal* men kill 50,000 Indian warriors? Please don't fight against the Spaniards anymore, Manco," pleaded Paullu.

Paullu chose to remain in Cuzco and be a happy puppet Inca King. He concluded that he had chosen wisely. Upon Rodrigo's return from Vitcos, Paullu realized that had he chosen to follow his brother to his forest retreat, he would now be in Cuzco anyway—as the Spaniards' captive instead of their puppet Inca King.

CHAPTER 42

Vira packed a saddle bag for her husband. As she stuffed it full of underclothes he wouldn't need, she shrugged her shoulders and turned to him in exasperation.

"How can you leave me now with the baby coming?" she asked desperately.

"I have to go, my love. But don't worry, it's not dangerous," he tried to comfort her.

"You will send Almagro away from Cuzco and take it for Francisco?" she asked.

"No, we're only going to talk to him. Diego needs to see that taking Cuzco was wrong. He has to try to understand."

"Wrong?" Vira's eyes flamed with indignation.

"But it was *right* for the Pizarros to take Cuzco from Manco? Cuzco is our *home*! Now Manco lives in the mountains like an outcast." She broke off for she realized that she was losing her temper again. She had been so emotional lately.

"Forgive me, Alvarez, I didn't mean to criticize *you*. I am just so angry. Whenever I think about Francisco Pizarro, I feel . . ."

"Hatred?" Alvarez completed her sentence. "I know. You don't need to apologize. I'm just glad that you are being honest and open with me." He sighed. "I would never expect you to feel otherwise about Pizarro after all that has happened to you and your family since we landed in Tumbez."

"There are some things about your *New World* that I *don't* hate, Alvarez," said Vira apologetically. "I like the way you marry only one woman and let her keep her own personality."

"Of course you like that," smiled Alvarez.

"I also like the way you listen to each other's ideas. My people are simply expected to bow down to our all-powerful Inca King."

"Well, Vira, I think we communicate better because we use writing to share our ideas and opinions. If your people had writing, then you also could share thoughts and ideas with others more freely. How are you doing at your lessons with Father Pedro?"

"Oh, that is all going fine, Alvarez," sighed Vira. "But what I'm really worried about is that we don't fit in with either group. We're not Inca and we're not Spaniards now, we are a mixture. We don't belong anywhere."

"We have the best of both worlds, my love," said Alvarez as he kissed Vira lovingly on her lips. "You spend far too much time thinking. I'm going to buy extra paper and ink for you, and help you write down your thoughts so they won't spin around like a storm in your mind."

Vira buckled the latches on Alvarez's saddle bag. They stood for a long moment in silence just holding each other. Vira wondered at herself and the power of this love she felt for Alvarez. She loved him more than she loved herself. She felt liberated but vulnerable: A complex mixture of emotion and wisdom that inspired her faith in her gods.

CHAPTER 43

F rancisco Pizarro didn't take the news of Almagro's defiance well. "That wretch," he yelled as he beat his fists on the desk. "He forces me to negotiate because he knows the King's edict is unclear. Why did King Charles fail to specify that Cuzco belongs to *me*?"

Francisco immediately dispatched an escort that included Don Alvarez de la Vega, Carlos de Galez, Father Pedro, and Father Sebastiano to safely deliver Gaspar de Espinoza to Cuzco. Espinoza, an elderly lawyer, was tasked with the challenge of facilitating the negotiations with Almagro. Because the King's edict failed to identify within which kingdom Cuzco was located: That of Pizarro or that granted to Almagro, negotiation between the two governors was required.

Espinoza's primary concern was the release of Gonzalo and Hernando Pizarro from their prison chamber within the Temple of the Sun. His secondary concern was if, once released, the two Pizarros would seek revenge against Almagro.

"How do you plan to approach Almagro?" asked Don Alvarez with concern for his old friend.

"My first goal will be to shed the light of reason," answered Espinoza wisely. "A man must be satisfied with what is actually his and belongs to him. This conflict has revealed Almagro's true nature to command and dominate in order to achieve his own ambition."

"Excuse me, my Lord," said Alvarez with a smile, "but that sounds more like a description of *Francisco* than Diego. Diego was in Cuzco when the King's first edict was delivered. He only traveled south upon Francisco's suggestion. Now he has returned to Cuzco. Remember, he's the one who delivered Cuzco from an Indian siege that lasted a year."

Espinoza nodded. He fully realized the complex nature of the situation.

Don Alvarez carried the royal parchment upon which Pizarro's demands had been granted by the King. The royal order demanded that Don Diego de Almagro immediately hand Cuzco, along with all its treasures, over to Francisco. It also commanded that all of Almagro's captives be released from prison. In return, Almagro would be granted a ship in which to sail to Spain for a meeting with King Charles. The orders specified that Almagro was to disarm his army within fifteen days and travel to Nazca to await his ship.

After more than a week of travel along the Inca Highway, the envoy of twelve men finally reached one of the fortresses of a suburb of Cuzco. The roof was burned and only its sooty walls were standing. Cuzco, once so beautifully framed by its suburbs, was now surrounded by a desolate ring of blackened ruins.

The guard announced the arrival of the visitors and at once a small troop of soldiers approached on horses. Juan de Guzmán, a faithful friend of Almagro, greeted Pizarro's messengers cheerfully.

"Welcome dear comrades!" he said politely. "I'll have your weapons, please, for the duration of the visit."

"What?" choked Father Sebastiano. "We are to be disarmed? This is a *trap!*"

But Don Alvarez trusted Almagro whose honor and kind heart he knew well. He assured his companions that it would be acceptable to comply with his request.

"Here's my sword and dagger," said Alvarez cooperatively.

After the rest of the men delivered their arms to Guzmán, they were led into Cuzco. Alvarez was saddened to see the battle wounds of the city. Wherever he looked he saw that the once luxurious city was marred by walls that had tumbled down and roofs that had been burned. But already new buildings were emerging from the ruins and there was lively traffic in the streets. To their surprise, well dressed Indians were walking the streets laughing and chatting.

"You are astonished at our progress?" asked Guzmán. "Almagro has created an Indian paradise. He governs Cuzco peacefully and has rewarded our Indian allies for their assistance. We have a new Inca King now! Almagro crowned Paullu to take Manco's place and the Indians obey him willingly. We sleep without fear now! Paullu is even studying to convert to Christianity!"

When they arrived at the splendid palace called *home* by Almagro, Guzmán invited them to make themselves comfortable until the evening meal was served.

That night, when the twelve members of the embassy, in full dress, entered Almagro's magnificent dining hall, they were delighted to see Hernando Pizarro in attendance. He was elegantly attired in yellow velvet adorned with jewels, and he moved about freely among the other knights that had been invited. It was not what they expected as Hernando was a prisoner.

The messengers were welcomed warmly and there were many questions about Lima and how Francisco was getting along. In spite of the forced friendliness, Alvarez detected tension just below the surface.

Guzmán drew Don Alvarez aside. "I don't know what terms the Viceroy may offer," he said in a low voice, barely louder than a whisper, "but I suspect that Almagro will not be able to accept them. Why should that ambitious tyrant pocket all of Peru's treasure for himself? Is this how he rewards his servants and faithful companions?"

As Guzmán walked away from Alvarez, Hernando approached. "They invited me to dinner," he snarled, "because that fool Almagro, whom his advisors lead by the nose, wishes to appear generous toward my brother the Viceroy. But I swear to you, upon my sword, that he'll repent the hour when he delivered me to his jail!"

"Where is your brother, Gonzalo?" asked Alvarez.

"Thank God, he escaped," answered Hernando. "You know he has a way with the women, right? Well, one of the *mamaconas* in the Temple of the Sun where Almagro's dogs are keeping us, fancied him. She helped him escape to a tunnel he had discovered some time ago. He told me he would go to Francisco in Lima. Did you see him along the Highway?"

"No," answered Alvarez. "This is the first I've heard of his escape. Truly, I expected you both to be in jail."

Suddenly the big doors with gold molding opened and old Almagro appeared accompanied by his son, Diego de Almagro *the Younger*, Rodrigo Orgóñez, and several of Almagro's closest friends. The old warrior entered with dignity wearing a black velvet gown with a golden cross upon his chest. He gave a noble impression but his wrinkled and worn, one-eyed face was the face of a suffering man.

Almagro headed straight for Alvarez. He walked with a cane and limped noticeably. He embraced Alvarez with an affection that was genuine.

"Don't mind me," said Almagro trying to comfort Alvarez about his obvious physical degeneration, "my feet were frost-bitten in Chilé. It kills me to walk."

Almagro turned and greeted the others coldly and stiffly, especially Father Sebastiano whom he regarded with deep distrust.

"I am pleased to introduce to you, gentlemen, my son, Diego," he said with pride. He presented a young man of perhaps twenty years of age. The youth was somewhat taller than his father and had the same broad shoulders. But Diego inherited the good looks of his Panamanian mother. A light of frankness and courage radiated from his eyes.

Father Sebastiano decided that it was time to disclose the purpose of the visit. Somberly, he stepped forward toward the old governor.

"We brought a document for your review from Francisco. We do hope you will agree to the terms and avoid any potential for civil war. No doubt, the natives would find it most amusing to watch us destroy each other."

An acidic silence followed his ultimatum and an air of hostility floated throughout the hall. Almagro reached out with a trembling hand for the parchment. He knew without reading it that it contained commands he could not follow. He also knew that to disobey would mean war.

He handed the parchment to Guzmán. "Why should a soldier know how to read? Reading is for priests and clerics," he said with a sad smile.

Guzmán read the document in silence as everyone watched. He turned to Almagro and reported, "You are ordered to abandon Cuzco, hand over your riches, liberate your captives, and disarm your military," said Guzmán. "In return, they offer you a ship upon which you may sail to Spain."

"No," said Almagro. "No," he repeated shaking his head. "You would send me into exile?"

The room buzzed with sudden chatter.

"What about *my* terms?" asked Almagro loudly returning silence to the hall. "The Viceroy shall grant me not merely *one* ship but an entire port city! And I will remain in Cuzco until the port city is prepared. His Majesty the King will have to settle this matter. I will *not* disarm my army." Almagro nodded his head at the entourage.

Again the hall buzzed loudly, this time with earnest agreement. Hernando Pizarro rolled his eyes. Rodrigo glared at him with unbridled hatred. The Pizarrists listened sternly.

"You mustn't let your personal interests impede the progress of Christendom!" bellowed Sebastiano.

"Then we are not obliged to give you Cuzco to satisfy Francisco's desire to found his own dynasty. What good would that bring to Christendom?" growled Guzmán.

The debate grew sharp and hostile. Father Pedro, fearing that there would be a fight, interrupted them, "I suggest, my brothers, not to partake in a supper when our moods are so excited. It is better that we withdraw to our guestrooms since we are exhausted from our weeks of travel through the mountains."

Everyone agreed. The Pizarrists rose to leave but when Alvarez arose, Almagro spoke desperately.

"You would leave too, Alvarez? You have become my enemy now?" he cried. "You don't think that you and I would quarrel, do you? Please stay and eat with me."

Don Alvarez agreed to eat dinner with his old friend. He motioned to the others to proceed out of the hall as he sat down with the Almagrists at a long table. Old Almagro, in the seat of honor, gave Alvarez the seat at his right. His son, young Diego was seated at his left.

At first the conversation was very stiff since all tested subjects ran aground unintentionally on offensive remarks. But when all had eaten and they left the table to drink more wine, Almagro grew eloquent. He put his bony hand upon Alvarez's arm and gave him a long explanation.

"Your opinion matters to me, Alvarez. You are my dear friend. I have often said that after my son, you are my favorite. Don't condemn me as the others do. You know yourself, how faithfully I always served Francisco. We were supposed to be *partners*! You know how many times I came with my soldiers to his aid. When he was in danger and the boot was on his throat, I was there. How often did I travel to Panama for supplies or to Sevilla to persuade the King to give more generously? And he, whenever *he* had the chance to do something for *me*, he conveniently forgot. When he was named Viceroy, he strutted in his glory at the royal court and neglected me completely. Not a single word did he utter on my behalf. When I complained, he would disarm me with eloquent promises that the day would come when I would receive my great reward. I continued to have faith in him and serve him obediently. But again he forgot about me. A friend of mine appealed in my favor to His Majesty and he granted me a territory of 200 miles to the south, but he didn't describe the boundaries. Is there any reason then why I shouldn't possess Cuzco?"

Almagro sighed. Don Alvarez did not mention that Francisco Pizarro was currently organizing an emissary to the King with the most costly jewels, gold and silver artifacts, and Indian slaves to sweeten his request to list Cuzco within the territory allotted for his governorship.

Almagro emptied his cup again and continued. "I have a son, and as you see, he's a fine fellow. It's for him I strive to have some property. Do try to understand me, Alvarez. I want young Diego to be happy."

Almagro's eyes brimmed with tears and Alvarez felt his throat constrict with emotion as though he would choke.

"Thank you for your friendship and confidence," said Alvarez. "We've been through so much together over the years. No matter what happens, you'll always be my friend."

Alvarez rose and embraced him. "Don't talk like it's all over, Diego," encouraged Alvarez. "You never know what can happen. Remember, you're the one who never loses hope. How many times were we ready to give up and you were able to keep us going?"

Alvarez smiled warmly. The drinks and food had hit him hard after the strenuous journey. "I'm so tired, Diego, can you excuse me? I must get some rest."

"I'll only say goodnight to you," replied Diego playfully, "if you tell me what happened that night before I left for Chilé. What trouble did you and Lopez find?"

"It's a long story, Diego, but let me assure you, it has a very happy ending. I'll tell you all about it tomorrow, my friend," answered Alvarez with a wink.

"All right, Alvarez, but I want details!"

Don Alvarez and Almagro shook hands. As Alvarez turned to retire to his guest room, he wondered what would become of his old friend.

In response to the continuous urging of Espinoza, Almagro ordered that Hernando be set free as long as he promised to remain peaceful. Poor Rodrigo was mortified by this news. When he was told that Hernando was a free man, Rodrigo raised his head theatrically and grabbed his long dark beard with his left hand. With his right hand, he pretended to slice open his own throat.

When his dramatic show of disapproval was completed, he shouted with scorn at Almagro, "What a shame, my friendship with you has cut my throat!"

Within two months, the negotiations between Almagro and Espinoza collapsed and war was declared against the Pizarros. Everyone had known all along that the Pizarros would be the last people on earth to either forgive or to forget.

CHAPTER 44

"Little Princess," urged Pani. "It's time for you to go, Doña Conchita awaits you. Her servants are here to take you to the palace."

Vira had slipped into a dark blue satin and lace gown. It was weightless compared to the wool and gold robes she was accustomed to wearing. She dreaded her visit with Inés. Her first meeting was so uncomfortable that much time passed without the women meeting each other again. They only spoke to one another when necessary. Also, Vira had no desire to be anywhere near Francisco Pizarro without her husband at her side and Alvarez had not yet returned from his trip to Cuzco.

Pizarro's Indian servants awaited her outside with a most incredible palanquin. Instead of being carried by litter bearers, this litter was carried along by a horse and two wheels! A beautiful brown horse was attached to the front carrying poles. The poles in back of the litter rested on an axel with a large wheel at each end. Vira had only seen wheels on small toys her brothers played with when they were children. Never in her life had she imagined that wheels could be made so large and could actually be used for something so important!

With hesitation, Vira climbed the steps into the newfangled litter. She was impressed by the elaborate design of the interior. Velvet curtains were pulled back with braided cords. The cushions were of an exquisite fabric. Vira wrapped the mantilla around her shoulders and shivered although the day was warm.

"Come with me, Pani," she begged.

Pani joined Vira in the palanquin with enthusiasm. A huge, adventurous smile spread across her face. Vira laughed lovingly at her. The Indian sitting on the horse lifted a small whip with his left hand and spanked the horse lightly on its rear end. With a jerk, they started towards the palace.

"This sure is a bumpy ride!" exclaimed Vira as her voice quavered from the vibration. Pani just laughed.

Inés awaited them sedately in the big, red, carpeted marble hall. She was surrounded by a bevy of beautifully dressed court ladies. She wore a dress of white lace with red flowers fastened to her belt. A hibiscus blossom was placed in her dark hair. She received Vira with a bow and addressed her as though she were giving her official information.

"Where is your husband," asked Vira looking around nervously.

"Oh, don't worry about *him*," answered Inés with more than a little scorn. "He's out *all* day, *every* day. If he's not in the fields working like a wretched Indian or toying with masonry at some new *awful* Spanish eyesore, then he's out playing that exasperating *bowls* game! He doesn't even come home to eat. I abhor the sight of him in that stupid white hat and ugly white shoes. What a joke he is! Anyway, never mind *him*! There is a woman here who says her name is *Sapaca*. She says Inca Manco sent her here to find you."

Vira jumped joyously and embraced Pani as tears began to fall. "Sapaca! Thank you Inés!"

"Wait," warned Inés, "don't thank me yet. You haven't seen her. I have only seen her through the window. She is very sick."

"What's wrong with her?" asked Vira in shock. "Bring me to her, let me see her."

Inés led Vira down the marble stairs to the courtyard where in the center of the green lawn, two guards stood with spears on their shoulders guarding a woman who crouched on the ground. The woman was simply dressed in a white gown and her head was covered with a scarf. Only her face showed: It was disfigured and covered with abscesses and scabs. Open ulcers had destroyed the tissue that had once formed her lovely nose. One of her eyes was covered with a bandage. But it was Sapaca.

"Sapaca!" shrieked Vira as she pulled free from the loving grips of Inés and Pani and dashed toward the unhappy creature. She ran toward Sapaca but was stopped by the guards. Although she struggled against their grasp, deep in her heart she was glad they stopped her. She felt ashamed and guilty that she was glad not to go any closer.

The guards were gentle. "You cannot go any closer, Señora de la Vega," they told her. "That woman is very sick."

Sapaca knelt upon the ground and sobbed while Vira spoke kind, consoling words to her. Both women cried tears of heart break.

"Sapaca!" groaned Vira. "You'll come home with me. Pani and I will nurse you back to health. Everything will be all right now."

Sapaca lifted her face wet with tears and for a moment there was a faint flash of her former charm as she said in resignation, "You always *did* cry too much, Vira!" Together the girls smiled and looked at each other.

"I'm going to die, Vira. There is a place I can stay until my time comes. There are some people who remember us. Manco's spies found me in Jauja. I wouldn't let them tell him that I was sick. But there are good people here and I am safe and comfortable. Vira, you're so beautiful. Your dreams have come true. I should have stayed with you. I'm sorry."

"No, Sapaca, don't be sorry. *I'm* sorry. What happened to you? Where have you been all this time? What happened to your baby?"

"She was a little girl, Vira, a beautiful and perfect little girl. I don't know where she is. They took me to Jauja and made me stay in a temple. They forced me to give myself to every man they brought me. It was horrible: I, a member of the royal Inca family and the wife of an Inca Prince. I was continuously brutalized until I became ill. They threw me out into the street with nowhere to go. But some kind people helped me and sent messengers to Manco. His spies came for me but when they saw my sores, they told the Indians to carry me to Lima. Now they won't let me out of the place I stay because they are afraid I will cause a plague. They only let me come here because they heard you lived in this city. I'm sorry. My life is over. But now I can die in peace knowing that you are well and that you still love me."

"I do, Sapaca, I love you."

The guards moved forward and took Sapaca gently by her arms. "We're sorry, Princess, but she might be contagious. We must return her to the *Tambo*," said the Indian guard with sincere regret.

Vira unlatched a gold necklace Alvarez gave her and tossed it to Sapaca. "Viracocha will protect you," she cried. "I will try to visit you soon."

Vira stood in the garden for a long while. She was confused and exhausted. After a time, an arm embraced her tenderly. Inés came to her side and led her protectively into her receiving room as though she were leading her own child. She helped her to lie down upon the sofa and whispered to her affectionate words.

"Don't let this strike you down, Vira. Don't lose your proud spirit, for this is the only thing that has remained for us. The *white strangers* stole our freedom. They took our honor and made us their concubines. Let's show them that they will never hurt our pride or crush our self-respect. We will use our weapon of defiance. Let's fight them till our last breath!"

Vira didn't speak.

"I hated you at first," confessed Inés. "I was taken by an aged monster and you were taken by a handsome warrior. Your husband actually *cares* about our people. My husband invents ways to torture them."

Vira's features did not lose their look of despair, but she relaxed. The words of Inés found an echo in her soul. She felt pride and gratitude whenever she thought of how Alvarez saved Cura Ocllo and Kusa Akchi.

"Thank you for your kind words about my husband," she said looking up at Inés with sincere gratitude.

"I envied you and hated you, Vira. But now I don't hate you anymore. I have suffered and now I understand that others have suffered as well. I was alone in a dark world. Now we understand each other and can share our sorrow. Father Pedro told me that I nourish my own soul when I am kind and that, when I am cruel, I destroy my own soul. I want us to be sisters again." She kissed Vira on both cheeks and walked her to the palanquin where Pani was waiting.

When Vira stepped down from the fancy horse-drawn litter at the front door of her home, her heart was heavy. In spite of all its elaborate furnishings and servants, the house was empty without Alvarez.

Then she heard his footsteps. She ran in the direction of the sound to find Don Alvarez walking toward her. He was travel stained and tired but he was alive and uninjured. They rushed into each other's arms and for a time didn't speak a word.

A week later, Sapaca was buried in an unmarked and common grave outside of Lima used only for the corpses of the unfortunates that perished from contagious disease. The necklace given to her by Vira was buried with her, hidden against her broken heart. It was the only remnant of her past she possessed.

CHAPTER 45

The Viceroy summoned his troops to assemble in the Lima city plaza. It was time to organize the campaign to march to Cuzco and take it away from his old partner, Diego de Almagro. As the troops assembled in formation, they were formally placed under the capable command of Hernando Pizarro. To Francisco's surprise, Father Pedro and Don Alvarez de la Vega refused to participate.

"Why do you refuse to march to Cuzco?" asked Francisco as he removed his white hat from his head and wiped the sweat from his face with a towel he kept hanging around his neck just for that purpose.

"I came here to fight Indians," answered Alvarez, "I have no cause to kill my own countrymen."

"And you?" he asked Father Pedro as he placed his hat upon his head once more. "You're always the first to volunteer. Why do you back away now?"

"I have journeyed with you into every battle," answered Pedro with respect, "that was fought for the Cross. In this battle you will fight *against* Christians. This is *civil war* and I cannot go. It is not that I back away in fear, it is that I must step aside in protest."

"Oh well," muttered Francisco, "don't worry, I'm not going either. Good then, we'll play bowls tomorrow." Without another word, Francisco walked away from his old friends.

"We must punish the *traitors*," declared Father Sebastiano.

"Let God punish the *traitors*," stated Pedro with finality. "Be cautious, I hear that the men in Cuzco believe *we* are the traitors. It is *greed* that inspires Francisco to want Cuzco, not God. Ownership of Cuzco does not interest God and your arguments are bereft of God's inspiration. *For* us or *against* us, God will be present."

"You forget, Pedro," thundered Sebastiano, "that we are here to escort Francisco into his success! What *he* wants, *we* want. Our great plans will only come to fruition through *his* triumph!"

"I see," said Pedro dryly, "you prefer to spill the blood of your own people than concede a small area of land in which to let them live. Call it what you want and go for your own reasons, I will remain in Lima."

Sebastiano was furious; however, he recognized the position in which Pedro set his shoulders. Further argument was futile and, anyway, Francisco didn't seem to care. He wasn't going to Cuzco either. Father Sebastiano thought that to trouble overly with the insignificant friar might give the impression to the soldiers that he *mattered* to him. So, instead, he stormed off after Francisco.

"I guess you told him," said Alvarez to his friend with admiration.

"No," retorted Pedro sarcastically, "none of *my* words reach *those* ears!"

It was April. Hernando Pizarro arrived with his soldiers to fight for control of the Inca's sacred capital city. At a place called Las Salinas, approximately two miles west of Cuzco, his forces came face to face with the forces of Diego de Almagro. Hernando had amassed an army of over 800 Spaniards from reinforcements of men and supplies that had arrived in Lima. Several thousand natives, loyal to Hernando, accompanied him. Over 200 of the men were cavalry and mounted on war horses. They wore a full set of armor and carried sharpened lances and swords. The armored foot soldiers carried shields and brandished swords. But Hernando's greatest weapon was the 100 new harquebuses, the three-legged guns that fired lead projectiles able to penetrate the thickest armor. Rodrigo didn't know about the new harquebuses that could shoot farther than the old model.

Almagro had 500 men of which 240 were cavalry and 260 were foot soldiers. They had six cannon and over 6,000 loyal Indians under the leadership of Inca Paullu. Rodrigo, saddled atop a magnificent light grey stallion, led the soldiers to battle while Almagro followed, carried on a litter.

"Look what has become of our negotiations. This battle is a disservice to God and King Charles!" complained Almagro to his litter carriers who didn't bother to listen to his garbled sounds. "The reward they get for fighting and dying for the Pizarros will be *nothing*. Look at me! I'm an old, one-eyed man sitting uselessly on a litter. My feet are black and damaged by frost and I can no longer ride into battle. All I can do is sit here and watch the destruction."

"I can't believe this is happening," murmured an Indian woman as she watched from the hillside near Almagro. Many of the native women assembled to watch the *white strangers* kill each other.

"I hope they all die and both sides *lose!*" whispered some of the young boys.

On the cold, dreary battle ground beyond Cuzco, both sides lined up in their chosen formations. Lances were raised and swords were unsheathed. Rodrigo, completely unaware of the danger he and his troops faced from the new harquebuses, shouted encouragement to his men as he rode past the lines of his men on his beautiful horse.

Hernando gave the signal to attack. The harquebusiers fired their guns and Rodrigo watched in horror as his men fell. Even his fine war horse fell beneath him. How could this happen? He measured the distance carefully. He knew exactly where to line up his men.

After the guns were fired and Rodrigo's men crumpled to the ground, panic struck Almagro's forces. Courageously, Rodrigo ran straight toward Hernando's front line and struck bravely with his sword. But there were too many men around him now and he was without his horse. There was not even a moment when the battle swung in Rodrigo's favor. Hernando's new soldiers were fresh and trained to fire the new harquebuses into the lines of men with great accuracy.

In a move of cruelty that fulfilled Rodrigo's prophecy, one of Hernando's soldiers grabbed Rodrigo from behind while several others stabbed him with their swords. A brawny soldier pulled back Rodrigo's thick black beard and cut his throat with a dagger. He kept slicing until Rodrigo's head was completely removed from his body. In a macho display of victory, another one of Pizarro's soldiers impaled Rodrigo's bloody, bearded head on the tip of his sword and raised it high for all of Almagro's men to see that their commander was dead.

Almagro's troops broke apart and men began to flee into the mountains caring only to save their own lives. Young Diego de Almagro and Guzmán fled into the mountains. Their only hope was to contact Manco's Indian warriors and seek sanctuary with the Inca. Inca Paullu, who was able to foresee the outcome early on, had strategically changed sides in the midst of the battle and had ordered his Indian warriors to begin killing Almagro's men.

Almagro was mortified. Right in front of his good eye, his men were running. His prized commander was dead and his head was shish kabobbed on a Pizarro sword. Desperate to flee to safety but unable to find anyone to carry his deserted litter, Diego grabbed a stray mule and mounted it with great difficulty. The mule bucked and sat down several times and it was fortunate that no one who understood Spanish was around to hear such language.

Almagro rode toward the fortress of Saqsaywaman just above Cuzco. The sage words of Espinoza rang in his ears, "*When Governors quarrel they find themselves deprived of what they had previously claimed. Instead they inherit great misfortune, prison, and often death.*"

Hernando's soldiers were too busy killing, looting, arguing, and chasing women to chase after Almagro. Many of Hernando's soldiers began to fight each other over the spoils of Cuzco. The entire city fell into confusion. Indians chased Indians, men chased men, and men chased women. Amidst the turmoil, someone took the time to hang Rodrigo's handsome head with rope in the center of the main plaza.

It had been a bad day for Diego de Almagro. He lost 120 of his loyal soldiers: Men who had marched with him to Chile and back again. Hernando lost only nine of his men. Almagro, knowing that it was hopeless to hide in the fortress with no food and water, finally gave himself up and was imprisoned within the Temple of the Sun in the same chamber where he had imprisoned Hernando and Gonzalo.

A cold rain began to fall. Before it was able to wash away the bloodstains of Peru's second civil war, it bathed the city in red water.

CHAPTER 46

"*Por Dios*! Send me back to Spain," suggested Diego Almagro. "Don't make this decision by yourself, Hernando, it's too important. Let King Charles be my judge, or let me go to your brother in Lima. I'll sign any papers you give me and I'll do anything you want. Just don't kill me here! I can't believe this! I helped *conquer* this empire! I'm your brother's *partner*! None of his success would have been possible without my help! You can't do this to me!"

"Stop behaving so despicably," warned Hernando. He hated the groveling. "Have some pride old man."

As days turned into weeks and the weeks into months, Hernando left Almagro in jail. All the while, Almagro was told that Francisco was on his way to Cuzco to meet with him and negotiate a settlement. But that wasn't true. Hernando was using the time to prepare judicial proceedings against Almagro so that he could execute him legally.

"I may have only one eye to see," growled Diego, "but I know what is going on here. I see you clearly, you devil," he told Hernando. "*You*—you spent too many days staring at the sun while easing along the waves in ships. For two years you were gone! Who fought by Francisco's side during your *absence*? I did. Where were *you*?"

Hernando walked out of Almagro's prison cell feeling aggravated. He hoped the paperwork he was collecting to build his case against Francisco's old partner would keep him out of trouble with the King.

The mayor of Cuzco, the town crier, and the executioner entered Almagro's cell. "There is nothing I can do," said the mayor. "It has been ordered that you must die. We are simply carrying out orders."

"You tyrants!" yelled Almagro. "You're stealing the King's land and you're killing me for no reason! Had I executed that reeking moor when I had the chance," lamented Diego, "none of us would be here now."

As Diego watched, the executioner prepared the garrote.

"I will die like Atahualpa?" asked Diego in terror.

"Would you rather burn?" asked Hernando with a wicked smile.

The executioner raised the garrote and lowered it over Diego's head. Slowly and deliberately, he began to tighten it around Almagro's neck. With each twist, the bulging, dying face of Atahualpa flashed through Almagro's memory.

As the humiliation of defeat consumed him, he recalled the rejection when his mother sent him away as she peeked at him through the crack in her door. It seemed like only yesterday when his uncle chained his ankles and threw him inside that animal cage. Young Diego, young, handsome Diego: My beautiful son, please remember me . . ."

The next morning, Cuzco's town crier shouted out onto the streets of Cuzco for all to hear that "Don Diego de Almagro, Governor of the Kingdom of New Toledo, in the Indies of the South Sea and in the provinces of Peru, a native of Extremadura—is dead."

Francisco was informed by letter. When the letter was read for him, he dropped his head into his hands and cried. To Alvarez, he appeared to be stricken with grief, a response he witnessed once before when Juan died.

Chapter 47

"Do you think Francisco's tears were real?" Vira asked Alvarez after the evening meal.

"Only God knows," answered Alvarez. "I heard he's going to Cuzco to meet with his brothers. Whether he will praise them or punish them for killing Almagro, I don't know. It is rumored that he sent a message to his brothers to advise them to spare Almagro," continued Alvarez, "but I don't know of anyone who might have delivered it."

There was a knock at the door and Turi went to open it. When he entered the room, he was accompanied by Carlos de Galez.

"Could I speak with you privately Don Alvarez de la Vega," he asked formally.

"Of course," answered Alvarez, "come with me to my study."

The two men exited the room and walked stiffly to Alvarez's study where he conducted his military responsibilities. He spent most of his time lately playing games with Francisco. Francisco was tireless and could wear out the younger men at bowls and jai alai.

"Please, tell me the reason for your visit, Carlos," said Alvarez with an encouraging smile. "You are not usually so formal. What can I do for you?"

"Diego de Almagro's last wish was to give the territory granted him by His Majesty to his son," said Carlos.

"I know," answered Alvarez, "but Francisco will never allow it. When Diego was executed, Francisco confiscated all his assets."

"I know. That's why I have come to you, Alvarez. You have Francisco's ear. And I know you cared deeply about Almagro. Maybe you could intercede for the young Almagro."

"I don't know where he is or if he is even *alive*," argued Alvarez.

"I have had news," confided Carlos quietly. "Young Diego lives in Vitcos as Manco's guest, and he's not alone. Guzmán and some others are with him. They are planning revenge against Francisco for Almagro's death. Public opinion is rapidly turning against Francisco. Perhaps it would be wise; in an effort to allay the anger against him and protect the peace we have now in Lima, for Francisco to grant young Diego his inheritance. There are many who would like to see Francisco dead."

"I'll have to think about it," answered Alvarez carefully. He had successfully disagreed with Francisco before, but tensions were running high lately.

"That is all I request at this time, Alvarez," said Carlos as he stood and saluted.

As he turned to leave, Alvarez spoke to him, "Thank you for honoring me by sharing your news and concerns with me, Carlos. I will see what I will be able to do for my old friend's son."

Carlos smiled and left. Alvarez sat down at his desk and dropped his face into his hands. How had life become so complicated?

CHAPTER 48

Next to a small chapel stood a tiny cottage, insignificant in size and cost, encircled by a terrace where flowers bloomed. The flowers were not splendid exotic rarities, just the familiar carnations, white jasmine, and, in the shade of two pear trees, one on each side of the walkway, beds of violets. It was easy to see that the garden was arranged and tended by one who loved flowers and nursed them with a careful hand.

The interior of the cottage reflected the picture of an affectionate home. In the only modest chamber, the furnishings were simple and neatly arranged. It was decorated only with a crucifix on the wall and a painting of Mary, the holy mother of God.

Father Pedro sat on a wooden chair, leaving the one armchair for any visitor who might arrive unexpectedly. He preferred a modest seat, for he intended to serve his Lord humbly. He was busily turning over the leaves of a little prayer book he received years ago from a friend. The pages were hand illuminated and the book was one of the few treasures he possessed. He was so submerged in his reading that he did not even notice his guest until he was startled by a loud greeting.

"Good morning, Father Pedro. You should be more attentive. I could have walked right in here and killed you," said Hernando Pizarro.

Father Pedro rose quickly, closed the little book and placed it gently on the table.

"Welcome, Hernando Pizarro," he said kindly.

"Don't act like you're happy to see me," grunted Hernando filling up the whole room with his bulk. "I know your true feelings."

"My feelings are inconsequential, Hernando. I am always glad to greet a visitor to my home," Father Pedro assured him. "What brings you here this day?"

"I came to say goodbye," answered Hernando nervously. "I sail to Sevilla tomorrow to deliver a newly written chronicle of events to the King. Francisco seems to think I need to exonerate myself for the execution of Governor Almagro. As if the King doesn't know already that I am an Indian-fighting hero! A new load of gold for him will help His Majesty to see the Pizarro family through the flowers, so to speak."

"Anyway," continued Hernando, "I wanted to see what you did with the morsel of land King Charles granted you."

"A morsel can sometimes satisfy, my son. I would not change places with Solomon himself."

Hernando laughed ironically.

"Had you kept it for yourself instead of wasting it on that orphanage you fill with the unwanted spawn of Indian bastards, thieves, and murderers, you would have more than just this tiny cottage to show for your merit. I didn't believe the gossip. I had to come see for myself."

Pedro smiled. "And you see that it is all true and that I am content."

"Do you forget," Hernando cried, "that those wretched brats you waste your money on are the orphans of pagan criminals?"

"All children are innocent," replied Pedro. "I am here to dry their tears."

"Are not rats and snakes to be exterminated?" snarled Hernando.

"I do not concern myself with rats and snakes," answered Pedro dryly.

Hernando shook his head unbelievingly. "You find your answers in your books and letters. You will never understand a man like me," complained Hernando.

"I fear I do understand you, Hernando," retorted Pedro. "You do not believe in God. At least the natives revere the gods they know. You revere no one and nothing. What excuse will you offer when your life ends and you stand before God for judgment?"

Hernando looked puzzled. His always sarcastic and arrogant countenance became uncertain and he seemed to be seeking an excuse. "I didn't come here to let you scold me," he said coldly.

"Then why are you here?" asked Pedro as he began to lose patience.

"Look at me, Pedro," said Hernando. "In spite of my hidalgo origins, I have amassed great fame and wealth. Poor men are wretched and worthless. Rich men are respected and appreciated. I have robbed and killed for what I have. Even the King has rewarded me. I am proud of myself! Until Almagro . . ."

Hernando's voice broke off in mid-thought. He brushed a hand across his forehead which was now covered with perspiration. "I can't sleep any more. Almagro appears in my nightmares. I see him as he knelt before me begging that I spare his life and let his son receive his inheritance." He paused and looked down at his clasped hands.

Neither man spoke. After a moment, Hernando continued, "That's why I am here. I want you to liberate me from these horrible visions. Reconcile Almagro's ghost to his maker. Tell him to stop haunting me!"

"There are no ghosts to haunt us," answered Pedro. "What torments you is your own conscience."

"How can I find peace?" groaned Hernando.

"There is no peace without faith in God," answered Pedro.

Just then, a din of joyful children's laughter and talking was heard through the open door. Outside on the path to the house, a group of about twenty native boys and girls of various ages and sizes approached in single file. They were being led by a nun. Their hair was smoothly combed and they wore long white gowns that reached their ankles. All smiled happily and possessed the air of those that share a delightful secret. Pedro's eyes brightened and he put his hand on Hernando's arm.

"Excuse me please for a moment, Hernando, these are my children."

Turning from his high-ranking guest, Pedro opened his arms toward the children. At the nun's gesture, they sang a hymn in Spanish. By the look in their eyes, it was evident that they understood and believed in the words.

> Thou lettest old men, Thou lettest young men,
> Thou lettest boys in chorus sing;
> Matrons, virgins, little maidens,
> With glad voices answering.
> Let their guileless song echo,
> And the heart its music bring,
> Evermore and evermore!"

Looking like little angels they lifted their faces toward Heaven, but as soon as the song ended, their eyes sought the face of Father Pedro.

"Happy birthday, Father Pedro!" they shouted. It was easy to see that they loved him, this simple man dressed in his shabby brown garment.

The last notes of the song hung in the air for a motionless moment. Hernando stared self-forgetfully at the children, who quickly shifted their mood and suddenly became roguishly jolly. With pleading eyes, they waited for the nun to make the sign to be happy, and when she nodded, they ran to the priest, and dropped to his feet and embraced his knees. A few of the smallest ones climbed up into his arms and encircled his neck with their tiny arms.

Hernando Pizarro witnessed a scene which unsettled the very foundation of his principles of life. He saw that Pedro's face was transfigured. His brown eyes reflected the sunshine, but a part of their light came from the joy within him. Hernando had never seen a face so content. His wealth and power had never provided for him such obvious gladness.

Hernando's eyes softened with sorrow for himself. This was Father Pedro's wealth, these riches of love. Did this love pour out of him from the always flowing fountain of his own heart? For the first time, the knight felt something like envy for the poor friar. His own elaborate clothing seemed tawdry in comparison with the ragged brown gown when he considered how much happiness the Father had bought with the money he might have spent for his own adornment.

The children suddenly drew back from the priest and exchanged glances with shrewd little smiles. One of the little girls, who looked to be about ten years old, brought a loosely tied parcel and placed it upon the table. The bundle popped open by itself and a handsome new monk's gown was disclosed.

The Father stared with amazement at the fine robe and then at the children. They smiled at him mysteriously. The little girl who had carried the parcel approached him. She held his hand and explained with happy excitement in fluent Spanish.

"Our hearts were sad, Father, when we saw your ragged dress. You gave good clothes to us and your clothes were so old. The cold days will come and you would not be warm."

"But where did you get the money to purchase such a fine garment?"

The children danced and hopped about in their exuberance. "We didn't buy it, Father Pedro, we *made* it for you for your birthday!" shouted the children all at once. The priest's eyes slowly filled with tears of joy.

"And when did you have time to make this? I never saw you working on it."

"Oh, we didn't do it when you could see us!" explained the oldest girl. "We wanted to surprise you so we worked on it at night, after you went to sleep."

"We helped!" cried one of the boys.

Pedro found no words to speak. It was some time before he conquered his emotions.

"But where did you learn to make this fine material and sew the fabric together so masterfully?" asked Pedro. "And where did you get the golden thread?"

"Doña Veronica and her servant, Pani, helped us," said the nun, modestly approaching Father Pedro. "She is very generous. She came with her husband and taught the children how to spin and weave. She provided all the materials they needed and she and Pani did the intricate work."

"You had a secret conspiracy to make me happy?" asked Father Pedro smiling. He turned toward Hernando, "See," he said, "A conspiracy can be delightful. This new brown friar's robe, made with Indian wool by Indian hands, is to me what your 60 pounds of armor is to you, Hernando."

Hernando had seen enough. Gloomily and almost roughly he turned to leave. He pushed past the children and headed toward the gate. When he reached the gate, he stopped. The priest tried to find the words which would have an effect on his estranged friend.

"The goodness of God has no boundaries," he called out gently to Hernando. "I have heard that a drowning man is able to see Him. Perhaps this is why He has made you a sailor once again. Although you have gone astray, Hernando, God will rejoice upon your return."

"If I ever find the way, Pedro, it will be because of you," murmured Hernando. "Goodbye."

"May God go with you, my son."

CHAPTER 49

Hernando commanded a big galleon loaded beyond the point of safety with an incredible amount of gold and gems sent by Francisco to the Spanish King. In addition, on the last day, 200 Indian men and women with children were gathered from the streets and smuggled on board to be sold as slaves in Spain. These unhappy creatures were huddled in the damp hold on the floor and bound in chains.

"I think you should stay," argued Gonzalo. "We need you here to fight."

"You're just a boy, Gonzalo," chided Hernando, "Francisco is right. You don't know the King the way Francisco and I know him. The anger of the King is a messenger of death. I have to go."

Francisco hugged his brother and clapped him heartily on his back. The last time they had been together, he thought, Juan had been among them. He would never again meet his brother, Hernando, who, on arrival in Spain, would be incarcerated for the next 23 years.

"Be wary of the Almagrists," warned Hernando. "They want revenge for the execution. They say we took away their land and livelihoods when we rightfully claimed Cuzco for ourselves. The bastards! They backed the wrong horse."

"Goodbye, my brother," said Francisco. "Fare well."

"We depend on you now, Francisco," said Hernando with a smile. "Maybe it would be best to make friends with the Almagrists. Give them something to eat if they ask. But whatever you do, don't let groups of them gather around you. If they feel strong, they will surely try to kill you."

As Hernando's ship slowly sailed away, to begin its long diagonal course across the Atlantic Ocean to Spain, Gonzalo turned to face his oldest brother.

"Francisco, I want your permission to go after Manco."

"He's certainly a stain upon our victory, isn't he," replied Francisco. "Perhaps we should wait until Hernando delivers my letter to King Charles."

"I don't want to wait," urged Gonzalo. "He humiliated me and I want him to suffer. I already have 300 volunteers and Inca Paullu said he will organize an army of natives to assist me. Inca Paullu will go with me."

"That can help or hurt you, little brother," warned Francisco. "Remember that Paullu has changed allegiances in the midst of a battle. What will you do if he decides to fight *for* his brother instead of *against* him?"

"What," retorted Gonzalo, "and give up his throne in Cuzco? He would never risk losing his power to Manco. In fact, he's more intent on killing Manco than *I* am!"

"I have received numerous reports," admitted Francisco, "that travelers along the Inca Highway are frequently attacked by Manco's loyal friends. What makes *you* so confident, little brother, that *you* can catch him? Suárez and Villadiego failed. Rodrigo Orgóñez was unable. Even Hernando and I have tried and failed to find him in the wild landscape where he hides like a fox. I've heard that they torture travelers and impale them on sharp stakes. Does this not frighten you?"

In fact, Francisco's reports had caused such terror that many Spaniards didn't dare travel to Cuzco anymore. In retaliation, Francisco dispatched a cavalry under the command of Captain Francisco de Chávez to attack Indian towns and randomly slaughter Indian men, women and children. His most cruel soldiers torched their thatched roofs and set fire to their fields. His men ate the natives' llamas and stored food supplies and tortured them until they relinquished their hidden gold, silver, and women. Many Indians were chained together and dragged away to be sold as slaves. Abuse, extortion, and torture were everyday occurrences. But still, Manco's warriors continued to ambush Spanish travelers on the main Inca highway above Cuzco.

"If you are not afraid, then go," agreed Francisco. "Promise me you won't leave me in Peru all alone. I can only say 'goodbye' so many times."

In April, Gonzalo Pizarro led his volunteer soldiers on a 100-mile march from Cuzco to find Manco in Vilcabamba. After the attack by Rodrigo Orgóñez, Manco didn't return to Vitcos but ventured deeper into the Amazon rain forest. Manco was hiding in a place where Earth's longest mountain chain meets the largest rain forest.

Gonzalo's soldiers rode their horses as far as they could but, due to the terrain, had to abandon them to proceed any farther. The air was warm and thick with mosquitoes that buzzed about hungrily biting all exposed skin. The soldiers sweated underneath their 60 pounds of Spanish armor but wouldn't strip down to their cotton underclothes in fear of the Indians' rock projectiles and bamboo arrows.

Manco carefully organized his faithful followers and immediately planted coca, the sacred leaf. Before the arrival of the *white strangers*, only Inca royalty was allowed to chew coca. To reward his people for following him, Manco allowed everyone to chew the sacred leaves to dull their hunger and pain.

Manco arranged for salt, cloth, beads, bronze, and copper axes from highland areas to be traded for forest products such as exotic hardwoods, cacao, manioc, turtle oil, bird feathers, honey, and turtle eggs. Little by little, life became comfortable. There were new and wonderful aspects about the jungle which seemed to fascinate Cura Ocllo.

"Just look at these flowers," she said as she walked sedately toward Manco carrying an armful of orchids. "They grow everywhere! They're my new favorite flower!"

Manco laughed at her. She was still a little girl even though her baby was now two years old. Cura Ocllo's breasts were heavy with milk. "Where's Sayri Tupac," she asked with a tired smile. "It's time for me to nurse him."

"He's right where you left him," answered Manco. "He hasn't even fidgeted since you left. He's the sleepiest baby I've ever seen."

Cura Ocllo walked toward the nursery and began to arrange the orchids in gold vases. As she puttered around and hummed out loud, the baby stirred. Before he could even open his eyes, Cura Ocllo was over his hammock gently rocking him and watching him wake up.

"It's time to eat, my little prince," she cooed. Sayri Tupac opened his large black eyes and stared at his beautiful mother. Cura Ocllo took him lovingly into her arms and wrapped him in a clean cloth. She was content to care for Sayri Tupac as long as she had plenty of coca to chew. As she sat down and brought the toddler to her breast, Manco came to sit with her. He put his arm around her shoulders and kissed her cheek.

"Are you feeling better today?" he asked tenderly.

"Oh, I'm all right, I suppose. I don't know what's wrong with me," answered Cura Ocllo avoiding eye contact.

"You and Sayri Tupac sleep so much lately," stated Manco cautiously. "You look tired and you don't eat like you used to. What is the matter? Is it the forest climate? Do you miss the mountains and Cuzco?"

"I don't know what it is," replied Cura Ocllo sadly. "Nothing is as it used to be. I feel displaced. I feel lost. What will happen to Sayri Tupac? Will he live in the jungle forever? I'm troubled and I don't feel strong like I used to."

"I understand, my dove, try to be patient," comforted Manco. "Tomorrow may bring a fresh breeze to blow the fog away."

Manco and Cura Ocllo had only a limited entourage. But they did have many servants. Manco kept the masons, architects, and carpenters busy building new roads and buildings. The healers, priests, and diviners had a new temple to practice their arts. The farmers and herders also kept busy although the crops were of a limited variety now. In spite of the tranquil and productive lifestyle he had birthed along with his new son, it was still Manco's desire to defeat the *white strangers* and watch them leave his lands forever.

Manco continued to dispatch messages to all the Indians within the Inca Empire that the Spaniards were *not Viracochas*. He issued them orders to slaughter the *white strangers* and to join Manco in Vilcabamba as soon as possible.

"If we continue to work together," encouraged Manco, "we will eventually succeed in driving the *white strangers* back into the sea."

As Gonzalo led his troops through the undergrowth, guttural, deep roars were heard in the forest.

"Are there lions here?" asked Gonzalo nervously.

"No, my Lord, only pumas, but that not puma. I not know what creature make that bad sound," answered Runacha, one of Gonzalo's Indian guides.

"I think we are nearing Hell and that sound is Hell's guardian warning us to stay away," said one of the soldiers to another.

Strange, haunting trills penetrated the forest canopy and raised the hairs on the backs of the soldiers' necks.

"Is it true," asked Gonzalo, "that the forest people eat human flesh?"

"This true," answered Runacha. "If man from noble birth and high rank captured, Chief bring wives and children to celebrate. Tie man naked to tree. Use small cutting reeds and knives to slice morsel of meat. Juicy meat best from calf, thigh, and bottom." Runacha pointed to Gonzalo's body to show where the best cuts of meat were from. "Women and children," continued Runacha, "sprinkle blood on face and eat flesh. No cook or chew. Let man watch them swallow . . . he see they eat him fresh!"

"Do you speak the truth to me?" asked Gonzalo angrily.

"It is what they say," he answered. He was careful to conceal his smile as he watched Gonzalo consider his story.

When Gonzalo and his troops reached an area about twelve miles away from Manco's new Amazon royal city, they came across a new suspension bridge.

"We'll cross here," commanded Gonzalo.

As soon as twenty of his men had crossed, massive boulders came crashing down upon them. It was a trap. *Anti* archers, hiding in the thick vegetation, shot volleys of sharp arrows at the Spaniards and their Indian warriors. Within a short amount of time, over 36 Spaniards were killed and many others were wounded.

Gonzalo ordered a retreat. When they got back to the valley where they left their horses, Gonzalo sent messengers to request reinforcements from Cuzco.

"Where are your brothers, Paullu," asked Gonzalo.

"They are toward the back of the crowd on their litters," answered Paullu nervously.

"I want you to send them to Manco to negotiate a truce while we wait here. Choose your fastest runners to accompany them. Tell them to tell Manco that we'll give him a reward if he gives up."

Reluctantly, Paullu sent his servants to get Huaspar and Inquill, half-brothers to him and Manco but full brothers of Cura Ocllo. They arrived borne on their litters where Paullu explained to them the mission.

"He'll *kill* us!" exclaimed Huaspar.

"He'll *torture* us first!" added Inquill. "You know what he said he'd do to anyone who goes to the side of the *white strangers*. He'll blame us for bringing them here. He'll torture and kill us for sure!"

In spite of their complaints, Huaspar and Inquill were carried ahead in their litters to visit Manco. When they arrived at Manco's camp, Manco was furious.

"Did you not hear me promise to cut off the heads of any Indians I catch cooperating with the Spaniards? Why are you here? Did you not believe me? Do you *wish* to die? Do you think I was *joking*?"

"Manco, please," whispered Cura Ocllo to her husband. "You know the *white strangers* have no use for us, don't you see? They would *like* to see us all dead. Why should we give them any help? I beg you . . ."

"You must surrender and come with us, Manco," urged Inquill. "You will be rewarded."

"No. I will stay here and live free. *You* will die. Take them both away and bring me back their heads," ordered Manco.

As several of Manco's strongest warriors dragged Huaspar and Inquill to the edge of the camp, Cura Ocllo screamed.

"No, you can't do this, Manco!" she wailed. "They were children with me. Please don't kill them! I'm so tired of the bloodshed! Why should we help *them* kill us?" she pleaded as she chased after the warriors who took away her brothers.

"Better that I have their heads than they deliver mine to a Pizarro," said Manco to himself.

Without any more discussion, Huaspar and Inquill were beheaded. The warriors took the severed heads back to Manco but Cura Ocllo fell to the ground beside her brothers' headless bodies and refused to move.

"We must retreat, Inca Manco," urged Chutu. "The runners will tell Gonzalo Pizarro what you have done. They will arrive soon and they will not wish to talk. We must hurry!"

"I will not leave without Cura Ocllo," insisted Manco. "I don't know what is wrong with her. She has been terribly sad and listless lately. I fear her new lowland forest home does not suit her mountain nature. She cries often and is hard to console. We will wait for her."

"As you wish, my Lord," responded Chutu with deep disappointment.

They waited. Even after a considerable length of time, Cura Ocllo refused to move. When her servants approached to console her, she raged at them and sent them running from fear of their fierce mistress. Finally, against his wishes, the runners picked Manco up into their arms and ran with him. He tried to resist and called out loudly to Cura Ocllo as he disappeared into the forest, "My love, run away with us! Find me again as you did before!"

But Cura Ocllo didn't answer. She sobbed uncontrollably on the ground beside her brothers as though a dam had burst in her soul.

When Gonzalo found her, she looked like a wild woman. Her hair had come loose from its braids and her dress was smeared with blood. She was mumbling and holding the hands of her dead brothers. Although she made no attempt to escape, she defended herself savagely. She spat, scratched, bit and struggled against Gonzalo and his men with all the strength she had left, for her intense grief had weakened her.

Gonzalo's men plundered Manco's new town and took many captives. Cura Ocllo was tied with ropes and Gonzalo allowed his men to brutalize her as punishment for leaving him. All during the journey to Cuzco, Cura Ocllo tried to defend herself against the attacks of Gonzalo and his men. She finally resorted to smearing her beautiful body with her own wastes and any animal dung she could find to discourage her rapists.

Manco was crestfallen and disconsolate. Although he had reluctantly and barely evaded capture, he suffered terribly. "Take me to Cuzco!" yelled Manco. "That is where they will take her. I will negotiate with Francisco; I can't go on like this any longer. I need my *Coya*. I will surrender."

Upon hearing the news that Manco was ready to negotiate and perhaps even to surrender, Francisco sent fine gifts to him that included a beautiful pony and rare silk clothing. But Paullu, favored puppet Inca of the conquistadors, found a way to interfere with Manco's success. Paullu intercepted the men sent by Francisco Pizarro, slaughtered the pony, destroyed the precious gifts, and sent them back to Francisco with a vulgar message of hatred and threats that was supposedly from Manco. Through his manipulation and treachery, Paullu was able to convince the Pizarros that Manco would not surrender nor negotiate.

When Francisco saw what had happened to the presents he sent Manco and heard Manco's purported response, he decided to hurt Manco. He decided that the greatest pain that could be inflicted upon Manco would be to kill the wife he loved most. He would torture and kill Cura Ocllo in order to punish Manco.

Francisco ordered his men to strip Cura Ocllo, once a Sun Virgin, the young daughter of Huayna Capac, of all her clothing. After her already ravaged body was revealed to all, he ordered that she be tied to a wooden stake.

"Let the Cañari beat her, they're the ones who stole her from me and returned her to Manco," growled Gonzalo.

The Cañari warriors that were with him followed Gonzalo's orders. Since they were not the same warriors that had once saved Cura Ocllo from Gonzalo's home in Cuzco, they did not hold back in beating her with their fists as everyone watched. Cura Ocllo didn't make a sound and barely flinched at the cruel abuse.

"It isn't enough," said Francisco, "shoot her arms and legs with your arrows."

The Cañari, concern beginning to show on their faces, shot bamboo tipped arrows into Cura Ocllo's arms and legs. The arrows pierced her soft flesh easily and emerged from the other side. Rivulets of blood ran down her limbs and puddled in the dirt. It was a horrible and gruesome scene.

Finally, Cura Ocllo spoke. Her eyes were lit with a sublime light that gave her the appearance of being from another world.

"What sort of men are you," asked Cura Ocllo in Quechua, "that you take your anger out on a woman? Hurry up and finish me. Your appetites for suffering, blood, and gold will never be satisfied."

Many of the soldiers and Indian warriors that watched felt confused by what was happening before their eyes. The Spaniards concluded that the torture and murder of Cura Ocllo was an act completely unworthy of a sane Christian man. "After all," they agreed, "this war was not *her* fault."

Cura Ocllo's dead body was placed into a large basket and floated down the Vilcanota River.

"When Manco sees what we did with his precious *Coya*, he'll know exactly where he stands with us," snorted Francisco.

A few days later, Cura Ocllo's ravaged body was brought to Manco. He was grief stricken and despondent over the death of his beautiful and beloved wife. He wept and agonized over her loss and declared a festival of sorrow for thirty days. Many of his loyal followers were stunned by how much *chicha* he consumed. Although it was routine to drink as much as possible during festivals, they had never seen Manco consume such a great quantity.

Francisco returned to Lima where rumors had already begun to swirl through the streets that many of the Spanish inhabitants held secret meetings during which they planned the assassination of the Viceroy in retaliation for the execution of Diego de Almagro.

CHAPTER 50

Months passed and the much-longed-for baby was expected soon. The Peruvian winter was just getting started in June and it had been a drizzly and foggy Sunday morning. Vira was very tired and her heavy body made walking difficult. As lunch time approached, she worked her way to Alvarez's study where she found him chatting with Father Pedro and drinking a goblet of wine brought from Spain.

"We have advanced and flourished in every way," said Pedro. "But there is trouble. Punishment always follows sin and I fear the Viceroy's punishment is not far away. I heard that young Diego de Almagro prepares a conspiracy against him."

"Perhaps he should be granted his inheritance," suggested Alvarez.

"The Viceroy refuses. I heard he offered a small sum for compensation, but the young man wouldn't accept it. He is inconsolable over the execution of his father."

As Alvarez and Pedro invited Vira to sit and join them in their discussion, twenty armed assassins marched through the city to Francisco's palace.

"Long live the King!" yelled Juan de Herrada.

"Death to tyrants!" yelled Juan Rodríguez Barragán.

"For my brother, Rodrigo," shouted Diego Mendéz.

"For my father!" shouted Diego de Almagro.

As Alvarez poured a goblet of wine for his young wife, the assassins reached the palace and hunted through the rooms for Francisco Pizarro who was dining with his wife and friends. Upon hearing the noise of the approaching attackers, Francisco grabbed his sword and tried to latch his chest armor, but they were upon him too quickly.

In a failed attempt to negotiate with the assassins, Chávez, Pizarro's cruelest captain who bragged that he alone had killed over 600 native children, was killed on the stairs. Unafraid of the young, rebellious upstarts, Pizarro faced the open doorway to meet them and with the help of a few brave friends, he was able to hold them back for some time.

As Alvarez reached over and lifted Vira's feet from the floor to his lap to rub them, Herrada shoved one of his men forward through the door and, as hoped, Pizarro ran him through with his sword. With Pizarro's sword embedded in their comrade, the rest of the attackers were able to push their way into the room and surround him. One by one, Pizarro's defenders crumpled dead to the floor.

Alone and surrounded now by his attackers, the Almagrists closed in on him. They stabbed him with their daggers and swords wounding him until he fell heavily to the floor. Severely bleeding and flat on his back on the floor, Francisco made the sign of the cross over his own lips with his bloody index finger.

"Confession," he gasped.

"No confession for *you*, you tyrant," yelled Herrada, "for all we care you can confess your sins to the Devil in Hell!"

Juan Rodríguez Barragán hoisted a large pitcher full of water high above his head and brought it down with all of his might upon Pizarro's head. There on the floor of his palace, in a pool of water mixed with his own blood, in the City of Kings that he had built, in a country he had conquered, the 63-year-old conquistador breathed his last.

Suddenly, a terrible din broke the peaceful conversation in Don Alvarez's study. The door flew open with a bang and Inés burst into the room with disheveled hair and her clothes smeared with blood. Her face was distorted by fear and horror. She was holding hands with her little son and daughter and they were all crying.

"They killed him! They killed Francisco! He's dead," she yelled to all in the room.

Alvarez, Vira, and Pedro went to her and tried to calm her down. Pani took the two children to the kitchen for something to eat and to remove them from the terrible scene. Alvarez poured Inés a goblet of wine and made her drink until it was empty.

"The young Almagro and his friends," gasped Inés, "they barged into the palace and murdered Francisco. What is happening? What will we do now? Where will we go?"

"You will stay with us," said Vira trying to reassure her sister. "Don't worry, you are safe here."

"Oh, thank you, Vira! Ampuero has wanted to marry me for a long time but he couldn't as long as Francisco wanted me. Perhaps I will marry him now. But what will become of Francisco's children?"

"They can stay with me at the orphanage," offered Father Pedro. "I will take care of them and keep them safe from the troubles in this city. No one would look for them there."

"But you will stay here for now, all right?" asked Vira. "You cannot go out into the streets tonight. It's too dangerous. Come with me and I will get you some clean garments and show you where you will sleep."

"We've been waiting for a miracle," said Alvarez.

"But will it bring destruction?" asked Pedro.

The two men embraced as if they might not meet again. Father Pedro went to his cottage to prepare places for his new wards.

Vira showed Inés to her room and gave her many sets of clean clothes. As she turned to close the door, she felt a sharp pain in her abdomen.

"Pani," she called as she made her way to the kitchen. "Pani, you better heat some water."

"I already am, my dove," answered Pani. "I know Inés will want to bathe."

"No Pani, you better heat some water for me. I think I'm going to have the baby!"

"Now?" exclaimed Pani with a wide smile.

"Now," answered Vira as pain swept over her and made her sit on a chair.

"Señor! Don Alvarez!" she screamed. "Come quickly, you're going to be a father!"

Vira's little boy was born the next morning. The physician came and delivered him with no complications. Father Pedro anointed his little head with oil and appointed himself as Godfather.

"He is my first," announced Father Pedro with a smile. "I will look after him and teach him everything I know. You will never need to worry, for I will always be here to help you care for him. No matter what happens," he assured the new parents.

"Thank you, Pedro," said Alvarez. "I'm depending on you."

"I thank you also, Pedro. You are truly our best friend. I know he will have many questions for you about Jesus. And I know you will answer them all like you have done for me. Now I can thank Jesus for my many blessings. God bless you, Pedro."

Just then, the baby squirmed and yawned.

"He has your almond-shaped eyes," said Alvarez.

"But he looks just like you," said Vira. "He's perfect."

Alvarez kissed the baby boy on the head as Vira nursed him. She was exhausted and exhilarated as she reclined comfortably on pillows in her bed.

"What kind of a name should we give to him?" asked Vira. "He is not Inca but he is not Spanish either. He is a beautiful combination of our two worlds."

"The custom in Spain is to name a man's first born son after his grandfather," said Alvarez. "My father's name is Antonio. Do you want to name him Antonio?"

"Let's call him Antonio Manco," suggested Vira excitedly. "He will unite the Spanish with the Inca. He will bring peace to all of our people."

"Let's see," smiled Alvarez, "he'll unite the Indians, who fight against each other, with the Spaniards, who also fight against each other. Is that not a little ambitious, my darling?"

"I suppose. But I still like the name," said Vira with a radiant smile. "I love you, Alvarez. Thank you for my beautiful son."

"I love you too, my darling. And I thank you for my beautiful son. I think you did the hard part."

Father Pedro christened the new baby, *Antonio Manco de la Vega*, and uttered many beautiful prayers over his new God son.

Later, when Vira was alone with baby Antonio, she whispered with deep emotion in his ear: "Oh my darling son, there is a love in me that you can never imagine. But there is also a dark rage in me that you will never comprehend. Sometimes I am afraid that if the love is not sustained, my rage might be unleashed."

CHAPTER 51

When Cura Ocllo's battered body was delivered to the embalmers for mummification, Manco requested a small amount of her blood. Carefully and with much emotion, Manco himself dipped fine strands of *cumbi*, the fine wool from a baby alpaca, the best wool available to him in his jungle kingdom, into her blood to dye them. Manco dried the strands of wool and braided them into a strong cord. Three years later, he still wore the braided strands in his *llautu* in remembrance of the love that had been taken from him so cruelly. He knew that when Cura Ocllo died, the essence of all that had made him an Inca King had died with her.

The Viceroy, Francisco Pizarro, was also dead. The Almagrists took control of the palace in Lima but were soon defeated at the Battle of Chupas. No one trusted their neighbor and allegiances were challenged within every home. Almagrists fought against Pizarrists whether they were Spaniards, Indians, or mestizos. In time, and in response to reports of perpetual turmoil in Peru, King Charles dispatched Viceroy Don Blasco Núñez Vela to take control of the Inca Empire.

Francisco's assassins were hunted down and executed. Among them, young Diego de Almagro, was hung from the gallows for his crime. There was only one assassin left, Diego Méndez, Rodrigo Orgóñez's brother. Along with six of his friends, he sought sanctuary and protection from Inca Manco. Destitute, emaciated, and utterly defenseless, Manco took pity on the ragged group of Spaniards and allowed them to stay in Vitcos, only thirty miles away from his Vilcabamba estate. The men eagerly accepted his protection and generosity. He was their only hope for refuge from Pizarro's avengers.

For two years Méndez and his men taught Manco everything he wanted to know about being Spanish. They taught him how to load, aim, and fire the harquebuses and how to care for and ride the horses Manco's generals had confiscated after victories against the conquistadors. They taught him how to speak Spanish and instructed him in Spanish military strategy. In return, Manco gave them everything they needed. He built houses for them and appointed native women to attend to their chores and cooking.

Of all the things that Manco learned from his new Spanish friends, playing horseshoes was his favorite. In fact, playing horseshoes was the only activity that seemed to relieve Manco's ennui. Since Cura Ocllo died, he spent the majority of his days listlessly moping and depressed. He had very little energy and only performed the tasks that were required of him. Three years had passed since her death and he was only a shadow of the man he once was. Kusa Akchi, once his closest confident, was now only a sore reminder of all that Manco had lost.

So Manco often traveled to Vitcos to play horseshoes. Méndez and his entourage humored him and indulged him in as many games as he desired. But these were men of great ambition and courage and knew it would only be a matter of time before their luck would change. None of them desired to stay in exile forever playing horseshoes with a hopeless native has-been. Each man eagerly awaited the day when he could rejoin the outside world and leave Manco's Inca refuge far behind. As well as Manco treated them, they were tired of the life of outlaws. They wanted to return to their own people and reap the harvest of the New World as everyone else was free to do in Peru. And then King Charles sent Viceroy Don Blasco Núñez Vela to take control of Peru.

"We've waited years for a chance to save ourselves," said Méndez after hearing the news of the new Viceroy's arrival in Peru. "Listen to me. We must think this through carefully. If we dispose of Inca Manco, the King's last enemy in Peru, I bet the King and his new Viceroy would be grateful. Perhaps the King will even be charitable toward us and forgive me for killing Francisco. Perhaps," continued Méndez, "His Majesty would even reward us with titles, land, and gold."

"But we've been living off of Manco's hospitality for two years now. He keeps us safe and gives us everything we want. I don't want to hurt Manco. What has he ever done to us that was unkind?" argued his friend César.

"Manco holds the last official rebel stronghold in Peru," answered Méndez. "Does that mean nothing to you?"

"I don't like this kind of talk," concluded César. "He's my friend. He comes here just to enjoy our company. And I enjoy his company too. And I *very much* enjoy my woman he gave me. No, I'll not hurt Manco."

Méndez was undeterred by César's resistance. He had the attention of the majority.

"We'll invite him to visit us here in Vitcos for a horseshoe tournament. We can surprise him during a friendly game of horseshoes. He loves to play horseshoes! See, he'll die happy doing what he loves to do. Anyway, he's been miserable since Cura Ocllo was killed. We'll be doing him a favor and putting him out of his misery," plotted Méndez. "Or would you all rather take your chances in Spain against the instruments of the Inquisition?"

The Spaniards who had spent the past two years in Manco's sanctuary finally nodded in agreement. But it felt underhanded.

When an invitation arrived via *Chaski* runner from his Spanish friends in Vitcos, Manco went immediately to join them for games. The day was bright and warm. César had failed to hit the target stake with even one horseshoe all morning and Manco was enjoying teasing him. It was Manco's turn. Just as he swung back his right arm to throw the horseshoe, Diego Méndez stabbed Manco brutally in the back with his dagger. Manco felt the sting and looked around in confusion. He was thoroughly surprised and it took a long moment before he even thought to defend himself. But they were his *friends* and there were seven of them.

Titu Cusi, Manco's eldest son from one of his concubines, was ten years old at the time. Although he had spent some time growing up in Cuzco after being captured by Rodrigo Orgóñez in Vitcos, he had eventually escaped and found his way back to his family. He wanted to help his father but wasn't even carrying a weapon. When César panicked and threw a spear at him, Titu Cusi ran into the forest.

The assassins, now guilty of murdering a native king, ran to their horses and galloped toward Cuzco. But they took the wrong turn and failed to realize that they were being followed by Manco's faithful *Anti* warriors. That night, as the murderous parasites rested in an abandoned house, thinking that they had made a clean getaway, Manco's archers set the thatched roof on fire. When the sleepy Spaniards ran out of the door gasping for air, the jungle archers killed all seven men with arrows and left them where they fell.

Manco's loyal followers and bodyguards meanwhile carried him home to his estate in Vitcos. As everyone came to greet their King, it became obvious that something was dreadfully wrong. The litter bearers, carrying instead a long, flat golden shield, laid their burden gently on the ground.

Some *mamaconas* came and spread clean reeds from the river upon the ground. One of them gently placed Manco's head in her lap. As everyone gathered around, their faces were grim with sorrow. Titu Cusi sank to his knees beside his beloved father and pressed his cheek to his.

"He's still alive!" he cried. "Bring some water! Bring the herbs and wrap his wounds!"

Manco's dark eyes fluttered open and a spark of the old fire appeared in them when he looked into the face of Titu Cusi. His pale lips curved into a weak smile and his hand searched for Titu Cusi's hand.

"Father, they threw a spear at me and almost hit me! I was frightened and I didn't know what to do so I ran away. I did what you always tell me to do, Father, I looked for a mouse house!"

Titu Cusi smiled at the allegory his father always used to teach him to run and hide when a situation becomes dire and capture appears imminent.

"The mouse," smiled Manco at his son, "always gets away."

"I think they chased me, Father, but I ran for so long and I ran so far into the forest that they couldn't find me. Don't worry, Father, the *Antis* are chasing them and they'll kill those wicked men who hurt you."

"Good, my son."

"Why did they do this, Father? I thought they were your friends. You always play horseshoes with them when we come here to Vitcos."

Manco's breath was labored and a trickle of red blood oozed from the corner of his mouth. The cold shiver of death ran through him. There was so much left for him to do. His sons were young and Sayri Tupac, Manco's Crown Prince, was already growing up without his mother's love. Would the little boy have to grow up without his father as well? I need more time, thought Manco.

"Bring Sayri Tupac," gasped Manco as he tried to look around. A warm fire burned nearby and his loyal followers were gathered to see their wounded King.

"Here I am," answered a little boy. Sayri Tupac was the eldest child of Manco and Cura Ocllo. He was the center of his father's heart and the reason Manco still cared to live. The boy, tall for his age and well-muscled, was just as beautiful as his mother. His eyes were large and dark and his black hair fell into them. He had to shake his head to clear the bangs from his eyes.

"How many years old are you now, Sayri Tupac," asked Manco taking the boy's hand in his.

"I am five years old," answered the child proudly.

"Are you ready, my son?" asked Manco.

"What for, Taytay?"

"You will be Inca King," whispered Manco.

"This I know, Taytay, I practice riding your horse for the day I will wear the *llautu.*"

"This day has come, my son. I must go now to be with your mother and Viracocha. Do you see how my blood flows into the earth?"

"I will wear the *llautu* and hold the *champi today?*" asked Sayri Tupac.

"Yes, today you will be Inca King. *Qamña allinlla* my little one," he said as he smiled weakly, "and now you be good."

Manco closed his eyes and breathed heavily. As his people watched, *Amauta* Kusa Akchi bent over Manco's dying body uttering prayers.

"I will watch over the boy," promised Kusa Akchi as tears fell from his eyes and landed on Manco's tunic.

Manco's eyes opened again and he looked hard at his old mentor. "Whoever thought you would out-live me, ñawpa?" asked Manco with a silly, boyish smile.

Then, seriously and with great emotion, Manco looked Sayri Tupac in the eyes. "There is something you must remember, my son," he warned speaking louder now than he had before.

As the pale lids lowered over his dark luminous eyes, Manco spoke his last words to his son, "Always remember, Sayri Tupac, you must never, n*ever* trust the *White Strangers.*"

The End

BIBLIOGRAPHY

Ilona von Dohnányi, <u>The Sun Sets</u>. Unpublished Manuscript.

Dr. Sean P. McGlynn, <u>Pizzaroland</u>. Unpublished Manuscript.

<u>National Geographic</u>, "Lofty Ambitions of the Inca," Heather Pringle, Photographs by Robert Clark, April 2011 pp. 34-61.

Kim MacQuarrie, <u>The Last Days of the Incas</u>. Simon & Schuster Paperbacks, New York 2007.

John Hemming, <u>The Conquest of the Incas</u>, A Harvest Book, Harcourt, Inc. 1970

ABOUT THE AUTHOR

Sheila LeBlanc is the only daughter of Helen and Sean McGlynn. Born in Baton Rouge, Louisiana in 1964, she graduated from Robert E. Lee High School in 1982 and went on to study at Louisiana State University (LSU) and the University of Heidelberg where she earned B.A. and M.A. degrees in Cultural Geography. She studied and lived in Bonn and Heidelberg, Germany; Innsbruck, Austria; and Dungloe, Ireland. She lived in Englewood, Florida on Manasota Key where she collected fossil shark teeth on her favorite beach on Earth. She also lived for many years in Lakeland, Florida and now resides in Lafayette, Louisiana with her husband, Jeff, and daughter, Ryan Nicole.

Sheila currently works for John Chance Land Surveys, Inc. (a Fugro Company) where she handles routine regulatory work for clients in the oil and gas industry. She admits that her favorite character of Cantuta is Atahualpa and hopes that her readers will add Cantuta to their list of stories which exemplify the sad and ancient dilemma of man's inhumanity to man.